WILD GIRL

KINGDOM OF WOLVES

C.R. JANE
MILA YOUNG

CONTENTS

Wild Girl Soundtrack   vii

Kingdom of Wolves series   ix

Prologue   1

Chapter 1   9

Chapter 2   17

Chapter 3   30

Chapter 4   40

Chapter 5   50

Chapter 6   72

Chapter 7   87

Chapter 8   100

Chapter 9   124

Chapter 10   134

Chapter 11   147

Chapter 12   158

Chapter 13   168

Chapter 14   183

Chapter 15   197

Chapter 16   216

Chapter 17   225

Chapter 18   232

Wild Love   235

Author's Note   237

About C.R. Jane   239

Books by C.R. Jane   241

About Mila Young   245

Books By Mila Young   247

DEDICATION

For our amazing readers...

Go wild, for a while.

Follow your dreams.
Follow your heart.
Follow your wild.

We Were Happy

Taylor Swift

Better Man

Little Big Town

Hurt

Lady A

Murky

Saint Mesa

Secrets and Lies

Ruelle

Looking for the Rain

UNKLE, Mark Lanegan, ESKA

Cher

AIGEL

Renegade

Big Red Machine

All I Want

Kodeline

Wonderwall

Zella Day

The End of Love

Florence + The Machines

Now & Then

Lily Kershaw

Not Ready to Say Goodbye

Leah Nobel

Get the playlist on SPOTIFY, Wild Girl Soundtrack

KINGDOM OF WOLVES SERIES

FROM C.R. JANE AND MILA YOUNG

Wild Moon
Wild Heart
Wild Girl
Wild Love

These stories are set in the Kingdom of Wolves shared world, but our Wild series will follow Rune's continuing story with her alphas.

WILD GIRL

REAL WOLVES BITE...

My fated mate who rejected me has returned.

I should have known Alistair would find me.

But the dark secrets of my new home have been distracting me from the danger I'll always be in as long as he is alive.

A serial killer. My lovers' psycho ex. Not to mention my strange new powers;

It's been a lot for a girl to handle.

Two Alphas have also claimed me as their own. Now that I've been taken, they'll stop at nothing to get me back. But we should have remembered that there were scarier things in the shadows than my ex.

I need to be more wolf than woman now, because to survive, I'm going to have to embrace the wild in me.

PROLOGUE
WILDER

"*S*een Rune anywhere?" I asked one of the girls wearing the same dove gray dress Rune had been wearing during the ceremony. Her eyes widened as she stared at me, and I shifted impatiently, resisting the urge to snap at her to hurry the fuck up.

"Umm, no. Not for a while," she stuttered, looking around the room frantically like she could somehow find what I had spent the last twenty minutes looking for.

"Thanks," I said shortly.

"I could help you look?" she called out desperately.

"No thanks," I threw over my shoulder, not particularly worried about the fact that I'd left her a sputtering mess.

Across the room, I saw Daxon prowling around, obviously looking for Rune as well. Golden boy was looking a little rough around the edges as he searched.

Where the fuck was she if she wasn't with him? I'd been imagining them off in some room in this place and I hadn't been looking forward to walking in on them.

Fear flickered in my chest. Rune had a knack for getting herself in situations since rolling into town.

What if...?

"Where the fuck is she?" growled Daxon, appearing out of nowhere next to me. "I can't... I can't even smell her."

There was a manic edge to his words, and I side eyed him as we walked, hoping that he could keep it together. She was probably in the bathroom, and we'd all be laughing about mine and Daxon's over-the-top reaction after this.

Except something in my gut told me that wasn't the case.

"Daxon," a girl said breathlessly as we headed to the door.

Daxon ignored her like she'd never existed. I would have chuckled, but we were out in the hallway, and Rune was still nowhere to be found. And Daxon was right. I couldn't even smell her. And there was no missing that scent of hers. It was the most delicious fucking thing I'd ever experienced.

We pushed past the hallway teeming with people. The crowds parted as Daxon and I walked shoulder to shoulder down the hallway, a rare sight. After searching all the rooms on the main floor, we made our way out to the garden, practically sprinting at that point.

Daxon's hands had shifted, and I just hoped that everyone got the message to stay out of the way because Daxon would probably cut them down.

"Rune?" Daxon yelled as we got out to where the outdoor ceremony had been held.

We both sniffed the air at the same time. "She's gone," I whispered as the acrid scent of unknown shifters assaulted my nostrils. A group had been here, standing right there.

"He got her," Daxon said, not needing to explain further.

For weeks we'd been killing the men Rune's ex had sent to our town once he'd discovered her whereabouts. I'd thought the asshole would get the message.

Obviously I'd underestimated him.

Daxon abruptly shifted and tore off, following the path of the unfamiliar scent. Not for the first time, I cursed the fact that I could only shift on a full moon. It would be much easier to track the strangers.

I ran after him, appreciating that at least I had a portion of my supernatural speed in my human form. I trailed after him, catching a faint hint of Rune's scent as I followed.

When I got to the road, the scent abruptly cut off. I assumed she'd been put into a vehicle and it had taken off.

Daxon was there, an excruciating whine mixed with a growl reverberating from his throat. He shifted back and clutched at his chest as he let out a roar into the heavens that scattered the birds in the trees as they flew away in fright.

Rune was gone.

I sank to my knees, trying to get ahold of myself. *Think, think,* I urged myself. But everything felt muddled. Somehow I'd thought Daxon and I had it under control. That there was no way Rune's asshole ex would come after her, not after all the men we'd killed. But it had to have been him that took her. Who else would it have been?

Daxon let out another inhuman roar, and I snapped back to attention. I eyed him warily. He was shaking as he stood there, his eyes and his hands still shifted so that he resembled a monster.

His gaze flicked all around him, a wildness in his eyes that I'd only seen in feral wolves before. No sooner had I thought that then Daxon fully shifted and leapt out at me, a savage growl ripping from his throat as I narrowly avoided being shredded apart by his claws.

"Daxon," I said, my alpha voice leaking out of me with absolutely no effect on him whatsoever. Daxon lunged at me again, his jaw open as he aimed for my jugular.

The fucker was actually trying to kill me.

Just then a drunk stumbled out of the trees. He was wearing a rumpled suit and holding a half empty bottle of rum. I recognized him as Charlie Duncan instantly, a useless drunk from my pack who'd seen better days. He called out to me when he saw me, tripping over a root as he did so and falling to the ground.

Unfortunately for Charlie, Daxon's attention immediately shifted towards him when Charlie called out to us. Daxon twisted in the air and darted at Charlie who was struggling to get off the ground.

"Fuck," I swore loudly as I launched myself towards Charlie. I was too late though. My enhanced speed in human form was nothing compared to Daxon's speed in his wolf form. By the time I reached the pair of them, Daxon had already clawed Charlie's chest open. Blood was gurgling out of Charlie's mouth as he lay sprawled out on the ground, feebly trying to get away.

I grabbed two handfuls of Daxon's fur and pulled as hard as I could, cringing when I heard the sound of Charlie's skin ripping as I tore Daxon off of him.

I wrestled Daxon as far away from Charlie as I could, flinching as Daxon's jaw snapped down on my shoulder, and a shockwave of pain tore through me. I grunted, trying to hold on as tightly as I could to Daxon. Charlie was a useless waste of space, but he didn't deserve to die. Over the snarls of Daxon as he tore at me, I could faintly hear Charlie letting out pathetic little screams as he lay there.

The sounds of yells and people rushing through the woods hit my ears, and a few seconds later, some of my betas and Daxon's betas burst out of the tree line, their panicked yelps filling the air as they rushed to get Daxon off of me. My teeth gritted at the pain coursing through my body, courtesy of Daxon's razor sharp teeth and claws. I somehow pushed Daxon off as the six men surrounded and wrangled him to the ground.

Daxon was lost as he slashed and snapped at them. You had to admire the six betas. Daxon was tearing them up, but none of them let go. I grabbed Daxon's jaws, clamping them together as he continued to struggle.

"Anyone have some sedative?" I cursed as one of the betas temporarily lost one of Daxon's paws, and I narrowly missed having my nose clawed off.

"Are you sure?" asked Marcus, half-heartedly.

I snarled at him, and Marcus pulled a syringe from a pocket in his jeans. All the betas were supposed to keep a sedative close by just in case one of the pack lost control. I'm sure they hadn't figured they would be using it on Daxon though when we'd first instituted the rule.

He carefully uncapped the syringe, revealing a nasty looking needle. Marcus hesitated for a brief moment until Daxon's tail whipped him in the face. It must have been the encouragement he needed because he slammed the needle into Daxon's flank and injected the sedative quickly until the syringe was empty.

Daxon's thrashing continued without a hitch.

"Do another one," I commanded, panicking a bit as one of the betas got his stomach sliced open when Daxon kicked backwards.

"I didn't grab mine," Eric said, panicking. Looking around, I saw that none of the other betas had theirs either.

We were fucked. An alpha wolf needed at least three of the regular vials to even start slowing down. Daxon and I never carried a sedative because we were able to overpower everyone in the pack, so we'd never needed it.

Marcus's grip must have loosened when he saw what

happened to Tommy's stomach because Daxon was suddenly able to wrench himself free, and then he was gone, darting away into the treeline...right towards the reception.

"Grab some of the tranquilizer guns and meet me at the mansion," I ordered as I ran in the direction Daxon had disappeared. "And someone grab Charlie."

I had only made it halfway back to the mansion when the screams began.

I sped up, a litany of curse words spewing from my mouth. I didn't have time for this crap. I needed to find Rune. Every second I spent dealing with this just put her farther away from me. Agony tore through me, and I had to force myself forward. It felt like a piece of me was missing, something that I couldn't live without.

If I hadn't known the spectrum of my feelings before, I couldn't miss it now. I needed her. I needed her to breathe. I needed her to live. She'd somehow become my everything, and I wasn't sure I would survive if I didn't get her back.

I burst out of the forest and came to a brief halt as I saw the blood-soaked scene in front of me. Guests dressed in their finery were sprawled all over the grass, various gashes and bites all over them as they moaned and cried. I launched myself forward when I saw a flash of fur disappearing into the back entrance. Daxon was going to decimate both packs if he got the chance. I'd seen feral wolves in action before, but I'd never seen anything like this. Feral wolves usually attacked whatever they saw and then disappeared. Daxon was on the hunt, his bloodlust insatiable.

Marcus was suddenly sprinting next to me. He threw a tranq gun at me, and we rushed inside, shrill screams making my blood run cold.

The ballroom was a scene from a horror movie that I

didn't think I'd forget any time soon. Daxon was ripping through the room. Everyone was so shocked that they weren't even putting up a fight. Marcus and I pulled up our guns along with three of the other betas, trying to get a clear shot.

The packs may never recover from this.

My first shot went wide as Daxon suddenly darted to the left, intent on a group of quivering men who had fallen to the floor.

Marcus's shot hit Daxon in his front shoulder. Daxon fell briefly forward from the impact and that gave us the chance to fire off five more shots that all hit true. Thank fuck we'd made the betas practice so much. Daxon tried to move forward, but six shots of supercharged tranquilizer were too much even for him.

He fell forward, and we rushed towards him, lunging on top of him just in case.

Miyu and Rae appeared in front of us, tears tracking down Miyu's face as she stared down at her alpha. She was definitely never going to forget her mating ceremony, that was for sure.

"I don't understand," she sobbed as she looked around the room. I followed her gaze, wincing as I saw the destruction. I didn't even know where to start.

I didn't bother to explain what happened. There wasn't time.

The betas and I dragged the now passed out Daxon out of the ballroom and down the hallway. At the end of the hall, there was a door that led down to the basement. After typing in the code for the lock on the door, we stumbled down the stairs with Daxon's dead weight. His wolf was a huge motherfucker.

Few of the pack members knew about the group of cells

that lay in the basement. It had been used by prior alphas to torture enemies, but Daxon and I hadn't made much use of it. I suspected Daxon had his own torture cell somewhere, and some faint part of me found it somewhat ironic that Daxon had now found himself in one.

We hauled him onto a table and immediately went to work snapping chains laced with silver into place, which would weaken him enough to keep him secured even when the sedatives wore off.

I stared down at the wolf, exhaustion thrumming through me.

What the fuck was I supposed to do now?

"Two of you need to be down here at all times," I snarled at the nervous men around me. Their nerves were all shot, that was easy to see. They were about to prove just how useful they really were though, so they needed to get themselves together.

"Marcus, you're in charge of dealing with what's up there," I said, gesturing up the stairs where you could hear the faint sound of people crying.

So much for these rooms being soundproof.

"Where are you going?" he asked, a slice of panic threaded through his voice.

I was already up the stairs before I answered.

"I'm going hunting," I threw over my shoulder.

And I was. Whoever had taken Rune was a dead man.

I'm coming, baby. Hold on.

1

RUNE

I was thrust into consciousness by the force of someone shaking me. Strong hands grasped my arms, and the entire room shuddered from how hard the man jostled me back and forth.

Despite the abrupt awakening, it took me a moment to come to my senses and chase away the heaviness clinging to my mind and eyes. I tried piecing together my thoughts while taking in my surroundings from behind leaden eyelids.

"We gave her a huge dose, so she should still be out of it," the man said, a voice that didn't belong to Wilder or Daxon. But with it came a strong, woodsy smell laced with the unpleasant stench of perspiration.

"Just get it done," another distant but familiar voice responded.

My eyes fully shot open then, and in front of me stood a bulky guy with a short beard and bushy eyebrows that looked like they'd sprouted from his forehead. To his side towered another man I recognized all too well, and my heart seized in my chest. Dressed in an all-black uniform, was one of Alistair's enforcers. He clutched an iron rod in his hand, and my gaze fell to the brand at the end of the weapon.

A small cry slipped past my lips.

The first time I'd seen the enforcer hold on to that weapon was back in Alistair's home when he branded me. When he'd spelled me with a curse to steal away the one thing that made me a shifter... my wolf.

Terror shot through me, freezing me in place. I hastily swept the room with my gaze, and there on a metal chair several feet away was the monster, reclining, one leg crossed over the other, smirking.

He wore an eye patch over the eye I gouged out of its socket. I guess it hadn't healed the way it was supposed to.

Seeing him again was all of my nightmares rolled into one.

I felt sick to my stomach as reality collided into me. I thrashed in my seat, discovering I was tied up with my hands behind my back and my legs free. Frantically, I used my legs to scoot backward in the chair, the legs screeching across the concrete floor of what looked like an oversized garage or maybe a small warehouse. There was a black van parked at one end where the roller door was shut. Another door sat across from me, but out of reach. Fluorescent lights threw a yellow tone over the empty space. Where the hell were we?

The three men laughed at me.

"What am I doing here?" Of course, the answer was clear... he'd found me, and now I was going to pay. That was what Alistair did. He was the devil.

Everything was coming at me too fast. My mind was having trouble comprehending how it resulted in being tied up here. And then my last memory of Alistair finding me in the town of Amarok came crashing through me.

"Little Moon."

"Alistair," I breathed, grief slicing through my body.

He'd found me.

I spun and whipped out of there, needing to return to Miyu's wedding and get help. But all I managed was to slam right into a chest so rock hard, I bounced backward, falling into Alistair who stood at my back.

His arm wrapped around my neck, pinning me in place, choking me.

"My little moon, did you think I wouldn't find you?" he whispered in my ear, his voice carrying a darkening threat, one I was all too familiar with. One I had hoped to never encounter again. I should have known that he wouldn't give up on me. I should have never stopped running.

"You'll regret touching me," I hissed, stiffening against him before driving an elbow right into his gut.

A sharp stab pierced the side of my neck, then the force of his arm around my neck slackened.

I stumbled away from him, clasping the side of the neck, unsure what he'd shot me with. He grasped a syringe in his hand, smiling at me, but all I could think about was escape. How I would never go back with him.

"What the fuck did you do to me?"

Rage flooded me, my mind filled with the memory of how easily I defeated the other men in the woods who attacked Daxon and me while in my animal form. My wolf was pouring out of me before I could stop her, adrenaline racing in my veins with the thought of ripping out Alistair's throat.

A growl tore past my throat, my body jerking from the transformation, bones snapping, white fur spilling across my body. The burning pain of the change sliced over my skin, but vanished as quickly as it came.

Falling to all fours, I stood before the monster as my wolf, my *dove gray dress shredded at my feet. I growled my threat, my upper lips peeling over sharp teeth.*

"Well hello there, pretty girl," he said, not amused in the slightest.

I prowled closer, lifting my head, holding his gaze, never backing away. I was no longer the meek girl he once knew.

But with the wave of adrenaline also came an unfamiliar sharp ache at the base of my skull. The world tilted around me, and I wobbled on my feet. My sight feathered at the edges, and then the sensation snowballed within me, taking me down so fast I stood no chance.

The last thing I heard before I blacked out was his maniacal laughter.

"We're rebalancing the universe," Alistair says, climbing to his feet and strolling across the room toward me. "Everything needs to go back to the way it was, Little Moon," he continued, glaring at me with his one eye, promising retribution if I so much as crossed him again.

My chest tightened and a dark heaviness settled deep inside me like it used to do every time he looked at me like I was dirt. But so much has happened since I ran from him. I'd found freedom and love; things that I would fight to the end for.

"You're wrong," I answered, and in that moment, the room spun around me from the shot they'd given me. Whatever they'd used had been strong. "Things are being restored to how they should be. I'm never going back to you."

He snarled. "You belong to me. You seem to have forgotten your place, and I'll be sure to remind you."

My stomach turned as he neared me and grabbed my chin, his fingers digging into the flesh of my cheek and neck. Hot tears pricked my eyes, and I hated how angry he made me, how quickly he left me feeling helpless.

"I have so much in store for you. Things I'll enjoy immensely." He raised his other hand and pulled back the eyepatch, revealing a huge gash still across his eyelid, not healed the way it should have. The eyeball was pale like it had washed out. It was creepy as hell, and I wondered why it hadn't healed yet. "Eye for an eye is where we'll begin," he growled. His grip was strong, forcing me to sit still as he closed in, his breath heavy on my face. "I've missed having someone to play with."

I swallowed the huge lump in my throat, fully aware he meant he missed torturing me. Sadistic asshole.

A disturbingly ugly look crossed his usually handsome face, and he released me, pushing my head backward in the process. He dusted his hand down his black shirt.

I was tired of letting him scare me, or backing away. I wouldn't go back to that girl who'd been scared of all the shadows around her. And I'd rather die than be his slave ever again. "I don't belong to you," I snapped. "You made that clear a long time ago."

The back of his hand swung out and clipped me across the side of my face, his knuckles against my cheekbone feeling like acid. I flung backward so hard, the force sent me falling in my chair. I hit the floor with a crack, my face on fire. I cried out from the agony, feeling like my skull might have split in half.

His shadow fell over me, and he fisted my hair then wrenched me back up, chair and all. I cried out from the pain scorching my scalp. My breaths surged past my lips rapidly, the room spinning. Something wet dripped down the side of my face, and red drops of blood splattered down onto my chest and legs. Only then did I realize I was completely naked. The bastard didn't even cover me after I'd turned back from my wolf form.

He'd abused me for so many years, and I let him do it, too scared to ever stand up to him. Now that same fear brought back memories of how my life used to be, how I was dead on the inside to survive such an existence. My pleas had no impact on this monster, not then and not now.

Alistair was in my face again, and he grabbed my shoulder, his fingers digging into my flesh, his nails piercing skin. "You little cunt. You let another man fucking bite you. Is that what you want? Are you desperate for a bite, Little Moon? Willing to spread your legs to anyone to get it?"

A deep embedded anger soared through me, and I sensed my wolf shoving to come out, to tear him apart, but with it came that spinning sensation in my head.

He struck me again, this time across my jaw, and I tasted blood instantly. I hated that I cried out and let him enjoy my weakness, but my vision blurred in and out and my head hurt so much.

"P-please," I ended up begging him. Unless I got a chance to transform, I desperately needed saving right now.

I peered over to the enforcer who watched me with no emotion on his face, then to the other meat-head watching with a smile, enjoying the show of me getting beaten.

They wanted to join him. I could see it on their faces.

My thoughts went to Miyu's wedding, to Daxon and Wilder offering me each their hands... They wanted me to choose one of them, but I opted to run. And now I regretted that moment with every thread of my being. I would make that choice over walking into Alistair a million times over. That thought played over and over in the back of my head.

Alistair stood tall, eyeing me. I was ashamed, but there was still something that flickered inside of me, that wanted to call out to him. Even after everything.

I pushed that feeling as far down as I could and used my

anger to burn the feeling to ash. "You'll regret ever touching me," I warned.

He didn't move at first, he just held my gaze, and unlike in the past, I didn't look away. I had no intention of being shoved aside by him again. I'd show him that I changed, that I would never bow for him again.

Shadows crowded across his face. "Is that so?" he snarled, then turned on his heel and strode across the room to behind the van. Moments later, he returned carrying a hessian sack.

"This is what happens when anyone betrays me," he hissed while sticking his hand into the bag and pulling something round out. It took me a few moments to work out what he held. But when he tossed it at me, and a severed head landed on my lap, the stench of death engulfing me, I shrieked.

I shook violently and shuffled backward in my chair, the head tumbling off me and onto the cement floor. It rolled and landed with her face in my direction.

"You will pay for your sins," Alistair promised. "Just like Nelly did for helping you."

I couldn't look away from her dead open eyes, from the horror imprinted on her expression from her final moments of death. She was the only person who was kind to me at Alistair's home, the only one who offered me the occasional advice, a smile. Things I held onto on days I wanted nothing more than for death to collect me in his dark embrace.

And now...

I lost all confidence, lost the strength I held onto, lost my mind. Her death ripped me apart. "No, this can't be..."

Alistair towered by my side and snatched my hair, yanking my head back. I was trembling and my mouth fell open with a silent scream as my voice disappeared. All I could feel was the pain of her death, the fact he'd killed her because of me.

That wasn't what I expected, nor what I wanted. "N-Nelly. H-how could you?"

"This is a lesson you'll never forget," Alistair snarled, like he was savaging me with each word. "Brand her now," he snapped to his enforcer. "You know, Little Moon, I wish you'd shown this side of yourself before instead of being a doormat. Maybe things would have been different between us." He winked at me sickeningly with his one good eye.

My heart shattered like glass, my body trembling uncontrollably, and I shut my eyes as tears raced down my cheeks. That time, my screams again found their escape.

2

DAXON

*I*t felt like I was encased in lead. As if my limbs weighed a hundred pounds, and I groaned when I tried to move.

I was...weak. Weaker than I'd ever felt before.

My stomach growled with hunger. I was so fucking starved.

My gaze flickered open. Everything around me became blurry...out of focus. A soft growl burst from my chest as I tried to move, and nothing happened.

My mouth was watering, my teeth extending as my hunger grew.

Blood. I needed it. Craved it. Was desperate for it.

"Easy, boss," a familiar voice warbled warily from somewhere nearby. I snapped my teeth and struggled to move towards the sound of the voice.

A face flashed briefly in my mind, and I stopped trying so fucking hard for a moment as I struggled to grasp who I'd just seen.

An angel. That's what she'd looked like. I willed the face

to appear again, but my hunger was all-encompassing, like I'd been starved for months.

"What do you need?" the voice asked again.

"Blood," I growled out. "Give it to me."

Listen to me. I sounded like a fucking vampire. What the fuck was wrong with me?

So hungry...

Footsteps moved away from me briefly, and I heard the sound of a door opening and closing.

"I can hear you breathing," I scoffed to the room. I may not have been able to move my head, but I was aware that at least one person was behind me, just out of sight.

"I'm going to kill you when I can move," I purred, like the psychopath I was.

"Fuck, alpha. Please, come back to us," another familiar voice begged.

I closed my eyes, the hunger pulsing at my throat so powerful I wanted to claw out my neck. I had a headache forming at the base of my skull.

That fucking perfect face flashed in my vision once again, and a hitched howl tore out my mouth like I was in mourning.

A door opened and footsteps returned. I opened my eyes and inhaled greedily when I saw a quivering hand outstretched in front of me holding a bloody steak.

"I have a blood bag too, Daxon," the first voice said before tossing the steak into my throbbing mouth. As the blood from the raw meat slipped down my throat, I sighed in relief. I tore into the steak as best I could with the guy's hand still holding it since I still couldn't fucking move.

I must have eaten at least five raw steaks before my hunger released enough for me to be able to focus more on my surroundings. I belatedly realized that I was lying on some sort of cold metal table.

Chains were attached to each of my limbs, and I quickly grasped they weren't just normal chains. Some fucker had put chains laced with silver on me. No wonder I felt like I'd had my soul sucked out of me. The silver was keeping me weak.

As things continued to come into focus, I saw who the man was standing in front of me. It was one of my betas, Carlos. He looked like he was going to piss his pants as he stared down at me. Which was appropriate, since he was going to pay for this.

Except right then the face appeared...and this time I knew who it belonged to.

Rune. I gasped as everything came pouring back. She'd been taken. My body arched in agony as I laid there. It felt like I'd forgotten how to breathe.

With strength I shouldn't have had, I pulled on my arm in desperation and a loud bang echoed around the room as the chain broke away from the table.

"The key, now!" I ordered Carlos, pulling on the chain attached to my right wrist even though I felt like I was going to pass out at any moment.

I heard the familiar click of a gun and my attention swung to my left where one of Wilder's idiot betas had a tranq gun cocked and loaded...and aimed at me.

Without hesitating, I grabbed the stool next to the table with my right hand and launched it at the guy's head. It hit him with a loud clunk right in the forehead, and then he collapsed onto the ground in a heap. Not sure he was going to recover from that one.

Whoops.

"I'm not going to repeat myself, Carlos. If you don't let me out now, it's only going to get worse for you," I threatened my beta once again.

Carlos's gaze swung to the stairs before he gulped and pulled a key out of his pocket. "You went feral, Daxon. Wilder made us lock you up. You were attacking the whole pack."

I stilled for a moment, trying to remember all of that. But all I could see was a red haze when I tried to think about anything after I'd found out that Rune was gone. I'd been standing at the edge of the road and then... Nope. Couldn't remember anything.

Carlos wizened up and unlocked the chain on my left hand that I'd just about pulled from the table, before getting to work on the chains on both of my legs. He steadfastly avoided looking at the body next to us.

As soon as the cuffs were off, I could feel the energy trickling back into my limbs. I rubbed at my wrists, hissing in pain at the red welts that adorned them thanks to the cuffs.

"Where's Wilder?" I demanded.

"He's already gone after Rune. He left as soon as..."

"As soon as what?" I asked absentmindedly, hopping off the table and grabbing the pile of clothes resting nearby.

"As soon as we got you under control," Carlos muttered.

It was right at that moment Wilder burst into the room. He came to a surprised halt when he saw me standing there, but he quickly recovered.

"Done trying to kill everyone?" he remarked.

My hand sharpened into a claw, and I licked the tip of one of my long nails where some dried blood lingered. "For now," I replied.

Wilder's eyes glittered with the desire to attack me, but

he held himself back. We were both ticking time bombs, our usual restraint decimated with the disappearance of Rune.

My mate.

Except I couldn't really say that, could I? Not since she'd rejected my mark.

I shook the thought off. She would be my mate. I was going to make sure of it.

"I thought you were already gone," I asked with a frown.

"I was, until I realized someone in this town is probably the best way to find out exactly where she's been taken," he responded, pulling out his phone and looking at a message on the screen.

"You think someone here gave her up?" It made sense. Although it was feasible that a message could have gotten out about Rune's whereabouts, the men who Wilder and I killed had seemed to know an awful lot about Rune's actions. I felt like a fool for not thinking of that before.

I certainly would have questioned them a bit harder before killing them.

"I don't even know where to begin," Wilder muttered warily, frowning at whatever message was on his phone.

"Let's just start hauling everyone in for questioning," I responded airily as I headed up the stairs.

"Daxon," Wilder barked. "You're covered in blood. You need to at least wash off before we start questioning people. They're already terrified of you."

"They're going to be even more terrified of me when I finish," I said through gritted teeth.

Wilder was in front of me in a flash, grabbing me by the neck and pulling me forward.

"Not a good idea right now, buddy," I warned, just itching for a fight.

Wilder's hands only tightened on me.

The urge to descend into that blissful numbness where I was guided by nothing but my hunger and bloodlust was strong.

I'd always prided myself on control. When my father would close the door and bring out his belt or whatever his punishment of choice was that day, I would never cry. I'd let myself cry that first time, and after that, never again. It had been the ultimate frustration for the monster who raised me that those tears never came.

"Boy," he singsonged as he sipped at his whiskey. My mother was comatose in her bedroom already. She'd been in the kitchen trying to make dinner when he'd walked in. She'd turned to greet him, as he expected, and he'd hit her so hard she'd fallen to the hard wooden floor. I'd stood there and watched, as I'd also been trained, while she struggled to hold her whimpers in. Because if I did anything to interfere, it would only be worse for her. One strike. One cry. And then she would be safe in her room for the rest of the night.

Then he'd turn his attention to me.

One turned into many if I tried to stop him. She was safer in that room. Or at least that's what I told myself when the guilt threatened to eat my insides alive.

I wondered what had set him off today? Or was it, in general, the strain of having to pretend to be a good guy all the time that turned him into this twisted monster behind closed doors? I was exhausted from pretending he was a good guy, from having to hear every day what an awesome man the alpha was when they all should have been plotting his demise.

"Should I finish making dinner, sir?" I asked, trying to keep my voice steady. He gave me a sickening grin, his teeth sharpening in anticipation as he eyed me. I'm sure plotting whatever sick, twisted games I would have to endure that night.

"Leave it, boy. I'm hungry for something else." He pounced

before I could take another breath. A few steps and then I was thrown head first down the stairs to where his torture chamber was.

My head hit the concrete wall at the bottom of the stairs and everything went black. Of course, that didn't fit with my father's plans. I woke up to a bucket of cold water soaking me, and I stared up at him blearily as the world swam around me.

"You're nothing," he snarled, snapping a horse whip against the ground next to my leg. I stayed perfectly still. If I didn't show fear, maybe, just maybe, he would go away. "You're weak. Not fit to ever be alpha. I could kill you, and no one would miss you."

The next strike lashed against my leg, splitting open my skin, and a sharp howl of pain slipped from my throat. I stared in shock at my leg, realizing that my father must have made some alterations to that whip, because I could clearly see my bone peeking from where my leg had just been sliced open.

A cruel laugh echoed around me. It was never going to end. This would be my life. Forever and ever.

He lifted the whip in the air, and this time I didn't even move as the whip sliced through the skin.

My soul fractured into pieces until all that was left was a demon who wasn't affected by pain...or anything else.

I came back to the present, and to Wilder staring at me in despair.

I was irrevocably messed up. My consciousness had been lost somewhere behind those closed doors, and I'd never bothered to get it back.

"Just go get cleaned up," Wilder asked desperately. "Don't make me choose between saving the pack from you, and finding Rune. I won't make the right choice."

I huffed, but even my inner psycho was desperate to find my girl. The bloodlust could wait. For now.

"I'll be back in thirty minutes. Get to work," I ordered.

Harsh sighs of relief came from the betas who had been watching the scene avidly. I didn't give them a second look and instead finished going up the staircase.

I was a little shocked at the literal chaos that could be seen everywhere. As an alpha, you had a responsibility to your pack. To protect them, to guide them, watch over them.

There should have been some feeling inside of me—guilt, self-loathing...anything—as I passed by the townspeople who were whimpering with fear at the sight of me. But I couldn't stir anything up. The only person who'd been able to make me feel for years and years was Rune. Without her, there was a void inside of me. A black hole that was intent on sucking up any latent emotion. I had a feeling that "feral" would be a tame word to describe what would become of me if Rune wasn't found. The Daxon I'd always showed to the world was getting torn apart by the minute.

I was easily capable of making the world burn. They'd only gotten a taste of it.

I strode out of the building and back towards town where my house was. The hunger was building again, and it was all I could do to keep it at bay. I couldn't afford to let loose right now.

When I got to the house, I frowned, sniffing something both familiar and unwelcome as I got to the door. Looking closely at the lock, I could see that it had been tampered with.

I opened the door and walked through, sniffing the air as I did so. Had she just been poking around...or was she still here?

I walked up the stairs, looking in each room as I passed. The smell grew stronger the closer to my bedroom I got. She was still here. And the bitch must have more of a death wish than I'd thought because even when we were together, I'd never let her in my private domain.

I stepped into the entryway of my bedroom, a dark smile slithering across my face.

Looks like I was about to get a little stress reducer after all.

Arcadia was strewn across my bed, completely naked, a come hither look on her face as she arched, thrusting her huge tits forward when she saw me standing there.

"Alpha," she purred, and I shivered...in disgust.

I stared at her clinically, a thousand memories flitting through my mind, all of them tempered by how she'd betrayed me. Except it no longer felt like a betrayal. It felt like a gift.

I knew what the rumor around town was. Part of my golden boy image was that I was the wronged man. The good guy who'd been betrayed by Arcadia, the town slut.

I'd been betrayed alright. But darkness called to darkness. I'd never been the good guy in the story.

But she'd always been the slut.

"What are you doing here, Arcadia?" I asked casually, thinking it was a pity that I was going to have to burn my bed now. Shipping a bed to this town was a bitch.

She turned over to her side, running her hand down the center of her tan skin, reeking of desperation. I scrunched up my nose, the smell sour and disgusting.

"We can be together now," she responded with a giggle.

My body stiffened, suspicion creeping up my spine. "And what exactly do you think has changed," I said in a soft, dangerous voice that she was too stupid to read into. I took a step towards her, my gaze locked on her features, looking for anything to confirm what I was thinking.

"That bitch is gone now," she beamed, with another giggle that was like nails running across a chalkboard.

Another step closer, and then another. I trailed one finger down the side of her face, and she leaned into me. Her pupils were blown out, a combination of lust and too much coke. They both distracted her from the fact that things were about to get very, very bad for her.

My psycho gave an eager laugh inside of me. "Did you get rid of her for me, darling?" I purred. "Did you make sure I could be with you?"

Relief flashed in her gaze and anger ripped through me.

"Yes. I slept with one of the enforcers her ex sent. I told him all about Rune. I did it for us." She gazed at me expectantly, like she was anticipating gratefulness and adoration.

My finger finished trailing down her face and then my hand was squeezing her neck. A cry choked out of her as she began to struggle against my grip, both hands coming up to claw at my hold. But her nails might as well have been little pin pricks for how little they hurt.

"What did you tell him, bitch?" I roared, tightening my grip. The scent of her fear permeated the room, thick and cloying...and delicious.

The sound of my back door crashing open put me on high alert, and I stood up straight, Arcadia's neck gripped tightly in my fist as footsteps raced up the stairs. Then Wilder was there, a wild look in his eyes as he took in the scene of me holding a struggling, naked Arcadia.

"What the fuck is wrong with you?" he roared as he raced towards me and tackled me to the ground, forcing me to momentarily let go of Arcadia. Her breaths came out in gasps as she struggled to get up as Wilder and I rolled across the floor, each trying to get the upper hand. I grunted when he caught me right in the nose, immediately breaking it.

Blood splashed across the both of us, and I clawed at his chest, tearing into his shirt and skin as he grunted.

Out of the corner of my eye I saw Arcadia struggling to crawl across the floor to the doorway. That wasn't going to happen. I threw Wilder off of me with a huff and then leapt at Arcadia, catching her by the ankle.

"So much for mate," Wilder said sarcastically as he leaned against the wall, rubbing across his already healing chest. "Out of sight and out of mind, right? And then you're back fucking trash?"

Arcadia let out a squeak of either indignation or fear, I wasn't sure which, and I threw back my head and laughed.

"She sold out Rune," I explained as I dragged Arcadia towards me. She whimpered as she tried to kick at me, but a second later I had her in front of me.

"Say that again?" Wilder demanded, the danger clear in his voice.

I picked Arcadia up and threw her back on the bed, grabbing some duct tape out of my drawer. You never knew where you might need to be prepared. Smiling grimly, I quickly taped her arms and legs to the bedpost until she was spread eagle across the bed.

On second thought, maybe that wasn't a good idea. I was seeing far too much of her now.

I snapped my nose back into place, shuddering in pleasure at the bite of pain, and then pulled my switchblade from my pocket.

"What do you want to lose first? Your big toe? An eye?" I asked her.

Before I could say anything, Wilder had her in his grip, shaking her so hard that I heard the vertebrae in her back snap.

"Where is she?" he growled as her eyes rolled back in

pain, and she passed out.

I sighed. Amateur.

I grabbed a cup of water and threw it in her face, over and over again until she was sputtering back to life.

"Where is she?" I roared.

"I just told him where to find her. That's it!" she wailed.

I grabbed her hand and sliced off her pointer finger.

Her scream rang through the air.

"Let's try this again. Where is she?"

She cried and stared pleadingly at Wilder. "You don't want to do this. You loved me." Her gaze turned towards me. "I was the mother of your child."

I saw red for a second, and when I came to, she was missing the rest of her hand and sobbing hysterically.

"The next words out of your mouth better be what I want or..." I raised my knife, and she screamed. "Chicago. He was going to take her back to Chicago. The Colder Pack."

"Finish her," I threw behind me as I strode towards the bathroom, concentrating on not shifting and tearing her to shreds. Chicago. We had to get to Chicago.

Silence permeated the room, and I turned around to see Wilder standing over Arcadia, his hands shaking as he looked down at her.

"I can't do it," he finally said with shaking hands. "I-I just can't." A myriad of emotions danced across his face. Hate, sadness, disgust...

"That's fine. I can," I said, before striding towards her, taking her neck, and snapping it. She flopped lifelessly to the bed.

I didn't bother to look at Wilder and see what he was thinking. Only one thing mattered right now.

I'd said before I would destroy the world if I didn't get Rune back.

I would also destroy anything and anyone.

3

I wanted to die.

I tucked my chin into my chest in despair. I wasn't sure I had it in me to go through having my wolf suppressed again. But she'd been forced deep within me, leaving me bare.

Tears poured down my cheeks, and each breath I sucked in had me shaking harder.

I no longer felt like myself. There was an emptiness where my wolf should have been. The energy, the sense of her warm fur against my insides had been torn from me. It was worse this time because now I knew what it was like to have her with me.

My shoulder blade burned like acid from where the enforcer had marked and cursed me once more, ripping away the one thing that made me whole.

My wolf.

"You don't deserve your wolf...especially not after what you did to me," Alistair growled.

I lifted my gaze to his scornful grin that told me exactly how much he enjoyed every moment of torturing me.

Panic flooded me, and the heavy boom of my heart seemed to make my entire body shudder, but nothing...nothing could fill the gaping hole in my soul from having the wolf suppressed a second time.

No, this couldn't be real. Please let this be a terrible nightmare. Not real. Not this again.

Alistair laughed at my agony and crouched down in front me before grabbing me by the throat. "Now, it's time for your little payback." He tapped the soft skin underneath my eye with the tip of his blade. "Do you have a preference on which one you want to lose? Left or right?"

"Fuck you!" I spat the words, my mind churning with fragments of the past, of everything I'd never have again. Every hair on my body stood on end and sweat snaked down my spine. I swallowed hard, fighting the terror swallowing me.

The harsh light from overhead burned into my eyes, my vision blurring with how viciously I trembled. My thoughts swung to Wilder, to Daxon, to how much I needed them, how they'd opened my eyes to a new world, to experiencing emotions I believed I never deserved.

They gave me what Alistair, my true fated mate, never had.

Love.

Alistair just took and took from me. He had from the moment we'd met.

A sudden, sharp piercing pain stung just beneath my left eye, and I flinched at the promised agony.

Shadows slid across Alistair's face, those darkened eyes sharpening, his tight lips spreading into a smile.

My mind bled with images of him gouging his blade into me, the pain, the blood, and how he'd break me to the point where no one could ever put me back together again.

Not Wilder.

Not Daxon.

And not me.

It seemed the men with the coldest hearts had the ability to destroy everything around them. Evil people who enjoyed torturing others didn't do it to just cause pain. No, they took pride in the agony they caused, then enjoyed blaming their victims. Serial killers collected something from their victims, but for Alistair, his bounty was in the adrenaline and high he got from keeping those he tortured close to him.

They were his trophies.

I hated him at that moment. Far more than I ever had before. No matter what he did to me, I vowed at that moment to never stop fighting. I refused to return to the girl I once was. With or without my wolf, I wouldn't bow down to him ever again.

When he pressed his blade harder, words trembled past my lips, "Moon Goddess, please."

"There is no goddess," he growled in my face. "At least not for you. Do you think someone as pathetic as you would be worthy enough?"

His hand tightened around my throat to the point where I could no longer draw breath.

My stomach clenched, every part of me tensing as I knew what was coming, and there was nothing I could do about it.

A figure strode into my vision from behind Alistair, and my first thoughts were that it was my savior, carving through the space to come for me. My strained heart soared for those few seconds, and I writhed to escape the monster's grasp.

"Alistair," the person stated in a deep voice I didn't recognize. And the realization hit me harder than I anticipated, cut through me like the blade edged inches from my eye. It wasn't Daxon or Wilder, or anyone else coming for me.

"Come back later," Alistair snarled, his nostrils flaring, his fingers squeezing my throat like he might snap it in half.

Lights danced in my vision while my lungs scorched, screaming for oxygen.

"It can't wait," the man continued, trepidation shaking his words because he knew as well as I. Upset the devil, and you'd feel his wrath. "The back of the mansion is on fire."

"What the fuck!" Alistair ripped his hand from my throat and spun to face the man.

I couldn't hear a thing they said as I frantically gulped for air, trying to fill my starved lungs, all the while my head spinning from almost being choked to death.

"Don't even try to go anywhere," Alistair commanded, looking at me, pointing his blade right in my direction. Then he and the man darted out of the oversized garage.

I gasped loudly, suddenly crying the tears I'd fought to hold back, the terror of what was coming for me ripping right through me.

I didn't waste the moment of freedom I'd been given because I knew how rare they were. I started to shuffle with the seat I remained tied to toward the garage roller door. It had to have a latch or button to open it. My gaze scanned the space for anything like a weapon to free myself from this damn chair, then my eyes landed on a screwdriver near the black van. That would have to do.

Struggling, I shuffled closer when the clap of fast footsteps came in behind me.

My stomach somersaulted, and I fought to twist my head, expecting the worst. Every inch of me trembled, even my throat.

When I did manage to finally look around and lift my head, it wasn't Alistair I saw.

It was my mother.

Dark hair bounced across her shoulders, panic twisting her expression.

My mouth might have fallen open at that moment as she was the last person I expected to see. After I'd been rejected by my fated mate, my mother had left, too disappointed in me, never wanting anything to do with me. Or so I'd been told.

So, what did she want? To help Alistair trample me for good?

"W-what do you want?" I asked, my voice bitter. The thing about mothers was that a real parent was someone who put their children ahead of themselves. Except my mother had given me to the devil, then turned her back on me. How could I ever forgive her for that?

Her pale eyes glinted like she'd been crying, which I struggled to believe were anything but crocodile tears.

"We don't have much time," she told me, and only then did I notice she was carrying a navy colored coat—or was it a dress?—over her arm. She rushed to my back and tugged at the ropes around my wrists.

"What's going on? Why are you helping me? What do you want?" My pulse thundered through my veins. If there was one thing I learned long ago was that trusting anyone from my past came with the danger of me ending up in worse shit than I'd started from.

"Oh, Rune," she sobbed, and for a moment, I almost believed her cries were real. "I don't have time to explain everything, but I was wrong to leave you with that monster. And now is the time you need to trust me, my sweet girl."

My head hurt trying to make sense of what she was

saying. Memories hovered at the edge of my mind of growing up with this woman who made me believe her, told me she loved me, read me bedtime stories, but in truth, I'd grown up in a house of lies.

"How can I ever trust you again when all I have from our past is evidence of why I shouldn't?"

"I don't blame you, and that's why I'm back." The ropes from my wrists fell away, and I got to my feet, rubbing at the rawness of my skin.

My mother stepped in front of me and handed me what turned out to be a loose fitting dress, a lopsided grin on her face. "Put it on, we need to leave now. I caused a small distraction, but it won't last long before they work out the fire was set on purpose."

I blinked at her then quickly dragged the dress over my head and let it fall down over my body, reaching my knees. It hung loosely around me, but I didn't care. "Why are you risking everything to help me?"

She'd taken my hand into hers and forced me to hurry toward the garage roller door. "Because I made so many mistakes. I let myself be swayed by the expectations of pack rules, I told myself it was fine as it was your destiny. That I couldn't do anything as your fated mate owned you. But no matter what I told myself, I couldn't sleep and the guilt was starting to destroy me. So, I'm here to do whatever I can to try and clean up my mistakes."

I wasn't sure how to respond at first, too scared to let myself believe her even as she tried to show me she'd changed. Yet even with her actions, I wouldn't permit myself to accept as truth. Not after she abandoned me to a monster. The pain and torture I'd been through should have made me go crazy by now, but I guess I was more of a fighter than I ever realized.

My voice remained quiet as my mind roared for the truth. I was trying to stay strong, but I couldn't prevent my heart from weeping silently at the words I'd waited so long to hear from my mother.

I winced at her touch on my bruised wrist, but I never stopped moving, and we soon reached the side of the roller doors.

She clasped the sides of my face, forcing me to face her, and I sensed the quiver in her hands. "I have a car and driver waiting for you outside. You will leave, but I have to go back before I raise suspicion."

She punched a pin code into the panel on the wall, and only then did I notice the blood on her knuckles, evidence of what she must have done to get that pin.

The rollers lifted up, opening, and bright sunlight filtered into the garage, chasing away all the shadows.

She spun toward me, fear etched across her expression, her eyes filled with tears. "This is your chance. Let me have this to make up for everything I should have done before."

"Hey, stop!" A gravelly male's voice boomed from the other end of the room.

We both spun around abruptly to one of Alistair's enforcers charging in toward us.

Cold seeped into the pits of my soul, and I grabbed my mother's arm and tugged her with me to escape.

But she pushed against me. "Go, I'll delay him," she said.

It felt like I was being torn in two, an ache burrowing so deep under my breastbone, I was convinced my heart might stop beating.

I refused to let go of her hand and dragged her past the rollers doors for our escape.

But she ripped her hand from mine and nudged me. "Go. I may not have been your real mother, but that didn't mean I shouldn't have protected you with everything I had."

My heart might have paused at that moment. "What do you mean?" Did I hear wrong?

She shoved me backward again, and I stumbled outside into the driveway, and out of the garage. The sun beating against me was like a hand on my shoulder, pulling me away from this vile place.

"I found you on my front doorstep, abandoned by someone when you were a baby, so I took you in as my own. I always loved you as a daughter."

A shadow fell behind her, and she swung around, drawing a knife from her belt that she drove into the man's gut.

She *wasn't* my real mother?

"Go," she bellowed.

My legs were moving before I could make any more sense of her admission. I darted along the long driveway, as far from the huge mansion as possible. He had homes dotted across the land, but I'd never been permitted to visit many of them. I'd been to this one though. A heavy stench of ash wafted in the air, and I saw a black plume of smoke curling up from the back of the house. My mouth curled up in a grin as I watched his beloved mansion burn.

My smiled dropped when I saw my mother fighting someone else in the garage. She vanished out of sight. I paused, everything in me screaming for me to go back and help her.

Her earlier words sang in my mind, and they called me back to her side. To help her, to make sure both of us escaped because Alistair would not take her betrayal well.

A hand touched my shoulder, and I whipped around with a scream in my throat. A man stood behind me in front of a yellow cab. "We need to go now! You're to leave immediately even if I have to put you in the trunk. I promised your mother."

He grabbed my arm and rushed me toward the cab, practically throwing me into the back seat.

The door slammed shut behind me, and he was in the driver's seat in seconds. My face was glued to the window, the whole world spinning from everything happening too fast. From discovering secrets that never should have been kept from me.

I couldn't stop the tears.

As we started to pull away from the curb, the last thing I saw was my mother thrown out into the driveway, a huge blade sticking out of her chest.

Even from here I could see her eyes staring lifelessly up at the sky.

She was dead.

Alistair stepped out after her, examining her still body, a blank look on his face.

I screamed and frantically pulled at the door handle, but it wouldn't open. "Let me out, let me out," I yelled, yanking on the door latch while desperately banging along the door for the lock in case I activated it.

"Sit back. We've got a long drive."

"Let me the fuck out now!" I screamed, pounding my fists into the window.

He didn't listen though. We sped up and raced down the road far from my past, and with it, I left behind yet another part of my soul.

I curled in on myself and cried heavily for losing my wolf, for losing the only woman I knew as a mother, and for being born in a world where everything tried to destroy me.

Soon after, I blinked open my sore and most likely puffy

eyes, and then glanced out the window to the forest we were passing. I kept thinking about the times my mother used to read stories to me at night, how much she'd enjoyed explaining the magic in Harry Potter to me, how back then I believed I was as special as she had made me feel.

Now, I didn't know what to think or feel, aside from feeling like my insides had been smashed into a million pieces, like shards of glass over and over, and the guilt coursing through me that she'd died saving me.

So much was starting to make sense now though, like why I wasn't pure blood enough for Alistair, and why she'd turned her back on me. She was too scared to admit the truth to Alistair that she'd given him a dud mate.

I let my mind wander, and I closed my eyes, wanting to escape reality. I must have fallen asleep because when the cab came to an abrupt stop and awakened me, it was night time outside.

"Where are we?" I asked the driver, staring out at a parking area that led to a huge bar situated on the side of the road.

"Your mother said to take you as far south as I would go, and this is it."

I swallowed hard and glanced up at The Midnight Rambler bar. "Do you have a phone I could use to call someone?"

"Sorry, look, my shift is over, and I have a long trip back home." He paused. "Unless you have some money?"

What an asshole. "No, I don't have anything."

I pushed the door open and climbed out. The cab driver took off instantly, leaving me all alone in the middle of who knows where. There weren't many stores or homes around here, and not many cars driving past for that matter.

Where the hell was I?

4

RUNE

*T*he inside of The Midnight Rambler smelled of perspiration, beer, and oddly enough...socks.

It had an old sailor feel as if I'd just walked on board a ship, and all the men were drinking away their sorrows, slumped over the bar or tables, grasping onto their beers like a lifeline. A few were chatting here and there, while overhead the speakers were pumping out Everybody Hurts by R.E.M.

Everything in here was depressing, including the music and dark brown walls covered in all sorts of sailing memorabilia. From plastic fish to fishing nets, and even a couple of life preservers. I started to worry that I'd walked in on someone's wake. But when no one paid me attention as I entered, I realized this might be a regular night for this place.

With my head low, I hurried across the sticky floorboards, to the women's bathroom at the other end of the room. I doubted they were used often enough to be as filthy looking as the rest of the bar.

I paused in front of the sink and looked up at my reflection in the cracked mirror. At my harrowed-looking eyes, my puffy eyelids, and how red-rimmed my irises appeared. I had bruising around my throat from Alistair's fingers. Blood streaked the side of my cheek from where he'd hit me and split open my lip. I belonged on a poster advocating against domestic violence, and there was no hiding how bad I looked.

All I had on me was this dress.

No money, phone, or ID.

I hoped Alistair's whole damn mansion burned to the ground with him in it. If I thought I hated him before, this was a very different level of hate, one where I seethed on the inside at the thought of him. If I got the chance, I would drive a blade right into his dead heart, and now I wished I had done that the first time around.

But all I could think about now was my mother...who really wasn't my birth-mom, so not only was I rejected by my fated mate, but by my real parents too.

Her last words filled my head, and in seconds I was back in the garage with her, staring at the heartfelt pain in her eyes. I wished I would have said more to her, told her I had forgiven her... I wasn't sure if I had, but if I had known she would die, I would have given her that closure.

Darkness gathered in my thoughts. They were destructive things, reminding me of everything I'd done wrong, all the things I'd lost, all the chaos in my life.

My fingers gripped the sink until my knuckles turned white. I couldn't get Mom's death out of my mind. The image played on a loop, and my heart raced.

Mom used to always say that fate had a twisted sense of humor, and she couldn't be more right.

A tear gathered at the corner of my eye before falling, followed by another and another, until I felt like I was nothing but pain. There was no room for any other emotion to exist.

I stumbled backward, my back hitting the tiled wall, and I sunk to my ass, my legs folding underneath me. I dropped my face into my hands and cried hard, my entire body shaking.

For the loss of the woman I knew as my mother.

For my suppressed wolf.

For the fear crowded in my chest, taking me to the point where I might pass out. My breaths drowned in cries, and I hugged my middle, eventually quieting down, knowing that I'd have to find a way to contact Daxon or Wilder. I didn't care which, but I didn't want to be alone for another minute.

A sudden blur brushed past me, and I expected someone to have entered the bathroom. I lifted my head and wiped my eyes with the pads of my fingertips.

A young girl, maybe in her mid teens, hovered in front of me. I say hovered because she was levitating off the floor. She wore a tattered dress, torn at the hem that fell to her knees in rough edges, and stained across her chest with something dark, like maybe blood. She had bare feet, dirty like she'd been running in mud.

I stilled, my pulse hammering through my veins, and my breaths raced as I stared at a ghost in front of me. What else could it be?

She glanced down at me and folded her arms across her chest. "Sometimes good things will fall apart so that better things can fall back together."

I blinked at her a couple of times, my mouth parted from the shock of seeing a spirit. This was a first for me.

"Are you talking to me?" I managed to find a response, which wasn't exactly enlightening after she just offered me insightful advice, albeit advice that I was pretty sure I'd heard on the Hallmark channel.

She threw her arms into the air. "Who else would I be talking to? The toilet? Do you know how long it's been since someone could see me? But it seems you're just as broken as me so that's no fun."

Her belly bowed as she leaned in closer to me, saying, "Not many ladies come to this establishment. Why are you crying in the dirty bathroom, wolf girl?"

My hands trembled as I pushed myself up to my feet, figuring as a ghost she must be a little all knowing and able to easily tell I'm a wolf shifter. "Are you haunting this bar?"

She laughed. "I've been here long before this was a bar. This was once a doctor's office to one of the most evil surgeons the land has ever seen." She peeled back the fabric of her dress over her shoulder and down to reveal half her breast. A vicious cut ran the length of her chest sideways and through her breast. It still looked open, the blood black, although obviously it no longer bled.

I continued to gape at her in astonishment, unable to do much else.

She shrugged and covered herself back up. "The scariest creatures on our planet are men. So if you're crying over a lover, forget him as he'll only destroy you. You should be planning your revenge for whoever hurt you, not crying."

She spun in the air, then paused in front of the mirror as if glancing at herself, except she had no reflection.

"What's your name?" I asked.

"Lillian Baker, but my friends used to call me Lil."

"Why can I see you?" I asked, well aware that if I'd been able to see ghosts before, I would have remembered.

She whipped around, and I reared back into the wall again from how fast she came at me. "Only you know the answer to that question, princess." And just like that, she disappeared into thin air before my eyes.

I stood there for a few moments, half expecting her to pop back into existence in front of me, but she never came. The idea that I hallucinated the whole thing played on my mind, but then so did her earlier words.

What if everything that happened to me did so for a greater purpose? For me to be put together as someone stronger, braver, better?

Wouldn't that be nice.

My teeth began to chatter like I was freezing to death, and my head hurt a little too much to make sense of ghost logic or whether I was really imagining things now.

I hurried to the toilet, then washed all the blood from my face. Feeling partially normal, I patted down my hair and looked into the mirror at myself, appearing less scared than when I first walked into the bathroom.

I squared my shoulders, knowing I couldn't hide in here forever. What I needed was to call my men to come get me.

Back in the bar, nothing had changed from the somber ambience I'd witnessed earlier. I strode over to the bar where two men perched on stools, cradling their beer. I stepped up toward the empty corner of the bar, and I dragged myself onto a stool. I lifted my hand to try and get the attention of the bartender drawing a long beer for a customer. It took a minute, but he finally glanced my way.

"What will you have, darling?" His voice was gravelly and carried a heavy energy about him like I should be wary. I guessed working in such a place did that to people.

"Could I use your phone, please?" I asked.

"Can't hear you, give me a moment, and I'll be right there," he answered loudly, yet not a single person looked my way. Are these people even awake?

I spun my stool to take in the rest of the room when I spotted Lillian floating in the middle of a table, half her body sticking out from the table. She was tapping the three men around her on the head, singing a song I didn't recognize. It reminded me a lot of Ring-Around-the-Rosie in the tune, but the words were different. How long has she been haunting this place? She must be bored to death. I smiled at my thought, seeing as she was already dead. I obviously had a lame sense of humor when I was traumatized.

When I continued my scan of the room, I noticed two young kids in the far corner seeming to play a game of hopscotch. None of the other guests were paying them any attention. They were wearing dated clothing that looked to be from the 1800s or something. More ghosts. How many ghosts were here exactly, and why could I see them?

"Now, what will you have, Miss?" The bartender's voice startled me, and I twisted around in my seat to face him.

Towering over me, the man was covered in tats, his long hair white and pulled back into a ponytail, looking every part a biker gang member. He had to be in his fifties, and had been in a lot of fights in his time judging by the scars on his brow and jawline.

"Can I please--"

"Don't beg, the guy will laugh in your face. He hates weaklings," Lillian whispered in my ear and then flopped down on the stool next to me.

I glanced at her, not sure what she expected me to say.

"Are you all good then?" the man asked and started to walk away.

"No, actually. I need to use your phone to call my boyfriend to come pick me up."

"Not too bad, but I doubt it'll work. You know he once

turned away a nun looking for shelter in the rain because she wouldn't buy anything?"

I cut her a quick look, and she was making a cross sign over her chest. "Cross my heart and hope to die." Then she cackled. "See what I did there?"

I held back from rolling my eyes, clear no one else could see her or they would have reacted by now.

"Buy something and I'll consider it," the man stated.

"Please, I don't--"

"Trust me, girl, don't beg."

I bit my tongue and tried to think of another way to phrase how fucking desperate I was to get help. Ultimately, if this fell through, I'd ask every man in this place, though I suspected that might not necessarily work in my favor, considering I'd just left a monster. Alistair's reach was far, and any of these people could be in his pocket.

"I'll make you a deal," I said. "You let me make one quick call, and then when my boyfriend arrives, we'll order lots of drinks and food."

"We don't serve food here," he barked back, the nerves in his temple twitching, his patience thinning. What was wrong with this man? Now I started to understand why this place resembled a mortuary. No one wanted to anger Hulk over here.

"Then we'll order drinks and even a round for everyone in the bar," I countered.

"Smart girl, that's going to get his interest," Lillian cooed, clapping as if proud of me.

The man didn't respond right away, but scrutinized me with his glare like I was somehow going to do wrong by him. Frustration billowed within me as I'd had enough of dealing with shitty people. The world was filled up enough with darkness and hatred.

Maybe I'd just had enough of being walked over by so many that I snapped back with a response, "It's just a phone call I'm asking for, not to sell me your firstborn child."

"Eeehhh. Wrong thing to say," Lillian whispered. "He's got trust issues and his wife of fifteen years tried to murder him while she cheated on him with his brother. He now hates women. I probably should have mentioned that."

"You think?" I hissed under my breath.

The man's face heated up, turning almost red. Hell, I'd hate to see what he'd be like if he got mad over something serious.

"Get the fuck out of my bar before I toss you out. Trust me, you don't want to test me."

The cruelty of his voice was like a whip against my flesh. And still no one in the bar so much as lifted their heads in our direction, making me think they might have all been drugged to make the bar appear busy.

"Get your ass moving," he barked, to which I fumbled to get off the seat.

"Oh, crap, get out of here," Lillian called out.

But the huge man was already storming around the counter, his arms clipped tight against his side, fire burning in his eyes with fury. He was coming right for me. He jerked an arm forward to grab my neck.

The movement made me panic. Echoes of the past thundered in my thoughts, and the instinct to cower took over. A tremor shuddered through my stomach.

I jutted an arm out to block him, to stop him. "Don't touch me."

His fingers barely brushed across my forearm, when I shot my arm straight out and from my palm flew a spark of white light, dust falling in its wake just like the kind that I'd leave behind from my pawprints while in my wolf form.

The currents struck the man dead straight in the solar plexus. The boom of his scream flooded the bar, seeming to even startle the zombie-patrons who twisted around and inspected the commotion.

He dropped to his knees, clutching his chest, his hand fisting the fabric.

It all happened so fast. I stood over him as he fell to his side, crying like a baby. Then in a heartbeat, he collapsed and didn't move.

"Shit!" I rushed over to his side and pressed two fingers to the side of his throat, finding his pulse beating fast and healthy. Okay, thank the Moon Goddess he wasn't dead.

Where once the silence was deafening, he suddenly gasped awake, and now only his hollers of pain filled the space. A couple of men from a nearby table approached him, one of them calling for an ambulance.

Frantically, I took this chance to run behind the counter and use the phone sitting up on the wall. No one was calling for my execution or coming at me with pitchforks, so I figured no one had seen me take down the goliath...only the aftermath.

The phone picked up on the third ring. "Yes," Wilder answered, his voice strained.

"Wilder, it's me, I need you to come pick me up, please." There's an edge of desperation in my tone.

"Rune, shit. Babe, where are you? Are you alright?" His panicked voice sped up. I could feel his tension through the phone line.

"I'm okay for now. Not sure of the location, but I'm in a bar called The Midnight Rambler. Please come quick."

"Don't go anywhere. Hide if you have to, but I'm coming now." The phone hung up.

I returned the phone to the cradle and turned to the

commotion in the room where they had the bartender sitting at a table now.

Lillian sat perched up on the bar counter, her legs crossed. She was studying me with a huge grin. "Oh, I see now." She tapped her chin, smiling at me. "You're not a normal wolf girl after all, are you?"

5

WILDER

I hadn't told Daxon that Rune had called me. He'd been torturing one of Alistair's informants that we'd come across in a town outside of Chicago. The town had been filled with pack enforcers, and he'd quickly gotten to work while I'd begun searching for specifics on Alistair's location.

Not telling him was an asshole move, especially since Daxon's version of torturing included killing almost everyone he came across, but I was desperate to get to her. Desperate to be alone with her.

Speed limits didn't exist as I raced towards the bar where she'd called from. A quick Google search told me it was a little over an hour away in the middle of nowhere. Or at least I was hoping that the bar I'd found was the same Midnight Rambler as the bar Rune was at.

Earlier in my drive, there had only been fields of wheat as far as the eye could see. I'd preferred that, being able to see for miles in each direction, to the woods that came after. The trees were so thick, it felt like someone could appear around the next curve at any moment and take me by surprise.

Driving this fast was just asking for disaster, but I didn't care. There was nothing that was going to keep me from Rune. Not even a car crash.

I hit the outskirts of a town that had seen better days. It was one of those places where you could blink and miss the entire thing if you weren't paying attention. I went on high alert, expecting to see more of Alistair's enforcers at any moment, scouring the streets for Rune. Daxon and I had underestimated just how many soldiers Alistair had at his disposal. It was amazing to me just how many idiots were willing to die for a megalomaniac.

There were only two streetlights in the whole town, and I'd started to become panicky when I didn't see the bar as I passed through the first one. I had just stopped at the second light, which never should have been red based on the lack of traffic in the place, when I saw it, off to my left.

The broken neon sign advertising The Midnight Rambler could have been the most beautiful thing I'd ever seen. My heart started going thirty million miles a second as I screeched to a stop and fled the car, not bothering to lock up behind me. The keys could have still been in the car for all I knew. I had one mission. One goal in life.

Rune.

I ran to the door and burst through, frantically looking around for any sign of Rune. The place was a true dive bar that looked better suited for some tourist trap beach town than the middle of Illinois. There was fish decor everywhere. And it was deathly quiet besides the soft strains of some old rock song playing from a hidden speaker.

I saw Rune then. She was seated in a chair, with no one around her. And it looked like she was talking to herself.

Looking around, it appeared that the few people in the bar were eying her warily...maybe because she looked crazy carrying on a conversation with herself.

Crazy or not, the moment I saw her it was like the stars exploded in the sky and the world was put back into place. That emptiness inside of me...it shriveled up and disappeared. It was like I could breathe again. Rune was the girl of my dreams, the girl of my existence. I couldn't ever lose her again.

A rough cry that sounded more like a dying animal bleating for help burst out of me as I threw myself across the room, desperate to feel her in my arms.

She froze for a second at my touch, the sharp acrid scent of fear momentarily filling my nostrils until she realized it was me. Rune immediately relaxed against me. She buried her face into my neck, with what I hoped were relieved sobs shaking her body as I held her as tightly as I could.

I wasn't sure it was possible to let her go ever again. Someone moved out of the corner of my eye and my teeth bared in a sharp growl, all of my protective instincts on high alert to protect what was mine.

Mate. The word beat into my skull, sliding into my veins until the word was pulsing in my heart...pulsing in my soul as a matter of fact. It was so unlike before, when I'd flinched away from the very thought of Rune as my mate. This time I welcomed the word with every fiber of my being.

Whoever had moved flinched away at my warning growl and I buried my face into her hair, taking a deep inhale of her...

Her scent was off. The warm caramel that had driven me mad for weeks was all but gone, cloaked in the sharp, heavy scent of what I recognized as magic. She'd had a similar scent when she'd first arrived in town, but I hadn't recognized it for what it was since it had been so long since I'd encountered magic. If you were to smell Rune right now, you would be hard-pressed to realize she was a wolf.

The fact that the scent was back meant...

Hatred shot through my gut, so thick and strong it invaded all of my senses. They'd done it again to her.

The tickle of her tears sliding down my neck brought me to the present. I would deal with him later. Alistair would die.

But right now I had my angel back in my arms.

I let myself absorb the feel of her soft body against mine. Even when I was crazy about Arcadia, it had never been like this. It had never felt so perfect, like her body was made to be my exact match, like I was holding something immeasurably precious in my arms.

She lifted her face up to look at me, and I hungrily devoured her features. There were bruises on her face and her eyes were red-rimmed and swollen, but I was pretty sure I'd never seen anything more glorious and beautiful in my entire life. Another scent hit me then. Need. It leaked out of her, dampening the scent of her magic and pain and making my dick take notice.

"You're here. You're really here," she whispered as she stared up at me. She pressed against me, a soft keen from her perfect mouth brushing against my skin. From somewhere nearby I heard someone groaning, the scent of her arousal obviously filling the room. It was so strong even humans would feel its effects. And I'd clocked as soon as I'd come in that none of the people in here were anything but humans.

It was hard to keep my head in the moment, her arousal was somehow getting stronger. All I wanted was to be inside of her, claiming her...making it so no one else could ever touch her or look at her.

I knew my thoughts were crazy, but something about having her in my arms after not being sure I'd ever seen her again, and the sweet scent of her arousal was doing something to my brain. Twisting it and manipulating it until I resembled more of a feral caveman than a man at this point.

Mine, mine, mine, my wolf growled. The urge to kill everyone in the room thrummed through me until I wasn't sure I could actually stop myself. I turned my head and once again bared my teeth like a crazy person, warning everyone away.

Rune moaned, rubbing herself against me like an animal in heat.

Fuck...was that what was happening? Was she in...

It couldn't be, not with her wolf suppressed.

My mind went fuzzy as another wave of arousal hit my senses. More moans echoed around the room. We had to get out of here. Every person in here was in real danger of dying if we didn't. My brain wasn't in control anymore.

Sweeping Rune into my arms, I walked out of the bar, shooting death glares at everyone in the bar, warning them off just in case they were getting any ideas.

It was easier to think outside. There was a light breeze blowing, and it took the edge off the all-encompassing lust we both seemed to experience. In the back of my mind, there was the thought that we should be talking about everything that had happened. We should be getting back to Amarok. Hell, I should be telling Daxon that I had her.

No, fuck that guy. Rune was mine.

Rune moaned again and the wisps of rational thought disappeared. I desperately searched for a place to go. There was a run down motel across the street. We could...

A door opened to one of the rooms and a fat, bald man sauntered out, sweat stains on the pits of his dirty wife beater. That was a no.

Another desperate keening sound assaulted my ears.

"Wilder," Rune moaned, as she pulled at my shirt, trying to climb me like a tree. Something I was more than willing for her to do. For a second I was tempted to tear her clothes off in the middle of the street, have her ride me right here so that everyone around would know she was mine.

I'd lost my mind. It was official.

Mine, mine, mine.

A strong breeze blew by, giving me a second of relief from the desperate need to tear Rune's clothes off.

We had to get out of here. Alistair and his men could be nearby.

I held my breath as I sprinted to the car, practically throwing Rune in and buckling her seat belt, even though I wanted to just keep her in my lap. I darted to the driver's side and leapt in, quickly starting the car and racing down the street, running right through the two red lights of the town. Both windows were down, and I had my head as far out the window as I could, trying to take deep gulps of air in an attempt to not run off the road.

A torrent of words that I'd never heard Rune say before were flowing out her lips as she begged me to fuck her, to fill her...fuck, I couldn't hold back any more.

We were out of the town limits and five miles beyond that into the thick forest when I pulled the car desperately off to the side of the road and unsnapped Rune's seatbelt with a growl.

I dragged her from her seat, as we began to devour each other. Frantically, I grabbed the lever to lean back my seat so I could fit her on top of me. I was a big ass motherfucker, and even with the seat pushed back there was hardly any room for me to maneuver Rune on top of me. Rune was panting, small cries bursting out of her beautiful fucking mouth as she tried to move against me, desperate for relief.

This wasn't going to work.

I jumped out of the car, pulling her with me as I hurried into the forest. This wasn't smart, my brain was blaring it at me as loud as it could how we needed to get as far away from that town, and Illinois in general, before Alistair caught up to us.

But the rest of me was more than happy to ignore the warning.

Once we were out of sight of the road, I practically threw Rune against a tree. I groaned as she arched against me, our tongues tangling. Her hands roamed over my chest, fumbling with the buttons of my shirt desperately.

"I'll take care of you, baby. Hold on," I promised her as she whimpered with desire. I'd never participated in a female wolf's heat before. I'd experienced the initial effects before with various pack members, but I'd always been able to keep my head and leave the room before I succumbed.

This was different. This was a cliff I had no choice but to jump off. And I was glad to do it.

She was hoisted up into my arms, her legs wrapped around me, her dress hiked up around her waist. Using the trunk of the tree behind her for balance, I slid my hands up her soft, smooth legs, finding the apex of her thighs. I hissed as I got further up; she was so wet, she had moisture dripping down the inside of her legs.

I was going to have a coronary at this rate. A brush of my fingers higher up, and I realized she was completely bare. Ordinarily, that would have been a turn-on, if not for the fact that she'd just escaped a kidnapping from her abusive ex.

A growl ripped from my throat as my mind immediately went to what could have happened for her to not have underthings on.

"Rune?" I gasped as she tried to pepper my face with kisses. Still using the tree to support her, I grabbed her face between my two hands, forcing her to look at me.

"Rune...did anything..." It was impossible for me to even finish the sentence. If I was a Bitten, I would have shifted already, ready to destroy the world. As it was, I could feel my wolf going crazy inside of me, and the urge to kill was so strong that I could taste it.

She stilled against me, understanding my question enough for her lust to dampen. "No. He didn't get a chance," she whispered, and my eyes closed, relief flooding through my body. Thank fuck.

"I can feel his hands all over me though. I can see clearly in my mind what he wanted, what he saw when he looked at me." She pulled me as close to her as she could, her lips whispering against mine as they moved. "Make me forget. Make it so all I can feel and see is you."

I stared down at this girl, this beautiful, perfect girl who I was crazy about.

Mine, mine, mine, my wolf growled again. And I agreed.

"Gladly," I growled against her lips, and her arousal sparked back to life.

We kissed as if our souls required it. I lost myself in the feel of her skin, the taste of her mouth, the sound of the soft whimpers she made. Suddenly, her arousal spiked, at least I thought it was her arousal.

Except when I opened my eyes, I saw that there were wisps of a silver mist-like substance streaming from her. I stared at her, flabbergasted. She must have been unaware of what was happening because her lips were still moving against mine.

Without warning, Rune went stock still, and her body bowed backward, a low growl emanating out of her. She gasped and the silver mist intensified. Her hair floated upwards, and her body began to vibrate gently against mine until everything abruptly stopped and she gasped.

Her eyes flickered open, and there her wolf was, staring out at me, so majestic and lovely that I felt the urge to bow in her presence.

A tear streamed from Rune's piercing blue eyes, and I had the inane urge to lick the drop of water off her face.

"She's back," Rune whispered in awe. "I can feel her again."

My heart leapt in my chest, a mix of awe and unease churning in my stomach. I'd never heard of anyone breaking that curse, let alone twice. And Rune's wolf wasn't just beautiful, she was powerful. Powerful in a way that felt ancient, life changing...dangerous.

It was becoming more and more obvious that Rune wasn't everything she seemed. Finding out she was a wolf had just been the beginning of Rune's mystery, that I was sure of.

What exactly was Rune?

Her scent hit me then. And this time it wasn't just her arousal I was smelling. It was like her regular scent had been amplified times a million. Combined with her arousal, it was more mouthwatering than I could comprehend. I'd thought she'd smelled good before. But this...I was losing my mind.

Again, that small voice in the back of my mind tried to alert me that something was off...there was something I needed to pay attention to, but it was practically impossible at this point for me to listen.

She looked at me, her pupils almost completely blacked out with hungry lust, a sight that I'm sure was reflected in my own gaze. A bleating whimper escaped her, and I moaned softly in response. "You're fucking gorgeous," I purred, my voice not even sounding like my own.

She tried to say my name, but it was lost against my mouth as I launched myself against her, kissing her lips, her chin, her cheek...nipping at her jaw. Rune moaned and rolled her hips forward, her hands resuming their quest to undo my shirt. I reached down between us and leaned away from her just enough so I could tease her clit, smiling as she gasped against my mouth. We were pressed too closely together for me to touch her the way I wanted...no, needed to.

My hands tightened on her hips, and I lowered her to the ground, the primal part of me loving the idea of having her while being surrounded by nature. It was a weird thought, but my wolf was firmly in control right now. He was beyond desperate for us to get inside of Rune, to own her, to mark her, to have her forever.

"Rune, tell me you want this. I need words," I forced out, knowing that I wouldn't be able to stop once I got inside of her. My wolf had overpowered me from the inside.

"Yes. Fuck. Yes," she all but screamed.

My brain shut off then, and I suddenly had to taste her. I moved down her body and pushed her dress up, not hesitating for another second. I groaned as I sucked and tasted her wetness on her inner thighs, spreading her legs apart so I could get to what I wanted.

"Fuck, Rune," I murmured before I licked her slit. A cry broke from her parted lips, and she slammed her head into the ground, squeezing her eyes closed as I lapped and teased at her clit with my tongue and teeth. Fuck, I'd never tasted anything so exquisite. She'd always tasted amazing before...but now. Now it felt like I was eating ambrosia, a nectar sent straight from the gods to capture and enthrall us all.

She bowed into my mouth, and I groaned as I licked and sucked, desperate to get her as crazy for me as I was for her right then. Her hands yanked on my hair desperately as she thrust herself against my face. All of a sudden, I felt her tense up, and I realized she'd sat up some. She reached down, and suddenly my shirt was ripped in half in what may have been the sexiest move I'd ever seen. Her hands tugged and grasped at my newly revealed skin. Full on claws suddenly tore into my skin and I just moaned, in danger of coming early from her show of aggression.

She abruptly bucked her body, sliding her legs down until they were around my torso. Rune flipped our bodies until I was the one on the ground, growling that she wanted to taste me. That was it, I was done. A lick of her hot mouth against my dick and I was finished, thick ropes of cum erupting out of me straight into her mouth.

Rune kept lapping at my aching cock, and I realized quickly that I was still hard. Rune smiled at me sensually like this was her lucky day, both of us not comprehending that something was off. She wrapped her fingers around my dick as her tongue licked at the top like it was a lollipop. It was official. I was going to die. I sucked in a deep breath of her scent, and the smell almost dragged me over the edge again.

"I have to get inside of you," I growled, my voice sounding choked even to me. Rune glanced up and gave me a wicked smile, her eyes still so blissed out there wasn't a strip of blue visible. "Come here," I ordered as I reached down and pulled her up until I could get at her lips once again. I rolled us back over, and her hand tightened on my cock. Fuck. This girl may have been mine, but it was obvious she owned me in every way.

Her dress was still on, but I was too impatient, too eager to get inside her. Instead, I shoved the thin dress further up her hips, before grabbing her hands off my dick and thrusting them above her head as I positioned myself at her entrance. I slammed into her without warning, inhuman growls echoing out of both of us. She wrapped her legs around me again and dug in her heels, somehow managing to get me even deeper inside of her.

But it wasn't enough. I needed to touch her. All of her. I let go of her hands, growling so she knew I wanted them to stay above her head. Reaching underneath her, I pushed her dress up, somehow maneuvering it off over her head, finally revealing her gorgeous breasts...the prettiest pair I'd ever seen. Cupping them with both hands, I took one rosy nipple into my mouth, swirling my tongue around it desperately. At the same time, I began to rut in and out of her, savoring every slide of my body against hers.

I lost myself in her. That was the only way to describe it. All that mattered was Rune. I couldn't feel the rocks digging into my knees as I moved. The sweat dripping down my spine only enhanced the moment. Her body, her soul, her everything. I wanted it all. I had never wanted to be a part of someone as much as I wanted to be a part of her. I wanted to drive her wild, fuck anyone else out of her mind until there was only room for me.

She moaned as our hips slapped together, the decadent, filthy sound echoing in the air around us. Her fingers dug into my shoulders as I slid my hands down her hips, reaching around to grab her ass and guide her movements so we could fuck harder.

"Come for me, baby. I want to feel that perfect pussy choke my cock," I begged in a gravelly, desperate voice. I was close, and there was no way she wasn't coming with me.

She gritted her teeth as she thrust her body against mine in a frantic rhythm. I took her nipple in my mouth, dragging my teeth against the hardened peak, trailing my hand around to her stomach and downward. My thumb found her clit and she gasped, moving even faster, as I began to fuck her even harder. All of my finesse was gone, I just needed to feel her climax, needed to bring her that release before I found my own. I abruptly bit down on her shoulder, my wolf having enough of this fucking nonsense of not claiming her.

Mine, mine, mine.

With my bite, she stiffened and cried out, her body shuddering like she'd just needed that little edge of pain in order to finally let go. She clenched me tightly, and with one final thrust, I reached my own climax, letting go of her shoulder as I did so. A tendril of blood slid down her shoulder, and I eagerly licked it off her skin until I was lapping softly at her bite. She let out a hiss, and I reluctantly moved away, but only so our lips could meet. We gasped against each other, just breathing each other in. I sucked in her soft breaths, still somehow desperate for her, even after two orgasms back to back.

I finally gathered Rune in my arms and moved us until I was leaning against the tree. She nestled against my chest. I could feel her heart racing, its beat matching my own. Her scent hit me again, and I felt myself immediately start to harden.

Again.

My eyes flew open. Yeah, I had good stamina, and was usually up for a few rounds. But it had literally been a minute since I orgasmed. I may have been supernatural, but I wasn't Superman.

Something was off. In heats it was common to come multiple times. The scent of your female could arouse you again and again...but there was still usually a bit of lag time.

Her scent was making me dizzy. Despite the fact that we were in the open air, with even a little bit of breeze. It permeated the air, thick and heavy. With every breath I took, desire pulsed through me.

I bucked against her, desperate to slide into her warm heat again...and then I heard the sound of a wolf howling in the distance. I ignored it the first time as I started to slide in and out of her once again with her in my lap.

And then more howls joined with the first. Their sounds, combined with a sharp bite of wind across my face, momentarily allowed me to think.

The strength of her scent, the overwhelming lust, the never-ending nature of it all... This wasn't a normal heat.

Fuck. We had to get out of here. Now. I slid out of her, a pained cry coming out of both of us. I set her down gently and grabbed my ruined shirt desperately. I rubbed it around in the dirt and then thrust it against my face, taking a deep breath of the earthy smell in an effort to block out Rune's scent.

It didn't work very well.

I scrambled into my discarded jeans and then grabbed Rune's dress, offering it to her.

"Slip this on, sweetheart," I told her soothingly as she tried to rub against me. She made no effort to move and I cursed as I gently pushed her away, holding my breath as I moved my shirt away from my face so I could slide her dress back on.

A growl echoed through the woods, followed by more. My blood ran cold. I recognized that sound. I'd heard it once before and I'd never forgotten it. They were hybrids. Hired guns sent out to capture and kill feral wolves. I knew from experience though that they hunted non-feral wolves as well. The hybrids were half-vampire/half-shifter. No one knew where they'd come from...since vampires couldn't reproduce. But they were terrifying motherfuckers, and if they'd caught Rune's new scent, which was impossible to miss, we were in deep shit. Guess I should have brought the psychopath with me after all.

Rune's scent hit me again, and I cried out in dismay and lust. There was another growl from closer by and the fear the sound brought reverberated down my spine and allowed me to grab my dirt covered shirt. I wrapped it around my face to help dim the scent. We had to get out of here. Now.

I scooped Rune up and sprinted back towards the road awkwardly, trying my best to keep my face away from her as she nuzzled against me.

If the hunters didn't kill us, Rune was going to kill me.

But honestly, what a way to go...

We got to the car, and Rune whined against me, breaking my heart and making my dick as hard as a rock. A growl sounded nearby again. Fuck.

I had to stop myself from being able to smell her.

I couldn't control myself, couldn't think. There was no way I could last in a car with her, even with the windows down. And it could cost us both our lives. Her scent after sex was so much stronger, so undeniable. It took a second, and then I felt like an idiot. This was going to hurt like a motherfucker. But it was the only way that I was going to be able to get rid of my sense of smell. Thank you, *Black Widow,* for the life advice I never knew I would need.

I threw Rune in the car, ignoring how badly my cock wanted her, and zipped over to the driver's side. Desperate, I smashed my nose against the steering wheel, effectively severing the nerve to my nose that allowed you to smell, while also sending the sound of the horn echoing into the forest.

"Fuck," I gasped through gritted teeth, the pain reverberating through my entire skull. All I could see were stars as the world spun around me. The pain felt like it was never-ending, but at least I couldn't smell anymore. It was a strange concept to have just given yourself a traumatic brain injury but still be able to think better than you had in hours. I shook my head, trying to clear my vision. The nerve would heal, I couldn't control my supernatural healing. And I'd have to repeat the process. That was going to suck.

Once my head was clear, and I could see well enough to operate my car, I threw the car into drive and sped down the road. Rune was now moaning next to me, her hands sliding down her body desperately, in a way that was both sexy and terrifying all at once. "Baby, I need you to snap out of it," I told her, hating myself and the whole world because she was basically writhing in pain. When a wolf was in heat, she needed constant attention.

Rune began to sob, wrapping her arms around herself tightly and staring at me as if I was breaking her heart.

It felt like hell. And worse, my nose was already starting to heal, meaning I'd have to throw my face against something soon.

My mind churned, wishing I'd paid more attention in Shifter Biology when they'd talked about a wolf's heat. I moved my hand to her forehead and hissed when I realized how hot she was.

"Fuck!" I hit the steering wheel in frustration as I looked in the rearview mirror and saw a truck approaching in the distance. It could have just been a random truck but my gut told me otherwise. The truck was going almost as fast as I was, and my car was pushing a hundred.

Rune abruptly tried to crawl into my lap, latching onto my jeans like she was possessed.

"Baby, please," I begged as I gently pushed her back into her seat.

Suddenly, it came to me. Pain was what was needed when wolves went out of their minds during a heat. And not like a slap on the ass either. They needed something to break through the mindless haze. It wouldn't make the heat go away. But it would push away some of the brain fog so she was at least somewhat aware of what was going on. And I desperately needed her to know what was going on.

My hand shook as I pulled my pocket knife out of my pants. I felt like throwing up. I wasn't sure if I could actually do this. The decision was made for me though when I saw that the truck was getting closer and closer to us, and I was going as fast as this car could go. Rune threw herself at me and I didn't let myself think. I stabbed her in the leg.

Her shocked cry reverberated through the car, inching down my spine and forcing me to dry heave in disgust with myself...all while driving the car a hundred miles an hour down the road.

This was hell.

I peeked over at Rune and saw her staring around in confusion. "What's going on?"

"Rune, sweetheart. What do you remember?" I asked. There was a faint flush to her cheeks, and she was shifting uncomfortably while holding her wounded leg, so I knew she was still feeling the effects of the heat. But for the first time, her eyes were clear, a strip of blue peeking out from beside the blown out black of her pupils.

Before she could say anything, we were rammed from behind. Our car flew forward, sliding all over the road before I somehow managed to steady the vehicle. I looked over at Rune to make sure she was alright. She was plastered against her seat, a look of terror all over her beautiful face. Her chest was rising and falling rapidly.

A ping all of a sudden hit the back windshield, shattering it into a million pieces of glass.

"Fuck," I growled as Rune screamed and I started to swerve the vehicle all over the road to make it harder to hit us. Another bullet hit the driver's side back window and it shattered as well, showering us with more glass. I opened the glove box and pulled out my gun as I pushed the car towards a hundred and ten miles per hour.

Please, Moon Goddess, I pleaded inwardly. *Help me save Rune.*

It was the first time I'd prayed in awhile.

Trying to keep at least one eye on the road, I aimed my Glock behind me and shot off a few rounds. The truck swerved to try and avoid the bullets. We would have gained a little bit if it weren't for the fact that I briefly lost control of the car and almost took us off the road.

"Baby, I need you to take this," I pleaded to her as I moved the car around a corner, not an easy feat at this speed.

A bullet went into the seat two inches above her head, and I swore and started to do evasive maneuvers across the road. Two more bullets went into Rune's seat, and I grabbed her with one hand, trying to push her down as low as possible.

I glanced over at the bullet holes in the seat, shocked to see that they were almost in a perfect line.

The fuckers were playing with us.

"Rune. Take this gun. I need you to shoot at the truck. I have to watch the road."

"I've never shot a gun," she cried as she took the gun with two hands, a wild look in her eyes.

"Baby, you can do this," I reassured her, even though it felt like my heart was going to beat out of my chest from the fear and adrenaline coursing through my body.

She steeled her features, a determined look in her eyes. Taking a deep breath, she peeked around the side of her seat and aimed the gun. "Okay. Just shoot at the truck. You can do this," she muttered to herself. And despite the shit show that we'd found ourselves in, a grin curled up my lips. She was fucking cute.

I realized belatedly she'd closed her eyes when the shot veered wide and hit a tree we were whizzing by rather than the truck.

"Okay, sweetheart, open your fucking eyes," I told her as gently as I could.

"Sorry," she squeaked, and then she gritted her teeth and started firing shot after shot at the truck.

Her aim was actually pretty good, and the truck had to start swerving to avoid her shots.

They fired again, hitting the seat on the other side of where Rune was peeking out, and she ducked down lower in the seat.

I knew from stories that the hunters were supposed to be expert shooters. It was almost like they were playing with us...or they wanted us alive.

Scratch *us*. It was like they wanted *Rune* alive.

This wasn't happening.

"Baby. You're going to take the wheel now, okay?"

"Okay," she said breathlessly, practically shoving the gun at me like it had burned her. She grabbed the wheel, leaning awkwardly over the middle console as she tried to keep the car on the road while I continued to push on the gas pedal. Like we'd learned already, there wasn't really a way for her to fit in front of me to drive.

They shot at us again, this time firing at the bumper. It was only a matter of time before they tired of whatever game they were trying to play and shot out a tire. I turned and fired over and over again as they tried to swerve out of the way.

"Yes," I hissed when I saw the driver of the truck rock back, and then the truck veered off the road as one of the other occupants of the vehicle leapt over him and tried to grab the wheel.

I shook my fist in the air as their truck ran straight into a tree, the sound of metal crunching viciously like music to my ear.

I turned back around and took the wheel back as we sped away.

"Rune, you did good, baby," I told her, as I squeezed her against me.

She was shivering, a mix of fear and adrenaline I was sure. And fuck...now that I was paying attention, I realized that the scent of her arousal was starting to become suffocating again, which meant that my nose had healed.

Son of a bitch.

"Take the wheel again," I asked her, and she looked up at me questioningly before grabbing it again.

I picked up the gun and smashed it against my nose

again, blood splattering everywhere as I let out a loud expletive.

Rune yelped in surprise as I took huge gulps of scent free air.

"Okay, I've got it," I said after a minute, while simultaneously grabbing my phone and dialing Daxon's number through watery eyes.

"A little busy here," he growled when he picked up, and Rune winced next to me when a man cried out in the background. I could only imagine what Daxon was doing to the guy.

"I found Rune," I told him.

There was a loud crash. "Where are you? I'm coming right now!"

"Just meet us at your cabin."

"You already have her? How long? You're a piece of shit, Wilder."

I couldn't help but grin even though my face felt like I'd been hit by a truck.

"Just meet us there," I told him.

"Get her here now." He cursed again. I heard a shot fired and assumed he'd finished off whoever he'd just been torturing.

"And Daxon. Be prepared."

"I'll kill every last one of those motherfuckers," he growled, assuming I was about to tell him something terrible had been done to Rune.

"She's in some sort of mega heat. I've had to literally break my fucking nose twice just to be able to drive."

There was a long silence. "Oh," he murmured, obviously shocked.

Rune chose to moan at that point, her heat building

again. The sound of a vehicle firing up came through the phone, and I knew Daxon was on his way already.

"And there's something else," I told him, dread snaking down my spine as I thought about what we'd just escaped.

"The hybrid hunters scented Rune. They're after us."

"Fuck," Daxon seethed.

Fuck indeed.

I hung up and sped off into the fading light as Rune let out another sound that was like sex incarnate.

It was going to be a long drive.

I was shaking in the seat, hugging my legs tightly. I couldn't stop myself from glancing back, convinced more hunters would appear at any moment and gun us down.

Combine that with the raging lust throbbing through my body, and I was a mess.

Wolf hunters actually existed.

Because life wasn't brutal enough, there were also hybrids out there, hunting down wolf shifters. Just when I thought life couldn't get harder...

I'd managed to bandage up the knife wound in my thigh with an old shirt Wilder had in the back seat, but it still stung badly. Thankfully, Wilder hadn't stabbed too deeply into my leg, but it had bled profusely. The seat I was in was covered. The wound diffused part of the arousal that had overtaken me... the shock and pain clearing the insane fog in my head almost instantly. But it wasn't permanent. I was already starting to heal. I could feel the desire deep in my body, curling, waiting for the chance to push forward. The intense heat in the pit of my belly refused to go away, and every time Wilder touched me, I was convinced I'd die if he didn't fuck me.

It was terrifying to feel so out of control, yet I couldn't stop myself.

Wilder looked over at me from the driver's seat with a serious expression. For a second, I had hoped what we just experienced was some kind of mad joke, maybe a hallucination. But of course, that was me just being foolish.

I needed a distraction from how my body was reacting just from looking at the gorgeous guy next to me in the driver's seat. He looked beautiful even with the blood splattered all over his face from where he'd smashed his nose.

An insane burst of lust flowed through me, and I took a deep breath, trying to center myself.

"How do hybrids even exist?" I swallowed hard, picturing in my mind what a half-wolf, half-vampire monster would actually look like, and trying to remain calm while doing so. What I wanted to do was scream and cry and let everything out because I was so fucking tired of bad things happening to me. It was killing me inside to have lost my mother...right after finding out she wasn't my real mom, and to have just escaped Alistair's grip. I wasn't sure I could deal with anything else.

The world passed us outside the car, and Wilder was silent as he pushed loose strands of hair behind my ear that had fallen in my face.

"I have no idea about their origin. I've tried to find out and failed every time."

"But now that they've picked up my scent, they're coming for me. Of course. Have you encountered them before? I'm guessing you have." I heard myself rambling, but I couldn't stop as anxiety knotted up in my shoulders.

"Rune, babe, calm down. Yeah, I've run across them before. But for now, I want you to take a deep breath."

Pieces of my life had been scattered...broken, and I had no idea how to begin bringing them together again.

I shook my head, not wanting this to be another hurdle for me to overcome. Fear was clawing at my chest, but that wasn't anything new. Fear had been my constant companion for years. I was so sick of it. Even with all the changes lately, I'd always been running for my life. Part of me had forgotten what calm felt like, forgotten the sensation of not always looking over my shoulder, and forgotten how to enjoy life without expecting the worst.

Wilder kept driving, sneaking looks at me ever so often, letting me know he was there for me. If it wasn't for him right now, I'd be a complete mess. So, to stop holding onto all the anxiety, I ended up telling him everything from the moment Alistair kidnapped me from town, to my mother, and even what went down in the bar. He didn't respond at first, which of course, worried me.

"I'm really broken, aren't I?"

"No. Don't say shit like that," he reassured me, his hold on my knee squeezing. "There's so much about you we don't understand, but we're going to find out." He paused, glancing at me quickly, and smiled, the look on his face softening. Then he asked, "Was there anything strange you felt before you struck that man with your power?"

"Honestly, the fear that he'd touch me. I'd just run from Alistair, and to have another man coming at me...it terrified me. Something just snapped inside, and next thing I knew, I'd somehow zapped him. I don't even know where it came from." A thought came to me then. "But I did notice that the power was the same color as the footprints I leave behind when I'm in my wolf form," I mused.

"Hmm. It makes sense, actually, as you're drawing on the same source of power from within you. We'll figure out what this means, I give you my word." His voice was firm, and I desperately wanted to believe him.

My mind was spiraling out of control, and I didn't want to talk about myself anymore, so I asked him, "Tell me more about these hybrid hunters. When did you encounter one?"

He didn't answer right away, but stared straight ahead at the road. "More times than I want to recall. Those bastards are relentless and see wolf shifters like us as the evil upon this world that needs eliminating."

"But they're half shifters, that thought process doesn't even make sense."

Wilder just shrugged, obviously in agreement with me.

"It seems dumb to even say it, but I didn't even believe in vampires until now." That part still swirled in my mind. I told myself if wolf shifters existed, then of course other supernaturals would, but for some reason it still felt shocking.

Wilder overtook someone in the lane ahead of us, then began talking. "There was one time I couldn't forget if I wanted to. I'd been traveling out of town with two other pack members, going to rescue a female wolf shifter on the run from another pack wanting her as their broodmare."

I swallowed the thickness in my throat, honestly detesting the ugliness in this world; how females were treated as nothing was revolting. I could almost hear the screams of the women Alistair used to bring to his mansion, the haunting sound of their pain, his cruelty seeing no end.

"The girl rang for help through another pack, who contacted me about her situation. But I was younger and dumber then, going out there without backup aside from the two men with me...without taking a closer look at the situation."

"And, what happened?" I asked, hanging on every word he said.

A painful growl rolled over his throat before he responded. "We arrived, and the girl was strung from a tree by her ankles, her throat slashed. They bled her to death. She was never meant to be saved. They used the poor girl as bait to draw out more wolves. The contact at the other pack had done a deal with the hunters... To save his pack, he needed to lure out other werewolves. And the suckers of course were me and my two men. We were ambushed. My men ended up brutally killed, and I barely escaped, bloodied with broken bones." He pulled back his ear where a healed scar ran from within his hairline to the base of his ear.

I thought I knew every inch of him by now, evidently I'd missed a few spots.

"The only reason I didn't die that day was due to the kindness of a human driving past as I was stumbling along the freeway. He took me away from the hunters."

I gasped, imagining it all.

"I learned my lesson, and the next time I crossed paths with them, I repaid the favor, taking a couple of them out." The tone of his voice grew darker, and I could tell the topic touched a nerve. His knuckles were white with how hard he was gripping the steering wheel too.

"That's terrifying." I didn't recall Alistair ever mentioning these hunters, but of course I wasn't privy to all his conversations either.

We fell quiet after that and the silence was deafening. Was that my fate too, just like that poor wolf girl? Here I thought there couldn't be anyone crueler than Alistair. I needed a vacation before I went crazy, even if it was just for a short time.

"How safe are we in Amarok from them?"

"We've never been breached by hunters, so we're all safe for now. But I'll increase the guards the moment we arrive back." He'd fallen serious, and it was like I could almost hear the thoughts ticking in his mind as he went over everything he needed to get done.

The more I sensed his stress, the more my heart sped up, harsh breaths beating in and out of my lungs. While my panic actually helped with the lust, pushing it out of the forefront of my mind didn't aid me in feeling calm when I saw the burden Wilder carried.

I reached over and placed a hand on his strong forearm, needing him to know that I was there for him as much as he was for me. "We'll sort out all this crap together."

"You're so damn beautiful, inside and out." When he glanced my way, a smile curled his lips, and he leaned over to kiss the back of my hand. "Maybe try to sleep, gorgeous. We've got a bit of a drive."

I nodded and pressed my back into my seat, then turned to the window where storm clouds gathered overhead, stealing the moonlight. My heartrate refused to calm down. All I could think about was returning to town and feeling a sense of normalcy, a sense of being home. It's strange how the place I had stumbled across was more my home than the house where I'd grown up...even with the terrible reception I'd been given from most of the townspeople.

I must have fallen asleep because when I opened my eyes, we were driving into Amarok. Night cloaked the land, and excitement built in my stomach thinking about seeing the town again. There had been a few moments when I was with Alistair, where I'd believed I'd never set eyes on the place. I was actually smiling just thinking about seeing everything again.

We followed the curve of the road toward Daxon's house, and I tensed, waiting for Wilder to say something about dropping me off with Daxon. He never said a word though, just watched me with serious eyes.

A low keen sprang from my throat as desire threatened to overtake me. Looking down at my leg, I could see that it was almost healed. I'd probably lose my mind soon.

"I would give you the world if you asked for it," Wilder said suddenly as Daxon's house came into view. There was a strain to his words, an almost painful heartache. His point was made, and as much as I wanted to lean over and kiss him, I wouldn't risk losing control. He must have understood as he never tried to kiss me farewell either before we reached Daxon's place.

"You and Daxon...you're becoming everything to me." I didn't push it any further, as I was aware that this was a touchy topic for both of them. I'd seen the fights between them, and still recalled the way they both stared at me during Miyu's wedding, imploring me to choose one of them.

That was like asking me to tear my heart in half, then choose which part to keep.

The weight of such a decision would crush my soul.

Wilder parked outside Daxon's wooden cabin, the motor of the car still running. The lights were on inside, and I could see a figure moving behind the curtains. Daxon was home. My desire increased at the thought of seeing him in just a minute.

"If you want me to come and get you anytime, use his phone and call me. I'll come immediately." Wilder sounded anxious, like he was hoping I would tell him I wanted to leave right now.

"I know." Unbuckling my seat belt, I leaned over and pressed my forehead against his, trying to restrain myself from jumping him.

"I thought I was never going to see you again," he whispered hoarsely.

"Me too," I replied.

There was something almost shattering about the fact that he wasn't coming in with me. But I knew what would happen as soon as I stepped foot into Daxon's cabin, and I knew none of us were even close to being okay with that becoming a group activity.

"Okay, you better go." He smirked, trying to lighten the mood, and Moon Goddess, he was captivating.

A bright light beamed outside the house from the outdoor lights being switched on. I looked out and found Daxon standing in the doorway, holding the door wide open. Even in the dim lighting, I could see the shadows beneath his eyes, and in his gaze itself, I saw his heart-wrenching ache at seeing me. He needed me as much as I did him.

I climbed out of the car and blew a kiss to Wilder, then I partly limped to Daxon who ushered me inside, before shutting the door behind us.

He sniffed the air instantly and groaned, his jaw clenching at the sight of me.

"Daxon, you need to know something." The words slipped from my lips, and a rambling rush of explanations followed about my scent, about losing control, about the blade wound in my leg, and why Wilder stabbed me.

A snarl ripped from Daxon's throat, a raw, primal sound

that rumbled through his powerful chest. I had no idea if he even understood what I had just told him.

But hearing his animalistic side did something to me. It flicked on a switch that made me forget everything but him. He came at me, and I couldn't move, wouldn't move. I wanted everything those eyes promised.

"No taking it slowly. I hurt thinking I'd lost you. And now, I want you hard and my way," he growled. One hand moves to the back of my head, fisting my hair, tilting it back, the other on a breast, squeezing, burning me alive with need.

His mouth was on my neck, licking me in long strokes, and my lustful flood gates I'd fought to keep shut burst wide open.

"Fuck, I missed your smell. Your taste. Those adorable sounds you make when you're so turned on, you lose all control. I want it all."

My pulse hammered in my ears, my entire body tingling with the growing arousal from his words, from the way he started to claim me like we were animals in pure heat...which I guess we were.

I murmured words that made little sense in my head between gasping breaths. He released me just as quick, and his hard grip on my arm tugged me to spin on my heels and face away from him.

"I was so fucking worried. I was going insane."

I gasped at being under the control of this powerful, gorgeous man. And I fought the hunger that consumed me, made me lose my mind, but it slipped through my fingers like sand.

I'd always thought that the kind of man I wanted would be tender and soft, but I couldn't be more wrong. When I was near Daxon and Wilder, I lost all control and craved to be dominated by them. To have them spank me, fuck me, make me ache for so much more. What we had between us was animalistic and dirty. And I loved it.

He shoved me forward, pinning me against the wall, and tore at my dress, ripping it off my body. It fell away in shredded pieces. I stood naked, trembling with unbearable need.

Everything about the way he treated me, the way he tore the clothes off my body was rough, manly, and I shivered all over, drowning in desire.

"Daxon," I begged.

The sound of his zipper and the smack of clothes on the floor followed. Burning heat pressed against me as he came up behind me. What felt like a charge of electricity raced up directly between my legs, his simple touch causing such a deep ache, that I quietly moaned at how much I needed him... needed this.

"I'm going to mark you, make you mine, eliminate the scent I'm picking up on you for good. Trust me, baby. I'm going to fuck you so good."

I wholeheartedly trusted him, and I embraced everything he offered me.

His breaths washed over my ear and cheek.

My heartbeat pulsed hungrily against my ribcage. When his hand found the heat between my thighs, his touch unceremoniously forceful, he slid his touch along the liquid fire he stirred. I drew in sharp, short breaths, my hands plastered to the wall to hold myself still.

I shivered at how eagerly he took what he wanted, and I spread my legs wider for him. He pushed a finger into me, then a second one. I moaned, my insides throbbing with each rapid heartbeat.

The faster he pumped into me, the more I whimpered,

my hips responding with their own rhythm. Everything about Daxon had my body alert, reacting, starving for more.

"Is this what you've been wanting?" he growled in my ear, his lips brushing against my neck.

My cries escalated with how fast he pushed me to the edge, teasing me, pulling me to a place of no return.

He withdrew his fingers, and I was the one growling in protest this time. A snarl purred from my throat, and I had to have him at any cost.

Powerful hands grabbed me by the waist and swiveled me around to face him.

His muscles clenched as he stood in front of me and took in all my nakedness, devouring me with his eyes. Even the way he licked his lips left me shivering, the pulse between my thighs throbbing. Then there was the matter of his heavy cock, so big, wet at the tip, ready to stake its claim.

Fuck, he was really hard.

Daxon roared as he dragged me against him and our mouths crashed. My hands fell against the hard plane of his chest, my breaths lost somewhere along the way. All I felt was his touch all over my body, and the feel of his hardness pressed against my lower stomach. We kissed like long-lost lovers, like we believed we'd never find one another again. I wrapped my arms around his neck, pulling him closer, needing him before I burst from heat.

Strong hands fell to my waist and gripped me. In the blink of an eye, I was off my feet. I curled my legs around him as his tongue plunged into my mouth, his hands cupping my ass, squeezing it. My back kissed the wall, and he pressed against me, our bodies crushed together. We both moaned loudly while I completely drowned in his kiss. I forgot everything else, all my worries.

Adjusting his hips, the tip of his erection slid along my

slit. I moaned the moment he pushed into me, my body on fire. I panted the deeper he plunged, holding me against the wall, and taking, taking, taking.

I cried out with how incredible it felt, how much I loved the pain and pleasure he ignited within me.

His eyes never left mine, and I stared at this man, at the fierceness in his pale, hazel eyes, at his chiseled jaw. At the way he claimed me completely.

I grasped onto his strong, round shoulders, my body shuddering as he partially pulled out of me, then slammed back in. Once he found his rhythm, he pressed both hands to the wall over my shoulders.

"Hold on," he ordered. "I'm going to fuck you so good that your mark will stick. You will accept me."

I nodded and clung to him, while he fucked me, his hips pumping rapidly.

He roared once more, the sound of it rippling through me. He was so tight, his muscles tense, completely rock hard inside me.

"I've thought of nothing but fucking you since I found out you were safe."

I moaned louder, barely able to breathe, let alone find my voice. I curved my hips each time he came into me. His deep growls were intoxicating.

Arousal escalated like a waterfall, crashing unrelentlessly, and I stood no chance to hold it back.

He took me faster, and his arms looped around me that time. He groaned, both of us tense and so very close.

The world blurred at the edges when my orgasm hit me suddenly and came out of nowhere, so hard that I convulsed, screaming.

My reaction had Daxon growling, his body just as tense, and the moment he lost himself to his own explosion, his mouth latched onto the curve of my neck and good shoulder. Sharp teeth cut into flesh.

Pain burst across my shoulder, while I screamed his name, my body shattering for him. I spasmed, completely coming undone, while he throbbed inside me, filling me.

I couldn't even remember how long we lost ourselves in the orgasms, but when we finally came back down to earth, our bodies were tangled and sweating. He lifted his head from my shoulder while licking a drop of blood from his lip. My blood. He then cupped my face and kissed me fiercely.

"You're the world to me. I worship the ground you walk on. I love you," he said while kissing my whole face.

I smiled, exhausted, and draped against him while my heart beat faster. Hearing those words would never get old, and I melted on the inside every time he said it. It was everything I'd ever wanted.

Daxon and Wilder were mine. I never wanted to let them go.

Daxon held me up against the wall, no sign of weariness at holding this same position for so long. "I'm not ready to finish this or go back out into the real world. I'm just not finished with you."

I blinked at him, struggling to think as desire pressed into me. "I want more of you, now."

Our kisses grew deeper, harder, and I was more than ready for another round when he suddenly pulled back, shaking his head.

"Daxon," I moaned desperately. His gaze fell to my bandaged thigh.

He withdrew from me, and with his strong hands on my hips, he set me onto my feet. The ground felt unstable at first, but I found my footing. I stepped toward him, feeling like someone had cut me in half to be so far from him.

He was shaking his head again. "Something's off. Wilder told me. You did too." And he turned away from me, returning moments later with a lighter.

But I was already by his side, my hand on his hard cock. "Please, Daxon, it hurts to not be close to you."

He hesitated, holding my stare.

A sudden burn sliced across my arm, sharp and painful. I flinched, practically jumping from Daxon. He stood there, lighter in hand, the flame flickering.

"I'm so sorry, sweetheart." I blew on my arm where the burn mark was red and hurt like a bitch. "We need to be more careful from now on."

Daxon hissed, and I looked up to see the flame against his forearm. He gritted his teeth, letting it burn slightly longer before he paused. His eyes shut and he groaned deeply in his chest, like the pain was utterly unbearable.

I swayed on my feet, staring at him, the pain from the burn feeling like a heartbeat, thumping, distracting me from the desire deep inside me.

Finally, he opened his eyes and asked, "Do you feel my mark?"

Remembering his earlier words about marking me, just as Wilder had tried, I shook my head. I felt nothing, aside from the sexual hunger beneath the burning ache on my arm...But nothing else. No response from my wolf, and no marking bond between us.

Reading the response on my face, his reaction was instant, his body against mine stiffening.

"I don't understand how it didn't take? I can feel the bonding from my wolf."

It felt like someone had just taken a dagger and jammed it right through my heart to see the way his expression crumbled before me. I was shaking, and I hugged myself, feeling completely ruined that each time they tried, nothing happened from my end.

I blinked away tears, hating how a few short words bruised a perfect reunion. "Why can't we just stay as we are? Can't you see what's really going on here? I'm broken."

My chest heaved for breath, and it hurt to stand there feeling vulnerable while pain etched across his perfect face.

"That's not acceptable," he told me, hurt underlining his voice. "We'll find a way, even if I have to try for eternity, I will find a way to bond us just as we are meant to be."

I couldn't find my words, didn't know what to say, so I grabbed my discarded clothes and quickly dressed. I turned for the door, but Daxon grabbed my arm.

"You're not running away." He collected me into his arms. "No more running. We're going to work this out together."

I couldn't stop the tears this time, and I softened against him where he held me as I cried for so many wrongs that ruined too many things in my life.

Desire eventually overtook us both, and as our bodies once again moved together, I made a thousand wishes that somehow this wouldn't be taken from me too.

a loud knock stirred me from a deep sleep. I looked around in a daze, realizing that Daxon and I were on a large fur rug in front of the fireplace, both of us still naked. Flashes of the night before played through my mind.

There had been so much sex.

Thank goodness that my supernatural healing had kicked in with the breaking of the curse, because there was no way my vagina could have survived otherwise. As it was, I was sore.

My breath hitched when I realized that the heat had broken. I could truly think clearly again. Even though Daxon looked like Zeus come to life stretched out next to me, his body so perfect it looked photoshopped, I didn't have the overwhelming urge to jump him.

Progress.

The pounding on the door resumed. I stood up, looking for a blanket or something to throw over me. Daxon's torn shirt was all I could find. It had gotten ruined at some point and I threw it over me. Luckily, the tear was in the back, so I was mostly covered.

I walked to the door and looked through the peephole, breathing a sigh of relief when I saw that it was Wilder looking grumpy and utterly fuckable.

And that wasn't residual desire from the heat talking. Wilder just looked that good.

I threw the door open, scrambling sounding from behind me as Daxon staggered up, still half asleep.

"Rune, don't open the door without me," he drowsily said until he realized that Wilder was here. "Oh, it's you."

Wilder's gaze flickered dangerously as he stared at Daxon, who was still naked. Daxon, of course, stood there proudly. He slipped his arm around me, pulling me close and making no move to cover up. A growl that was more of a sexy purr slipped out as he nuzzled my shoulder.

Wilder stiffened, his eyes tracing where the faint outline of his bite could be seen. He sniffed the air and shame churned in my chest when I realized that he was trying to smell himself on me, to see if the mark had bonded.

"Come on in," I told him with a fake, bright smile, trying desperately to distract him.

I could smell his complete disappointment as it saturated the air.

What the hell was wrong with me?

Daxon pulled me against him possessively. "Maybe come back in a couple of hours, bro," he told Wilder.

"Fuck you," Wilder rebuffed as he pushed past us.

I flinched when I realized what he was walking into. The whole place reeked of sex, and things had gotten a little messy the night before. Furniture had somehow been destroyed. It was a miracle the place was still standing. I knew they were both aware I was "dating" each of them, but there was definitely something cringy feeling about knowing Wilder was seeing the aftermath of Daxon and I's night firsthand.

I squeezed Daxon's arm soothingly before I hurried after Wilder, trying to pick stuff up as I did so. This wasn't quite the morning after I'd pictured, but I couldn't deny that something inside of me was soothed having them both here with me. Making love with each of them was incredible, life-changing...out of this world. But there was still something missing when it was only one of them.

I was a terrible fucking person.

It was probably why neither of their mate marks had worked. Because I didn't deserve them.

"Rune, sweetheart, it's alright," Wilder said exasperatedly as I accidentally mooned everyone in the room by bending over to pick up a lamp.

An embarrassed giggle burst out of me as I tried to cover my ass, and then all of us were laughing, the awkward feeling in the air somewhat dissipating. Apparently, a good old-fashioned mooning wasn't out of style.

"Some of your clothes are in my closet," Daxon murmured as he passed me and walked towards the kitchen.

"You have some of my clothes?" I asked, confused. I definitely hadn't remembered bringing any clothes over. I was too much of a scaredy-cat to have gotten to the point where I'd asked for a drawer before I was kidnapped.

"Why wouldn't I?" Daxon asked with a smirk.

I opened my mouth, and then closed it. "Are you admitting that you broke into my room, took my clothes, and put them in your house?" I finally asked, not sure why the thought was turning me on so much. I didn't have very many clothes to begin with, so I should have been demanding he return them immediately. And I should be creeped out, right? I should definitely be creeped out.

Down, vagina.

"I was just preparing for the inevitable, babe," he said with a wink before striding past me cockily. I tried to keep my gaze from staring at his ass.

But I failed, big time.

Wilder snorted from somewhere nearby as Daxon reached down to grab the jeans he'd been wearing yesterday and slid them on. I stood there looking between Daxon and Wilder, back and forth...definitely looking like an idiot. I finally scampered away to the privacy of Daxon's bedroom, their soft chuckles following me the whole way. A shower was definitely in order to wash off the scent of sex that drenched my skin.

I started the shower and slipped off the tee, grimacing as I saw my reflection in the mirror. I was a mess. There were hickeys all over me. And some scratches too. My hair looked like a bird had made a home in it, and I had huge circles under my eyes. I traced where I had been branded again. The skin was silky smooth, like nothing had happened. I could still feel the phantom pain of the brand though when I thought about it.

How had the curse been broken again? How was that possible?

I belatedly realized that steam was filling the bathroom, meaning I'd been staring at myself for quite some time. I hurried and got in, moaning a bit as the warm water beat down on my shoulders. It felt like I'd stepped into heaven. The shower at the motel was clean, but it definitely wasn't luxurious by any means. Daxon's shower, however, was the thing shower dreams were made of. It had a waterfall feature and then two other spouts on the wall. You could press a button and seal the top as well, making it a steam shower. I leaned against the tiled wall, letting the water batter against my skin and listening to the comforting sounds of Wilder and Daxon talking in the living room. It was progress that they were just talking and not screaming at each other.

What I really needed was to soak in a bath, maybe sleep for a few days straight. I'd already felt destroyed after my time with Alistair. Combine that with the marathon sex...my heat, and I felt half dead.

But judging by Wilder's face when he'd arrived, there wasn't time for that.

I still couldn't believe that I'd gone through a heat. Growing up, I'd heard some of the female wolves gossiping about it. I hadn't really spent very much time thinking about it back then. It had always sounded...kind of terrifying. And after Alistair had rejected me, and I'd been cursed, it hadn't been a thought. Alistair and his men would sometimes joke about times they'd taken advantage of women in the pack during their heat. It had been one of the only times that I'd been glad not to have my wolf. At least I wouldn't have to endure that. Although maybe if I'd been out of my head with lust, it wouldn't have been so bad when Alistair had...

No, I wouldn't let myself think about that. I would only think about the fact that somehow I'd gotten lucky enough to have two men like Wilder and Daxon with me during my heat. Most of it was a blur, but I could still see bits and pieces. The things they'd whispered to me. The way their hands had felt on my skin. The way their cocks pounded into me, filling me over and over until I felt empty without them. My hand trailed down my body and I found myself touching my suddenly aching clit, their words echoing in my head.

"Need some help?" Daxon asked through the door in a

gravelly, lust-filled voice that made me jump and almost slip and fall.

"Just finishing up," I told him in a squeaky voice. Damn supernatural senses. I couldn't feel anything without them knowing.

I quickly finished my shower, promising myself that I would get to relax someday. Toweling myself off, I walked to Daxon's large walk-in closet. I gasped in surprise, because while I recognized some of my clothes, there were racks and racks filled with brand new clothes in my size. When had Daxon gotten all of this? There were literally thousands upon thousands of dollars worth of clothes in here. There were even bras and underwear stacked in neat little piles on a shelf.

Too tired to overthink everything, I grabbed a pair of underthings, along with a pale pink summer dress, and quickly got dressed. After I threw my wet hair into a messy bun, I took a deep breath and walked out to where the guys were waiting. Daxon was still dressed in nothing but a pair of low-slung jeans that showcased his mouthwatering abs, standing over the stove and cooking something that smelled divine. Wilder was sitting stiffly on the couch, looking through his phone. Both of them looked up when I walked in, their eyes widening appreciatively as they looked over me despite the fact that I was currently rocking the drowned hood-rat look.

A girl could get used to that sort of attention.

"Fuck," Wilder groaned, throwing his phone down on the couch. "You still smell heavenly."

"But my heat broke!" I said defensively, my gaze looking out through the windows nervously, expecting one of the hunters to suddenly appear at any moment. I sniffed the air, wondering if I could smell what they were talking about, but

I couldn't smell anything other than the scent of Daxon's soap on my skin.

Daxon handed me a plate loaded down with the most delicious looking omelet I'd ever seen and growled under his breath as he nestled his face in my neck and took a deep breath. When he stepped back, his eyes were glazed, the pupils blown. "You do smell incredible, love. Like nothing I've ever smelt before," he said in a raspy voice.

"We have to take her to Daria," Wilder muttered with a curse.

My wolf didn't like the fact that another woman's name had just come out of Wilder's mouth. Even though she didn't seem to want to accept his mate's bond.

She was a possessive bitch evidently.

"Daria?" Daxon looked at him incredulously. A smirk creeped across his beautiful face as he stared at Wilder knowingly. "Yes, let's do that."

"Who's Daria?" I asked. "And why do you think she can help?"

I had been starving before, but now my stomach felt like I'd swallowed lead.

"She has powers that will be useful," Wilder said vaguely, obviously not wanting to tell me the full truth. "We were...acquaintances in the past."

"Acquaintances, is that what we're calling it nowadays?" Daxon asked, his voice full of mirth.

I wasn't an idiot, I could read between the lines. Daria was an ex. Great, I was going to get help from an ex.

Hopefully she wasn't the Arcadia kind of ex.

All of a sudden there was a pounding on the front door. The laughter fled from Daxon's face and both he and Wilder let out almost synchronized growls.

"I know she's in there, fuckers!" Miyu's voice called

through the door. "You better let me in, or I'm going to beat down this door. And then you!"

"Can I kill her?" asked Daxon dryly.

"No, you can't kill her!" I screeched, horrified. He was definitely joking. Right?

Wilder rolled his eyes and grabbed me before settling back into the couch.

"I'll just get the door," growled Daxon, looking like he wanted to rip me out of Wilder's arms.

I giggled nervously as Daxon strolled sexily to the door, until I remembered that I'd been kidnapped during Miyu's wedding reception. The guys had been extremely vague about everything that had happened after I'd been taken. And that told me enough.

"Go away," said Daxon when he opened the door.

I could see Miyu in the entryway, she was staring avidly at Daxon's naked chest, not paying any attention to what he was saying.

Daxon coughed, and she shook her head as if in a trance before dragging her eyes away from his perfection and pushing past him.

"Rune," she screamed when she saw me. Wilder grimaced under me at the sound. And I didn't blame him.

Miyu didn't care that I was in Wilder's lap. She threw herself on me, squeezing me so tightly that I had trouble breathing. "I'm so glad you're alive."

I relaxed in her hold, soaking in the feeling of someone who cared about me.

"No one really knew what happened. People were saying you were dead, and that's why..." She sneaked a look over her shoulder to where Daxon was leaning against the wall, watching us impassively.

"That's why what?"

Daxon cleared his throat and Miyu rolled her eyes.

"The reception got a little out of control there for a minute," she finally answered, a shadow dimming the light in her eyes as if she was reliving whatever had happened.

"I'm so sorry," I blurted out.

Wilder and Daxon both growled at the same time that Miyu's eyes widened. "Why are you sorry?" she asked.

"It was my fault that your reception was ruined. It was my choice to come here, even though I knew he would never stop looking for me. I put the whole town in danger," I explained miserably. I was well aware that I was having a full-on pity party, but that sometimes happened.

Miyu scoffed. "We should have done a better job of protecting you, the whole town should have. And I mean, my mating ceremony will always be remembered now. None of the town sluts are going to forget any time soon that Rae belongs to me."

I snorted, because how could I not with that kind of thought process.

Miyu gave another furtive look at both Daxon and Wilder and then moved closer to me.

"Are you sure you're alright? Because I told Rae to be ready. We can get out of here, just say the word."

Another loud growl ripped from the two alphas in the room.

"Alright, I think you've overstayed your welcome," Wilder said, gently placing me down on the couch next to him and standing up. He picked Miyu up and threw her over his shoulder as he marched to the front door.

She began to beat on his back, but he didn't care. Daxon smirked as he watched, and I just stared, flabbergasted, as Wilder practically threw my best friend out on the front porch, slamming the door closed behind him and immediately locking it.

He stood there in front of the door, breathing heavily, before marching back towards me. Wilder scooped me up in his arms and leveled me with a kiss that left me breathless. "Just so we're clear, you won't be going anywhere. You're not ever leaving me."

Wilder set me down then and walked to the kitchen as I sat there, a mess of hormones and emotions. I could hear the sound of cupboards banging together as Wilder looked for something.

That was...intense.

"He's going to be impossible today," purred Daxon as he stalked towards me.

"Look who's talking," I murmured, as Daxon put his arms on both sides of me and leaned in until I was pushed back against the couch.

My insides started throbbing. If I were a TikTok video, there would be an emoji with a cat and a butterfly stamped on my forehead.

They both seemed to be really turning on the...whatever you called this. Alpha hotness?

"You still smell so good," Daxon whispered as his tongue slowly trailed down my neck. A little moan escaped me, and I heard a glass break in the kitchen followed by Wilder's muttered, "Fuck."

"Okay, we need to be going," Wilder barked as he came up behind the couch.

"Eager," Daxon sneered, his face still buried in my neck.

I gently pushed him away, not wanting the two of them to start fighting. Daxon groaned as if in pain as he moved from me and allowed me to stand.

It suddenly hit me then, that if my suspicions were

correct, I was about to meet one of Wilder's exes. And while I knew time was of the essence, and we'd certainly been wasting it this morning, I was not showing up to meet his ex looking like a drowned dog. Or wolf, as it were. I wasn't going to be a jealous bitch about anything, but I could at least try and look good.

"I'm going to go fix my hair," I murmured. "Be right back."

I left the suddenly brooding men and hurried back into Daxon's room to fix my hair. He may have stolen my clothes, but he had not stolen any of my hair tools, so a quick brush and an intricate braid was all I could pull off.

Finally, it was time to go.

The guys were both silent, lost in their thoughts, I guessed, as we walked to Daxon's truck.

"I'll drive myself," said Wilder, sounding despondent all of a sudden as he got into his car without another word.

I looked at Daxon in confusion, and he just winked at me as he opened his passenger door for me and I hopped in.

"What exactly am I about to walk into?" I finally asked, as my nerves began to spike as we drove. "Does she live far from here?"

"In the woods, at the base of Mount Cavat, about an hour away, there's a portal into Fairie," he said nonchalantly, like he'd just told me about the weather.

I swung around to stare at him in shock. I mean I knew I'd just discovered that vampires were real...and hybrids, but he was talking about fae, wasn't he? About a whole other world?

"She's a fae?"

Daxon smirked at the shock in my voice. "You should know by now that all the legends are true, my sweet."

"I'm learning that," I said slowly, turning back to stare at the never-ending road in front of us.

"What did you hear about the fae growing up?" Daxon asked. My heart panged miserably at the mention of growing up. I wasn't sure that I could trust my memories anymore, not after what I'd learned.

"Mother would tell stories," I said quietly. "Just stories at bedtime about fairies. I remember one talking about a human girl who was lost forever to the far king after she ate a few seeds at a party. Evidently, if you taste anything in Fairie, you're stuck there forever."

"What else?"

"There was another story about the far not being able to tell lies. But because of that, they were experts at giving you answers that weren't the whole truth. In the stories, they always liked to make deals as well. They would never do anything for free."

"Whoever the author of your stories was, they were right on all accounts." His voice got serious then as he grabbed my hand and put it in his lap. "When we pass through the portal, you need to stay by my side at all times. Don't accept anything from anyone. Don't shake anyone's hand. And don't make any deals with anyone. Let Wilder and I handle all of that."

"Okay," I promised in a shaky voice, thinking that the guys really were worried about my scent if this was what we were resorting to.

I was silent for the rest of the drive. Daxon didn't seem worried at all. He had the band *Sounds of Us* playing on the radio and he was singing along to their latest hit like he didn't have a care in the world. Wilder's car was in front of us, driving at least five miles below the speed limit for some reason.

Daxon finally got fed up with going so slow and passed him, throwing up a middle finger as he did so.

I could see Wilder snarling back at him, but he kept up with us the rest of the way.

Daxon slowed down, and I looked around, frowning, because I couldn't see anything around. He abruptly sped up and swerved to the left, right towards the dense forest.

I screamed in horror and panic, and Daxon yelled in delight as we headed towards our death.

What the hell was happening!

8

*W*e were an inch from crashing into the first tree when the forest abruptly disappeared and the truck landed with a thud as it hit the ground. I grabbed onto the dashboard in front of me, feeling like I was having a heart attack.

"That was a glamour," Daxon explained with a chuckle that told me he'd been trying to scare me. Asshole.

"Obviously," I squeaked, as I sucked in huge breaths, trying to calm myself down.

As soon as I felt like I could move without passing out, I unbuckled my seatbelt, and grabbed Daxon's shirt.

"What the fuck is wrong with you?" I snarled, my voice coming out low and garbled, my wolf intermixed with my usual voice.

Of course, Daxon was turned on by this, his pupils expanding and the heavy scent of his lust permeating the truck's interior and mixing deliciously with the scent of my fear.

That was odd.

There was a tap on the glass and I looked over my

shoulder to see Wilder standing at the window, an exasperated look on his face. I let go of Daxon's shoulder and opened the truck door without another word.

"Rune!" Daxon said, finally catching on that I wasn't amused. I ignored him and stretched out my arms, trying to get rid of the throbbing tension coursing through my veins. Not to mention the whiplash I'd just received.

Wilder touched my lower back briefly before pulling away, but I didn't check to see why. My attention was distracted by the fact that we were parked in the mouth of an enormous cave. The entire ceiling of the cave looked like it was covered in crystals and diamonds. Despite the fact that there was little light in the cave, the ceiling was sparkling so brightly it was almost blinding.

I belatedly noticed that the far wall in front of us seemed to be shimmering as well. If this was the portal to Fairie, they liked their glitter. They couldn't be that bad then, right?

Psychopaths didn't like glitter.

Daxon came up behind me, his touch hesitant. "I'm sorry," he whispered in my ear.

I glared up at him, but he looked appropriately miserable so it was impossible for me to stay mad at him.

"I'm driving with Wilder next time," I said primly. Daxon rolled his eyes in amusement, but a quick glance at Wilder told me he was still stoic, anxiously staring at the flickering wall in front of us.

"So how do we get through this thing?" I asked, Wilder's behavior making me even more nervous. I was also wishing that I had access to some hairspray and a curling iron right before this little trip. The fee in the stories I'd heard were always the epitome of perfection. I had a feeling that Wilder's ex was going to be a beauty. Of course, Arcadia was a beauty too. But the kind of beauty that would eat you if you got too close.

My inane thoughts were disrupted by Wilder approaching the wall and pulling out a knife from his pocket. I watched, entranced, as he took the knife and sliced a long cut in his hand. My stomach squeezed at the sight of his blood and I took a step forward, only to be stopped by Daxon, holding out his hand.

Wilder squeezed his hand until the blood was spread all over his palm, and then he pressed it against the wall. The sparkly gray color flashed a garish dark red, the same shade as Wilder's blood. My anxiety over what was on the other side of this wall only increased; requiring a blood sacrifice never equaled fun and flirty in my experience. Doom and death were more likely.

"We can walk through," said Wilder.

Daxon stepped forward, pulling me with him.

"Maybe my scent will just die down by itself?" I squeaked, feeling very unsure of everything.

"Just stay by me," said Daxon, his earlier levity gone.

"Rune," Wilder murmured, grabbing my other hand before Daxon could walk through the glimmering wall. "Promise me nothing can change what we have." His words were urgent...pleading.

I studied his face, wondering if it was possible for my heart to be safe with him...wondering if it was possible to really make that sort of promise.

My wolf cried out inside of me like his pain was her pain.

"I promise," I whispered back, and I hoped I meant it.

Daxon and Wilder both took my hands as we walked through the shimmering crimson wall. I gasped as a cold sensation passed over my skin, like I'd just been submerged in ice-cold water. For a second, I struggled to breathe. I couldn't feel their hands in mine. A feeling of dread, like I was going to die, tore through me. Hopelessness and panic combined and coursed through me.

Abruptly it was gone, and I found myself on all fours on the ground, huffing and coughing as if I'd actually been under the water that whole time.

"Rune," Wilder cried, panicked. I held up one hand, trying to get my breath back and get ahold of myself. It took a few minutes, but I was finally able to sit back on my haunches and look at my surroundings.

My jaw dropped.

We were in a land of monsters. The air was dense, filled with thick clouds that seemed to hover over us menacingly. Everything I could see looked designed to tear your insides out. The tree branches were shaped like sharp claws and I could see terrifying faces etched into their gray trunks, mouths filled with pointy teeth. The other plants weren't any better. Thorns and teeth everywhere. The flowers weren't bothering to hide the fact that they were deadly. The one that faintly resembled a rose just a few feet away looked to have drool dripping from its petals, except the drool was obviously venomous because every time it dropped to the dark green grass there was a hiss and a burst of smoke like it had just burned the ground. In the distance, I could see a lake that was blood red of course. There were humongous creatures with bat-like wings flying around it like vultures, as if it was actually a giant pool of blood.

My mouth opened to scream, and then I felt a hand grip mine and my surroundings disappeared. I was suddenly in paradise, a land of milk and honey that my mind had trouble comprehending. My breath came out in pants as I pressed my free hand on my chest, struggling to get ahold of myself.

"Rune, Rune...you're alright, baby. Snap out of it." I realized belatedly it was Daxon holding my hand with a worried-looking Wilder standing in front of me. I had the strangest urge to smooth out the wrinkles on his forehead from his distress.

"Did you see it?" I asked breathlessly. "Did you see what this place was a second ago? We have to get out of here!"

"I'm going to kill her," Daxon growled, and I looked up at him, confused as to what he was talking about.

"You were charmed, sweetheart," Wilder explained exasperatedly.

"Or cursed," Daxon muttered angrily.

"You're saying something did that to me?" I asked, the panic threading through my veins transforming quickly into fury.

"Someone was playing tricks on you," replied Daxon.

"You didn't feel like you were drowning when you passed through the wall? You didn't see the blood red lake, and the monster plants?" I gripped Daxon's hand tightly, sure that at any minute everything was going to change again.

I mean, what I was currently seeing looked like it had been ripped out of a travel magazine. Everything was so green and lush, the colors so bright it hurt my eyes to stare at any one thing for too long. The blood red lake from before had been transformed into a sparkling pool of blue water. And the demon birds flying above were now bright tropical looking birds whose beautiful song I could hear clearly even from where I was standing.

"We didn't see anything like that. It was all just an illusion. The fae are very powerful, and one of them must have wanted to play a little game with you. None of it was real," Wilder said soothingly.

"You can at least admit who did the illusion," growled Daxon.

Wilder shifted, embarrassed. And I realized they must have thought Daria was the one who'd done it. Perfect.

Honestly, these two assholes really seemed to like psychotic women.

Hopefully they were breaking the mold with me and I wasn't actually crazy too.

That could be debated most days though.

"Let's get moving. There will be a carriage waiting for us when we get to the main road, but we're a few miles out," said Wilder without acknowledging what Daxon had said. Wilder was freaking out though, that much was obvious.

"A carriage?" I asked, confused.

"Yes, that wouldn't have been in your story books," mused Daxon as we began to walk. I stuck close to him, especially when we passed any plants, sure that at any minute one of the beyond beautiful flowers was going to reach out and try to eat me. "Electricity and technology can't exist in Fairie. If you were to bring a phone in here, it would disintegrate as soon as you passed through the portal. They have magic though, so it's not something they miss."

One of the birds flew over our heads just then. Its long plume of orange and red feathers was like a trail of fire dragging behind it. Magic indeed.

The guys were both lost in thought as we walked, and I was distracted by the increasingly amazing things I saw along the way. That had definitely been a dragon sitting under the waterfall we'd just passed.

Both Daxon and Wilder were walking quickly, so it didn't take us too long to get to the golden-colored winding road. I felt a little bit like Dorothy from the Wizard of Oz as I stared down at the glittering gold bricks that made up the road. We waited there for a minute, assumedly for the carriage, before I gasped in shock as an intricate, white carriage appeared in front of us out of nowhere.

Neither Daxon nor Wilder looked surprised at the sudden appearance of the carriage. There were no horses attached to it, and the carriage hovered in the air a few inches above the golden road.

"Something's going to fly into your mouth," teased Daxon, and I realized I was just standing there in shock with my jaw dropped.

Besides the whole obvious changing into a wolf thing, there wasn't anything particularly magical about shifters. For the most part, a shifter lived their life much like a regular human, the recent weird things I'd been doing excluded.

So to be confronted with vampires, hybrids, and now magical fae, it was literally blowing my mind.

Pull yourself together, I told myself. The last thing I wanted was to come across like the naive, awkward creature I was in front of Wilder's ex.

I snapped my mouth shut and playfully growled at Daxon, grateful the more sunshiny aspect of his personality was out in full force at the moment to dispel the tension of this trip...and Wilder's sullen attitude. I was very much attracted to the newfound dark and dangerous part of Daxon, but we had enough heavy right now.

Wilder got into the carriage first and then helped me step up into it as well, Daxon following closely behind. There were bench seats inside for us to sit on that were so soft it felt like you were sitting on a cloud.

My body was still sore from the events of the last few

days and it felt like heaven to sit. I needed to figure out a way to get a bed made of whatever these seats were.

As soon as Daxon settled onto his seat next to me, the carriage door closed and we began to move along the road at a brisk pace.

The outside world whizzed by us, so fast I could only catch glimpses of what was out there.

"How long will it take to get there?" I asked, thinking I was going to get sick if we were in this thing for too long, comfortable cushions or not.

Neither of the guys answered, and I looked at them only to see that they both were looking very...uncomfortable.

"Are you getting sick?" I asked, but the question came out breathlessly because I'd just gotten a taste of the arousal that was thick in the air.

"You smell so fucking good," groaned Wilder across from me. He was holding onto the cushion beneath him with both hands, like he was trying to prevent himself from lunging at me.

Daxon let out the most erotic sounding groan that I'd ever heard and I flushed a million shades of red, thinking I could orgasm just by hearing that sound over and over again.

"Fuck," muttered Daxon, as my arousal joined theirs. I'm sure making everything even more uncomfortable.

He leapt from the seat and situated himself in front of me until he was kneeling in between my legs.

"What are you doing?" I gasped as he grabbed my dress and pushed it up so that my suddenly damp underwear was showing.

"Umm," I murmured, not sure if I wanted that, but then Daxon was hooking my thighs over his shoulders and my underwear was pushed to the side. Before I could say anything, he covered my slit with his mouth. Sucking and licking, his tongue separated my folds as he began to thrust two fingers into my clenching core. He pressed his face into me, his mouth and tongue demanding. Tilting his head up, he pushed my legs wider until I was basically straddling his face. I watched in shock...and awe as he sucked at me. He stared up at me with lust-ridden eyes.

All coherent thoughts left me.

I fisted his hair, pulling him into me, my hips writhing against him. "Daxon," I moaned. He devoured me. Like I was the most delicious thing he'd ever tasted. Like he never wanted it to end.

I couldn't hear if he was growling or moaning into me, but I felt the vibrations on my tender sex. Over and over.

My whimpered pleas filled the carriage along with the sucking sounds as he continued to devour me. Abruptly, I remembered that Wilder was right there, watching everything. My gaze locked with his. Wilder looked manic, on edge, like he didn't know whether he wanted to kill Daxon or join in. His cheeks were red and his breaths were coming out in gasps. A quick glance down and I could see a very large erection in his jeans.

Seeing evidence of his arousal did it for me. Suddenly everything tightened inside me as Daxon did something magical to my clit with his tongue.

Pleasure coursed through me in an almost violent rush. My hips thrust frantically against his mouth, desperate for more friction. Daxon licked and sucked eagerly as the tremors racked my body as I fell over the metaphorical cliff.

His fingers slipped out of me for a moment, but then his tongue pushed in. Fucking me.

He growled into my aching flesh, setting off another orgasm. The second one was shocking and almost painful in its intensity. I felt tears escaping as I helplessly convulsed in my seat.

The carriage came to a stop just then, and Daxon's movements paused. The air was filled with the sound of all of our combined breathing and the scent of sex was so overwhelmingly thick, any species would be able to smell it.

"Fuckkkkkk," Wilder cursed as he adjusted himself, his gaze still frozen on mine.

Through my orgasm haze, I heard footsteps approaching from outside, and I pushed Daxon away, struggling to fix my underwear back into place and pull my dress down. Daxon moved off his knees and slipped back into his seat. His mouth and chin still glistened with my juices, which he proceeded to wipe with a hand. But his eyes... Oh, those hungry eyes were locked on me.

I got my dress fixed just in time for the carriage door to open. There was a tall, thin...fae standing there. At least, I assumed he was a fae. He had long pointed ears which had always been a tell in those stories.

He was also freaking beautiful, with features that looked like they'd been carved from marble. He delicately sniffed the air, his cat-like eyes going immediately to mine. He gave me a predatory grin, and I shifted on my seat nervously...and still aroused.

"Don't even think about it," growled Wilder as he jumped up from his seat and leapt to the entrance, making sure the fae couldn't see me. Daxon was stiff in his seat, and I glanced at him. All signs of his previous lust were wiped from his face. His eyes were cold as he stared where Wilder was blocking the fae from view. Daxon looked like he was plotting murder.

Wilder stepped down out of the carriage, and I saw that

the fae was a few feet away now, staring determinately at the ground.

"With me at all times," Daxon reminded me in a tense voice and I nodded, my voice disappearing in my nervousness at what was ahead. At least the two orgasms in the carriage had distracted me for a while. Because I felt like a mess.

Daxon held tightly to my hand as I stepped out of the carriage. I gasped in shock as I stared up at the castle in front of me. It looked like it was made from glass. The walls were perfectly smooth and shining, not a blemish to be seen on the gleaming walls. There were countless turrets and towers, and the top of the castle was so high up in the sky that it was surrounded by clouds.

Talk about intimidating.

We began to walk towards the bridge that led to the castle doors ahead of us, doors that were at least twenty feet tall, at my guess. Wilder seemed to be intentionally walking right in front of me so he could continue to block me from view and Daxon was practically vibrating next to me as he gripped my hand tightly. There were fae guards every few feet along the bridge. None of them looked at us as we passed by. I took a glance down at the water underneath the bridge and lost my footing when it appeared to be the same blood-red color that I'd seen at first.

I blinked, and it was gone.

"Alright, sweetheart?" Daxon murmured as I regained my balance and began to walk again. I just nodded in response, my insides twisting up.

We got to the massive doors and the fae, who had continued to look at the ground during our walk, knocked three times. The sound of his fists against the glass echoed around us, sending shivers down my spine.

The doors opened at his knock, not making a sound as they smoothly slid open. As the doors moved, I saw an enormous room ahead, with what looked like a sparkling throne made of diamonds at the very end.

The room was completely empty, and like how the outside had been, was so bright I struggled to keep my eyes open.

There was a heaviness to the air though, and I could taste something metallic on my tongue as I breathed.

"It's the magic," Daxon murmured to me. "This is one of the most powerful places in all of Fairie."

"And this is where we're going to find Daria?" I asked.

Daxon just hummed noncommittally.

Perfect.

We walked down a long, ice-blue carpet that stretched from the door all the way to the enormous throne. It muffled our footsteps as we walked. As we got closer, I could see that the throne was made up of the same glass-like material as the rest of the castle, except there were diamonds embedded throughout it.

We were just a few feet from the throne when Wilder stopped so suddenly that I almost bumped into him. There was tension threaded throughout his body, and I couldn't help but place a hand on his back to try and relax him

It didn't work. If anything, he stiffened even further.

"Enough with the crap, Daria," Wilder growled suddenly to the empty throne in front of us.

The air filled with the sound of tinkling laughter and sparks began to appear right above the throne.

I blinked and there sat a stunning female...and she was completely naked.

It caught me off guard. Her skin was a silverish color, and she was lounging on the throne, her more than ample breasts thrust out as she made herself comfortable. She had long black hair, so long that it trailed to the ground and curved around the throne. Her eyes were a crystalline green color, and they trailed hungrily along Wilder's form, not paying any attention to Daxon and me.

"I hate this bitch," Daxon muttered under his breath, not that he could really talk because of Arcadia. Cough, cough.

"Hello, lover," she purred, her voice so sensual it seemed to caress my skin, making me feel hot and achy as I stood there.

She got up from her throne smoothly and walked around Wilder, trailing a finger across his chest. He stood there stiffly, not responding to her, but not stepping away from her touch either.

I saw red.

Without thinking, I made a move to lunge at her, and Daxon just caught me before I threw myself at her.

"Easy girl, we need her," Daxon said soothingly as he held me tightly against him.

The beautiful woman's attention turned towards Daxon, still ignoring me despite the fact that he held me in his arms.

"You've brought people to play with us," she said nonsensically, giggling again and hopping up and down in apparent delight.

"Over my dead body," drawled Daxon.

Her smile dropped then, and she shot Daxon a shrewd glance. "Daxon, isn't it? It's been a long time since I've seen you."

When he didn't say anything to her, her lovely lips pursed in anger. She stood there, staring at him awkwardly.

"You can quit with the bullshit, Daria. Your powers aren't going to work on me."

She pouted, a dangerous look in her eyes as her gaze finally landed on me.

"I suppose it's because of this girl, Daxon? Her scent's all over you."

"That would be correct," he drawled. "This is Rune."

"Rune," she purred as she looked me up and down, obviously finding me wanting.

"Rune, this is Daria. Queen of the Light Fae," Wilder said dismally, finally saying something.

Her eyes flashed to him. "Why, Wilder, I would almost think you weren't happy to see me. It's been almost five of your earth months, hasn't it? I know you must be dying for it."

"I've actually come for help," Wilder said, avoiding responding to anything she'd just said.

My insides burned. He'd been with this perfect creature right before I'd come into town.

A wave of self-doubt hit me. How could I compete with her?

"Whatever you're thinking, stop it. You're a goddess in every way. It's not even a competition," Daxon whispered in my ear.

Daria looked over at us at his words, and I was suddenly wondering just how good the fae's hearing was; the way her eyes were glimmering nastily at me suggested she'd heard every word that Daxon said.

"You're here for help?" Daria asked Wilder, those expressive eyes of hers narrowing in disbelief. "You'll be staying tonight though, correct." She said it more like a statement than a question. At this point, both of Daria's hands were on Wilder's chest, and Daxon was having to actually exert effort to keep me from lunging.

Wilder *finally* took a step back, so that he was out of reach.

"What's this?" she asked incredulously. Wilder's gaze flickered to me for the first time since we'd stepped foot in the castle.

Daria let out a harsh cackle, far different from the tinkling, melodious laugh she'd had at first. This one was menacing, and the hair on my neck rose as the heaviness in the room grew.

"I love her," Wilder said. I shifted in Daxon's arms, happiness and unease coursing through me.

He hadn't said he loved me before this. Of course, I'd known that he did. I'd felt it. But to hear him announcing it so proudly to his gorgeous, perfect ex...

It felt so good.

"What did you just say?" Daria whispered dangerously. She whirled towards me. "Has he told you he was in my bed every night for months? Did he tell you how perfect he thinks I am, how I'm the best he's ever had?"

A breeze suddenly whipped at my face as her words slashed against me.

I said nothing, just stared at her stoically. Of course, he hadn't told me any of that. We still knew next to nothing about each other, really.

I glanced at him and my insides leapt like they did every time I saw him. It didn't really matter to me, though. I hoped somehow to have forever to know him. It only mattered that my soul already seemed to know him, that my wolf knew him.

He was mine.

She laughed again, and it sounded even uglier this time. She turned towards Wilder again, throwing herself against him as her lips met his. It didn't matter to me that he wasn't returning her kiss and that he stood there, shocked.

Daxon was no match for me then. I shifted suddenly, pouncing at her and knocking her away from Wilder and to the ground. A growl ripped from me as the urge to *kill* washed over me. I was just about to tear out her jugular when I was pushed off her.

By Wilder.

"It's alright, pretty girl. I know I belong to you. Come back to me," he purred as he stroked my fur soothingly. My wolf perked up at his touch and gave him her full attention, stepping away from the fae queen and nestling against him. My tail whipped Daria in the face...because my wolf was petty like that.

"You little..." Daria suddenly said, and a blue pulse hit Wilder's chest, knocking him back a few steps. I dashed towards him, but he held up his hand to stop me. I turned and bared my teeth at Daria who had stood back up, her attention not on me, but on where she was sending her magic at Wilder. He stood there, staring back at her, no emotion on his face.

"Give it up, Daria. It's not going to work," he said, his voice hard.

Her lovely face fell, and the blue pulse of magic abruptly disappeared.

I transformed then, throwing my dress back on quickly. "What was she doing?"

Daxon smiled, but it didn't reach his eyes. "The light fae can control lust and sexual urges at will. Unless you're truly in love."

"Is that what she was trying on you at first?"

"She tried it on both of us. It didn't work." He gave

Wilder an appraising look, like he was seeing him as competition for the first time.

"It's going to be history repeating itself," Daria said softly, paying Daxon and I no attention as she stared longingly at Wilder. Her pain was tangible. I could see her heart breaking right in front of us.

"It won't be, because it's never been like this before," Wilder told her gently.

She continued to stare at him mournfully for what felt like forever, until she finally sighed and turned away. With a wave of her hand she was suddenly clothed in an elegant ice-blue dress, embroidered with diamonds like her throne. Her hair became intricately braided with a silvery ribbon threaded throughout it, and a crown that looked like it was one solid diamond appeared on her head. Daria sat daintily on her throne.

"What exactly is the issue with...Rune?" she asked Wilder, uttering my name like it was disgusting.

Before I could announce that I was of the opinion that we needed to leave right now, and under no certain circumstance was I trusting this chick to help, Wilder sighed in what seemed like relief. He then launched into the whole saga of the hunters...and my newfound scent.

Daria kept her face blank, revealing nothing as she listened to Wilder. There was only a faint glimmer in her eyes when he described the hunters shooting at us as we tried to get away.

"Well, that's all very touching, Wilder. But what exactly do you think I can do?" she said, a smirk appearing on her face that made me want to throat punch her.

Daxon growled like he'd had the same thought.

"I know there's something you could do, something to mask her scent. Please."

I shifted uncomfortably. The desperate tone in Wilder's voice made me stand up and take notice. I mean, the whole being shot at thing had definitely made me understand this thing with my scent was serious. But the worry he was exhibiting now was frightening.

"I don't do things for free," Daria said, after an uncomfortably long pause where she stared at Wilder like she wanted to eat him.

"I'll trade a favor," Wilder immediately said.

I wasn't an expert in business by any stretch of the imagination, but it was obvious to even me that it was never good to be negotiating when it was so obvious to the other party you would do anything they asked to get what you wanted.

There was no way that I was going to let Wilder enter into a deal on my behalf.

"Wilder, we're leaving," I commanded sharply, taking a step towards him.

He turned his attention to me. "You don't know what they'll do when they catch you. You can't comprehend it. You'll be begging for death by the end. I can't let that happen to you."

"We'll figure something out. We're not making a deal with the devil over this."

"It's the only way," Wilder said determinedly.

I turned towards Daxon. "Help me! Tell him we need to leave."

Daxon eyed Wilder speculatively, a million thoughts whirling behind those hazel eyes of his. They looked even more golden than usual with our glass surroundings reflecting light all around us.

"You know what you're doing?" he finally asked Wilder.

"It's the only way."

Daxon nodded, but I'd had enough. I lunged at Wilder

and grabbed his hand, trying to drag him towards where we'd come in. Every cell in my body was telling me that we needed to leave right now, that we would regret any deal with Daria for the rest of our lives.

"He's not giving you a favor," I told Daria fiercely, throwing her a look of disdain.

"I don't think that's your choice, little girl."

I gritted my teeth, a growl erupting from my own throat at the condescension in her tone.

"Although I have to agree with you, I don't think there's anything about you special enough to warrant saving."

"I'll do it," Wilder immediately said before I could respond, as if he wanted to prove just how special I really was. "But I won't have sex with you, and I won't kill anyone. And you won't do anything to Rune, but mask the new scent." Magic flickered in the air like his promise was already binding.

My stomach rolled at the thought of her even touching Wilder's spectacular body, and my wolf silently agreed.

"Trying to put stipulations on our deal when you're the one who's desperate?" she purred.

Wilder said nothing in response.

"Very well. I will agree to your terms."

She held out a delicate, smooth hand and Wilder hesitated before extending his. Power snapped in the air and a delicate, golden light surrounded their intertwined hands. After a second, the light disappeared and Wilder hastily pulled back his hand, looking a bit green as he did so.

"Let's get out of here," growled Daxon, the only way he'd communicated the entire time we'd been here.

"What's your favor?" Wilder quickly asked, and I stiffened, expecting the worst.

"Oh, I'll have to think about that," Daria said with a

smile. "It's not every day you get a favor from an Alpha wolf." Her smile dropped. "Although you would think the girl was the Alpha of the two of you with how you're behaving."

The urge to lunge at her threatened to overwhelm me, but Daxon put a steadying hand on my hip, like he could read my mind.

"I'll let you know when I decide." The fairy queen gave me a wink, like we were somehow sharing some kind of inside joke.

"Mask her scent," ordered Daxon, his entire body vibrating as he eyed Daria like she was a poisonous snake that was going to pounce at any moment.

"Very well," she said with a sigh, lifting her hand and waving it sharply.

A table made of a gleaming marble material rose slowly from the floor. She smoothly got up from her throne and walked towards it like she was walking down a runway.

"Well, get on," she ordered exasperatedly as if it was a no-brainer for me to jump on a random table in a fantasy realm that looked like it was used to perform sacrifices.

"Come on, little wolf. I won't bite...hard."

"That's it, I'm going to kill her," Daxon announced as Wilder moved next to us and put a restraining hand on his arm.

I hesitantly walked to the table and eyed it, my wolf snarling inside of me as if trying to warn me this wasn't a good idea.

Tell me about it.

I gave a questioning look to Daxon and Wilder, wondering if I should run for the hills.

Except...I trusted them.

The knowledge hit me solidly, burrowing in my heart

and flowing through my veins. I'd trusted only a few people in my life. And all of them had betrayed me.

I just hoped that Daxon and Wilder wouldn't join those ranks.

Wilder grabbed my hands and pulled me away from the table, leaning close to my ear. "I would never have done this unless it was the only way. I...I couldn't take it if something happened to you. I wouldn't survive." I looked up into his shockingly green eyes, full of worry, as he looked down at me.

"I'll do it," I murmured. He closed his eyes, letting out a sigh of relief and leaned his forehead against mine.

"Any time now," Daria barked, annoyance threaded throughout her voice. Wilder shot me a rueful grin and stepped away from me as I sighed and walked back to the table.

Daxon suddenly appeared right behind Daria, a glowing green knife pressed against her throat.

She gasped.

"Where did you get that?" Her voice was filled with horror, indignation...and fear.

"It doesn't matter. The only thing that matters is that this beauty really likes the taste of fae blood. In fact, it was made specifically to spill it. And if you try anything while you're doing this little ritual, I will kill you."

His eyes were unhinged and wild as he held the knife to her throat. It pressed into her smooth skin, a silver drop of blood trailing down her throat as he dug it deeper. She looked desperately at Wilder, but he just watched her impassively, as if the little scene did nothing to him.

Something inside me fluttered at the sight. There was no denying I was a little fucked up...that a part of me wanted the knife to cut even deeper.

"Do you understand?" Daxon sneered.

Her lip curled up in fury, her whole body stiff as the knife continued to press even deeper. "I understand," she finally said, the words coming out halted and dangerous.

"Good," Daxon said easily as he abruptly dropped the knife and stepped away.

"Get on the table, little wolf," Daria ordered through gritted teeth.

Taking a deep breath, I tentatively jumped on the cool stone table, just wanting to get this over with before anything else happened.

I laid down and stared up at her as she leaned over me, examining me closely. "You do smell delicious," she purred, and she smiled sinisterly at me, her incisor teeth all of a sudden looking larger and sharper than before.

It was all I could do to suppress a shiver.

A corked bottle filled with what looked like glowing blue smoke appeared in front of her out of nowhere.

She popped the cork and began to shake the bottle so that the smoke trailed out in streams. It hovered above me menacingly before abruptly falling towards me and enveloping me completely.

I lifted my hand, anxiety coursing through me as I stared at the sight of my hand and arm completely enveloped by the smoke.

Daria began to chant then, the words lilting and beautiful...and unfamiliar. The language must have been fae because I'd certainly never heard anything like it before.

My skin began to get hot, hotter and hotter until sweat beaded on my forehead and it felt like I was being boiled alive. I opened my mouth to groan in pain, but nothing came out. When I tried to move, I realized my limbs were frozen in place.

Fear shot through me as I stared up at her in horror.

Her face was perfectly blank...but her eyes showed how much joy she was getting from my discomfort.

Just when I felt like my body was going to burn into ash, the heat abruptly disappeared, along with the blue smoke.

I tried to sit up, a breath of relief escaping when I was able to actually move.

I got off that table as fast as I could. She had better be done, because if not, we were going to have an incomplete ritual. I was not letting her do anything else to me.

"Is it done?" growled Daxon, grabbing me and pulling me into his arms. He buried his head into my neck and took a deep breath, the air tickling my skin.

"How do I smell?" I croaked, my insides still feeling a bit singed after whatever had just happened.

"Like you again," he groaned in delight, taking another deep inhale like I was a chocolate dessert just placed in front of him.

"The scent is still there, she just has a cloak encapsulating it around her body so that it can't be detected," Daria said sullenly.

"How long will it last?" Wilder asked, coming closer but stopping just out of reach as he looked at me yearningly.

"It would take someone with immense magical prowess to get past the spell...or even detect it in the first place," she said proudly.

"Can we get out of here?" I asked, the memory of feeling like I was being burned alive still very clear in my head.

"We'll be going now," announced Wilder, eyeing me closely to make sure I was alright.

"Aren't you going to say thank you?" she seethed, outrage seeping from her.

"You didn't do it for free," Wilder answered. It seemed a

little dangerous to be that ungrateful around an all powerful fae queen, so I just hoped Wilder knew what he was doing.

"You know, Wilder. There was a time that you would have done anything for me," Daria stated throatily, a wild longing in her voice.

Wilder's cheek twitched like he was holding back what he really wanted to say and took a step closer to me, not bothering to answer her. He grabbed my hand and began to stalk away, Daxon following closely behind us.

I looked behind me as we rushed away, dread curling in my gut.

Daria was back lounging on the throne, no sign of the stone table...a look of victory all over her beautiful, perfect face like she'd gotten what she'd wanted all along.

She lifted up her hand and blew me a mocking kiss that burrowed into my skin.

It felt like a kiss of death.

The way back home was completely different from our initial journey. The land no longer held the beauty and majesty it had before. The land didn't sparkle. I took no notice of the incredible beasts flying through the air. The water wasn't crystalline.

We were all quiet and pensive, thinking over what had just occurred and the deal that had been made.

I wasn't sure of much anymore, but I was sure that we were going to regret the deal Wilder had made with Daria.

I marched down the main street of town, eying the diner Rune insisted on working at for the morning shift to get her mind off everything.

How could I blame her? I needed a distraction too. A damn vacation with her away from all the danger sounded really good about now.

I paused at the door and peered in through the glass window to find her coming my way, swinging her bag over a shoulder. Fuck, just seeing her had my heart racing, my cock twitching.

Daxon was in today, watching over her. Sure, her scent might have been masked, but that didn't mean we were free from the danger. It was nearly impossible to keep myself away, even knowing Daxon was there.

Rune emerged, the door chiming on her exit. She looked up at me with a beautiful smile when she saw me.

"Are you stalking me?" she joked, and it was refreshing to see her smile. My heart thumped faster just seeing it. It had been too long since I'd seen the joy in her eyes, the tempting smile on her lips.

"Hmm. Perhaps."

She cut me a grin and pushed the bag higher on her shoulder. I reached over and took it from her. "So, you admit to stalking me," she murmured.

"If that means I'll follow you to the ends of the earth to be with you and keep you safe, then yes, I'll be your stalker."

She laughed, and I reluctantly admitted to myself that it was good for her to have a few hours at work. It obviously had done her well. After our visit to the fae realm, she'd fallen quiet and barely spoke. I knew she worried about the deal I'd made with Daria. Fuck, I was worried too. Everything inside me told me I'd made a deal with a devil. But that was a problem I'd deal with personally when it happened. I refused to let that get in our way. We achieved the most important element first-masking her heat.

I leaned in and kissed her; it was hard not to when that was all I could think about all day. She tasted sweet, her scent flaring briefly as we touched. It wasn't the usual, beautiful intoxicating smell that drove me insane though. Her usual scent was diluted, which I guess made sense seeing she had a mask on keeping her heat at bay. Didn't change a thing about how much I fucking adored her.

She clutched my shirt, tugging me closer, the heady desire kindled with a single kiss.

She paused and looked up at me, breathless, her eyes dilated. "Let's go back to my place." My wolf reacted, demanding I claim her. To make her all mine...even though I knew exactly where that path would lead us. With her not accepting my bite once again.

And while I craved her more than anything else in the world, I had a different agenda for us today. "I have a better idea," I suggested.

"Go on, I'm listening." She fluttered her eyes, her wicked

grin doing things to me. My insides clenched as I thought about how close I'd come to losing her. I would end up destroyed if I ever lost her for good.

I smirked and slid a hand down to hers, our fingers intertwined. "Come with me." I guided her down the sidewalk along the main road, directly toward my place. Someday she'd be there with me all the time, but that was something I was working towards.

"I have an idea that will help us both," I told her, and she studied me, an adorable little wrinkle on her nose as she tried to work out what I meant. I loved how curious she was.

Let's be serious, I loved everything about her.

"Is this a guessing game?"

"Up to you. Or you can wait to find out."

She nudged her shoulder into my side. "You're always such a tease." She growled and then kept herself glued to my side as we walked, like she might climb me any moment, but I noted she was working to fight the instinct.

"Babe, you have no idea."

"Hmm." She pondered, staring up at the sky as we strolled, and then looking at me every so often as though she'd find the answer on my face. "You're going to have your way with me until morning?"

I burst out laughing. "That *is* always on my mind." I couldn't believe I was pushing back the offer of sex with this perfect woman.

We passed several women on the sidewalk who nodded their respect in my direction, but I didn't miss the envious looks they offered Rune. My girl was too busy staring at me to notice though. It did something to me to see how she was so captivated in me that the rest of the world faded away. I wished everyone in the pack could see how amazingly incredible this woman was. But fear of the unknown makes the most well-intentioned person act irrationally.

If I was honest with myself though, maybe I didn't mind that people kept away from her. I didn't like to share her with anyone anyway.

Upon reaching my house, I took Rune inside where I set her bag down on the kitchen counter, and then grabbed two bottles of water from the fridge before leading her out into the backyard.

"Don't tell me you want me to do yoga with you or something? I'm a runner... and that's not really what I'm in the mood for."

"I promise, what I have in mind is good for you."

She pouted, and the look was fucking adorable.

Out in the backyard, thick branches dangled over the wooden fence from the woodlands my property backed against. The yard stretched outward, offering privacy from the neighbors. Sure, the grass was longer than it should be, but it would provide us with some cushioning. I set down the water on the verandah and turned to Rune.

She glanced up, staring at me strangely through thick lashes. My heart pounded faster. Everything about her made me soft, made me fall harder.

"I never said it before, but thank you for being my hero," she said, holding herself still, like she was scared of the words as she said them.

Her words caught me off guard, and I swept her into my arms, our bodies crushed together, our faces inches away.

I closed my eyes for a moment, feeling like a fucking pansy as I savored how good she felt in my arms. At the same time I tried to beat down the rush of guilt and desperation I felt every time I thought about her being captured. Pushing the hair out of her face, I said, "If I was your hero, you wouldn't have been taken from me or endangered in the first place. But I can promise you that I'll be as close to a hero as I can be for you from now on. I'll catch you when you're falling, I'll kill everyone who wrongs you, and nothing is ever too much if it means fighting to keep you by my side."

She blinked at me and a tear rolled down her cheek. Her emotions were a rollercoaster. One moment she wanted to mount me, then she cried. But I leaned in and kissed the tear away, needing to be there for her, whatever she felt. Desire pulsed through me at the smallest touches, while my heart broke to see the hurt on her face at being told how much she meant to me.

I held her tight. Thoughts of taking her this very moment, stripping her, licking her all over flared through my thoughts. That wasn't why I brought her here, and I cursed myself as I broke apart from her. But I needed to help her protect herself, and that was a priority.

"No crying, sweetheart. Just know that you'll never be alone again." I took a deep breath, hoping she would be up for my plan. "I want to teach you something though," I blurted out.

She studied me with an arching eyebrow. "Okay, I'm listening."

"Good." With her hand in mine, I drew her out onto the lawn, my thumb stroking the inside of her wrist. Having her so close to me so often was like a time-bomb waiting to go off. All I thought about was pinning her to the ground and tasting those gorgeous lips. I was drowning in her scent, and I honestly had no clue how Daxon kept it together while she worked at the diner.

Standing in the middle of the yard, I swung her out in

front of me. "Alright. I'm going to teach you some fighting moves. Enough to give you time to escape."

"Oh," was all she said, like it had been the last thing on her mind.

I reached down to my boot and took out the small knife I always keep on hand. I spun it across my fingers and presented her with the hilt.

"For you," I insisted. "Daxon told me how savage and beautiful you were when you fought Alistair's men up in the mountain before Miyu's wedding. Your wolf is your armor, but sometimes you'll need something else too."

She accepted the weapon, her fingers curling around the leather hilt and flicking her wrist to get a sense for the weapon.

"I want to show you wolf moves too, but we'll do that later on."

She blinked against the sun in her eyes when she raised her head. "I'm going to be terrible at this."

"We'll see," I told her with a grin. "Half the key to hand to hand combat is having the will to win." I placed a flat palm over her heart. "And I know you already have that in spades. You couldn't have survived everything you've been through without it."

Her free hand settled over mine, her touch so tender, so small, but inside this beautiful creature lay a warrior. And I had every intention of bringing her out.

"Okay, then," she said and retreated a couple of steps, then flung the knife around in the air wildly, clearly having fun. Her breasts bounced in her blouse from her rapid moves, and all I could imagine were those perfect rosy tips in my mouth.

"Teach me," she continued, breaking me out of my spell.

My lips pulled into a grin. Goddess, I needed to get my shit together and focus.

I closed the distance between us and swung an arm around the front of her shoulders, pivoting myself behind her and driving her back against my chest.

She gasped at my sudden movement.

"When attacked from behind, the assailant will usually lock an arm around your neck. So you have several options. The two main ones are to grab your blade from your belt or bag as you want it as close as possible for easy access. Swinging it back to hit them in the gut is an awkward move from your angle, so go for the face. Throw your arm up with all your strength, striking him hard and fast. He won't see it coming."

She swung her arm in that same moment, just as I instructed, the blade glinting in the sunlight as it raced for my eyes. A slight rush filled me as I saw my impending death, and I ducked sideways to avoid being pierced. She'd pick this up quicker than I thought.

"Good," I said. "Another option is to ram your heel into their foot. Their hold will ease, and you spin around as fast as you can, then drive the blade right into his gut."

I spun her by her shoulders to face me, and she was nodding.

"What happens if one man holds me by my neck from behind, and another stands in front of me?"

I couldn't ignore the seriousness behind her gaze or how her words trembled when she asked as if she had experienced this first hand.

"Then, sweetheart, you ram your knife into the gut of the asshole in front of you, stomp the other's foot and run. There's no shame in running when you're outnumbered."

The breeze blew through her white hair, and she stood

there, lost in her thoughts. Piercing blue eyes glistened beneath the sun. If I could, I would have frozen time, preserving this moment where she might easily be mistaken for an angel.

"I wish I could take away all your pain," I told her.

She glanced up at me as if my words broke through her thoughts, and the smile she gave me became lopsided.

I grabbed her wrist and snatched the blade out of her fingers. "You've dropped your blade. What do you do if you're tackled?" I tucked the blade in the back of my belt. And in a swift move, I knocked her legs out from under her with my leg, and I wrapped an arm around her back as we both tumbled to the ground.

She huffed out loud, and I rolled her over instantly, pinning her onto her stomach, my body on top of hers. I went to grab her wrists, but she bucked against me, her sweet ass hitting me in the groin so unexpectedly, I groaned as she squashed the jewels.

I moaned, "W-well d-done."

She laughed beneath me, and I rolled onto my back, sucking in a breath as the sharp pain jolted across my balls. I was certain I was seeing stars.

Fuck! I winced, shuddering with a tightness like someone was squeezing them to death.

Suddenly, Rune was straddling me and holding the blade to my throat. When did she grab my knife?

Slightly surprised, but completely amused, I was half laughing, half groaning in pain, utterly smitten with her. To see how quickly she turned and knew how to take advantage of the moment had me feeling even crazier about her than normal.

I stared at her evil grin, as she knew she'd done well.

"No hesitation," I say. "When you get the enemy down, you strike fast."

She nodded. "Always kill."

"Good girl."

But she wasn't moving off me or removing the blade from my throat. Her gorgeous legs tightened around my hips, the heat from between them a fire burning through my clothes, calling to me, reminding me of everything I wanted from her. There was a bewitching sensation, where I felt the lick of pain from the knife, but my arousal still spiked. She pressed on my growing bulge.

"You like to see me this way? Under your control?" I asked.

She nodded, a blaze igniting behind her eyes, arousal bleeding through me. Her nipples hardened, pushing against the fabric of her shirt. She rocked her hips over my cock, studying me as the corners of her lips curled upward.

I needed her naked, riding me.

A cool breeze blew between us, and with it came a reminder that I couldn't get distracted. I wanted her to be powerful and never be captured again.

I grabbed the hand she used to hold a knife to my throat and pushed it away from me, squeezing. That beautiful expression morphed into one of pain and she cried out until she dropped the knife.

My heart clenched, but she had to learn. "What will you do in this situation?"

Before she could respond, I rolled over rapidly, sending her onto her side. Just as quickly, I swiftly tucked my arms under her and brought her to her feet. Then I pulled back a step, waiting for her response.

She was gasping for air. "Shit, you moved so fast."

"Use anything you have. In that case, headbutt the

attacker. It will give you a moment when he loses his focus and you can run."

She nodded and picked up the blade from the ground, studying it with a newfound determination.

Instinctually, I stepped forward.

I said, "Are you ready to become a warrior?"

She lifted her chin, resolution crossing her face. If there was one thing above all else that I loved about Rune, it was her fierceness. She never gave up fighting in this fucked up world. And she was going to need that drive to survive.

RUNE

*D*axon was on edge the entire time we walked down the street, tension practically emanating out of him.

"We don't have to do this," I told him softly, stroking his arm reassuringly.

He took a deep breath and sighed heavily, some of his stress seeming to dissipate at my touch. We were supposed to be on our way to the restaurant where we'd had our first date. It had been his idea. But now that we were actually doing it, he looked like he was prepared to grab me and run home if anyone looked at us wrong.

"Sorry, sweetheart. I do want to do this," he assured me, pulling me in closer to him until we were walking hip to hip, practically in sync.

Someone passed by us on the sidewalk and they raised their hand in greeting to Daxon. Instead of doing the whole sunshine thing that I was used to with Daxon, he flashed his teeth and growled at the offending townperson. The poor guy was so terrified that he fell backwards, inching away like a crab as he struggled to get away as fast as possible.

"Daxon," I chastised softly. I still didn't know what to think about this new Daxon. It made my panties wet, that was for sure. But I felt like I'd made Daxon into someone new, someone so different from who he'd been when I met him that he was practically unrecognizable.

Or maybe I was giving myself too much credit. If I was honest with myself, I hadn't asked him what was going on, because I was a little afraid of what the answer was going to be.

For right now, I'd told myself that this was just a phase.

A phase that I didn't really want to end.

I was for sure going to hell.

"He was looking at you," Daxon growled, and it took me a minute to understand what he was talking about. I was always doing that since I'd been back, getting lost in my head so much that it felt impossible for me to actually hold a conversation with anyone.

"That's hardly a crime. And anyways, I'm pretty sure he was looking at *you*."

Daxon didn't respond, just held me even tighter as we got to the restaurant. He opened the door for me and I took a step inside, only to be abruptly pulled away.

I looked back at him questioningly. The light from the restaurant fell on his face softly. In any other circumstance, I would have been obsessed with just staring at him, at how beautiful he was. But not right then. Daxon's face was full of terror as he stared at the packed restaurant. I watched as his hand drifted to the long, serrated knife he'd taken to wearing around his waist, as if he was going to grab it and start stabbing everyone.

"Daxon," I yelped as I pushed him out the door back into the street. I could feel the questioning stares on my back as the door to the restaurant swung shut behind me.

He leaned over, his hands on his knees as his breath came out in gasps. He abruptly stood and stared up at the starry heavens and let out a roar so loud and desperate that I swore the cobblestones in the road shuddered beneath us.

"Let's just go back to your place," I told him, speaking softly as if I was talking to a rabid animal.

And maybe I was talking to a rabid animal. His eyes were practically sparking as he stared at me, a crazy glint in them that spoke to the wild inside of me. My wolf was feeling a bit feral herself, and I was worried I was going to jump him right here in the middle of the street.

I didn't recognize myself lately. It was like I couldn't get enough of either of them. And with Daxon and Wilder practically glued to my side since I'd been back, I was becoming obsessed with them...in every position.

Focus, I told my hungry wolf.

"We can try again tomorrow," Daxon said eagerly as he grabbed my hand, both of us knowing that he'd just lied. I doubted he'd be ready to be around so many wolves the day after that either.

We walked down the street. I was practically sprinting to try and keep up with Daxon, whose fast, long strides were eating up the sidewalk.

We'd just turned the corner when he froze, a soft growl ripping from his throat as he stared to the right of us, down an alley that was shrouded in shadows. It was unnaturally dark, the light from the streetlights not making a dent in its depths, like all the light had just been sucked away.

"I need you to run," he murmured to me as he pulled out his knife.

"I'm not leaving you," I told him, my heart beginning to beat so fast in my chest, I felt a bit faint.

Was Alistair back? Was he waiting for us?

Or was it...the strong scent of pine hit me. Pine and blood. It was an odd combination, and one that for some reason struck fear inside me.

"What is it?" I whispered, pulling at Daxon's arm like I could somehow drag him away from the alley, and we could just pretend that this never happened.

"One of them is here," Daxon growled, his pupils slanting as his wolf came to the surface. "A hunter."

My fear increased. But so did my rage. I was so fucking sick of being hunted. The memory of being hunted down in the car, of feeling out of my mind with lust while bullets tore at the seats around me, it took over my mind.

That was the only explanation for my actions, then.

I grabbed the knife from the holder I had strapped around my thigh that Wilder had begged me to start wearing, and I lunged into the dark, like I'd never been afraid of it before.

"Rune," Daxon said with a curse, and I knew he was right behind me.

The darkness disappeared then, as if there'd been a curtain and I'd been able to pull it open. A man stood at the end of the alley, surrounded by discarded boxes that were waiting to be picked up by the waste collector. He was dressed in a worn leather jacket, his light blond hair long and wild as it danced in the light breeze floating through the alley. The guy was wearing a necklace with a strange symbol at the end of it, a zigzag with two triangles on either end. I wouldn't have noticed it in the dim lighting if it weren't for the fact that it was glowing.

The man smirked at us, probably because I'd done his job for him and willingly came. Two knives snapped out of the bottom of his jacket and my gaze widened.

I was such a fucking idiot.

Daxon pushed me behind him, the knife tucked into his belt to make way for the sharp claws his hands had transformed into. He held them up threateningly, but the hunter's grin only broadened, like Daxon had pulled out a rubber chicken or something.

Not sure why that had come to mind.

"Hello, wolfie," the hunter grinned. Before he could say anything else, Daxon threw himself at him, catching the hunter off guard. Both of them went crashing to the ground, the hunter letting out a long hiss as Daxon's claws dug into him. Blood began to seep out from beneath their bodies, darkening the ground around them.

"Daxon," I cried, running towards them, sure that there was too much blood for it to have been just the hunter's.

The hunter abruptly flipped Daxon off of him, both of them springing to their feet as the hunter brandished his knives and Daxon brandished his claws that were nearly as long as the knives.

I swore they didn't use to be that long...

Daxon had a long slash on his shoulder, but other than that, he didn't seem to be that injured. The hunter, on the other hand, had deep claw marks coming down his chest, but he didn't seem to be affected by them at all. He gave me a macabre smile, his teeth bloody and terrifying.

"I've been watching you," he practically purred as Daxon gave him an answering growl. The hunter flew towards me suddenly, and Daxon lunged at him, his claws shredding the man's side as he flew past. Daxon wasn't able to get his claws all the way into him or stop him though, because suddenly I found myself on my back on the ground, the hunter on top of me with a look of victory in his mud brown eyes.

I froze for a minute as he stared down at me

triumphantly, but it didn't matter, because Daxon tore him off me a second later, leveling him to the ground. Daxon reared back with his claws and then slashed him right across the face. The hunter howled with pain and the sound sent chills down my back.

There was nothing I could do after that. The two began to battle back and forth viciously, rolling all over the ground as both fought to get the upper hand. The sounds of their fighting echoed through the alleyway, somehow not attracting any attention from the street where I was faintly aware that people were still walking past.

I held my knife by my side, feeling stupidly helpless.

The hunter's cry echoed through the night as Daxon slashed across his throat. The hunter began to gurgle as blood went flying, spurts of it drenching me as I stood watching in horror.

"Daxon, no," Wilder yelled as he abruptly soared past me, tearing Daxon off of the hunter where he'd been about to level a death blow.

Daxon roared in response, flying to his feet and throwing himself at Wilder, his wolf clearly in charge and feeling the bloodlust.

The two tussled for a moment while the hunter groaned in pain. I watched as his skin began to mend back together before my eyes.

Of course the hunters would have the same or better healing power than a wolf.

Why did they hate us so much again? They were clearly the bigger freaks.

"Um, guys," I called out as the hunter sat up and shook his head, his gaze locked on mine once again.

I held up my knife shakily, thinking that I probably

needed about a million more self-defense classes under my belt right about now.

The hunter crouched, about to pounce at me, and then he was tackled from the side by Wilder and Daxon. I heard bones crunch as they fell on top of the hunter, and he tried desperately to throw them off, but he couldn't get out from under them.

Wilder finally reared back and punched him solidly in the head, over and over again, until the hunter passed out.

"Let's get him to my house," he growled as Daxon held up his knife. "We need to question why the hunters are after her. It can't be just her scent since it's being masked."

Daxon sighed frustratedly and grabbed the hunter, throwing him over his shoulder like he was nothing more than a sack of potatoes.

The sight was...sexy.

"Are you alright?" Wilder asked, concerned as he stroked my cheek, spreading the blood that had sprayed all over my face. "Is it weird it kind of makes me hot to see you covered in blood?"

I stared at him, shocked, ignoring the bolt of lust coursing through my body as he touched me.

I officially had a problem.

"If you two are done," Daxon growled as he strode past us.

I squeaked like I'd been caught doing something wrong and hurried after Daxon, keeping my eyes locked on the hunter's motionless back strewn across Daxon's shoulder, just in case he all of a sudden woke up. Wilder must have done something to clear the streets because we didn't run into anyone once we got out of the alley.

The trip back to Wilder's house seemed to take forever,

but finally, we were there. The hunter was just starting to stir as we walked up to the front door. Daxon made sure to bash the guy's head against the side of the front door as he went through it, knocking the hunter out cold once again.

I was a little doubtful that this guy was going to be able to do anything for us with all the shots to the brain he'd taken.

Wilder led us to the kitchen and pulled out a wooden chair from around his dining table, pushing it into the center of the room away from everything else. He left the room as Daxon tossed the hunter on to the chair, returning a moment later with some rope.

The hunter's head lolled backward at an awkward angle, and he remained passed out as Wilder tied his feet to the bottom posts of the chair and then bound his arms tightly behind him.

"He'll be able to escape those," Daxon commented, and Wilder disappeared out of the room again without a word, reappearing moments later with a bottle of silvery liquid.

"Liquid silver? Nice," Daxon remarked, and my eyes widened as Wilder promptly dumped half the bottle over the rope binding the hunter's wrists.

A scream ripped through the air as the hunter woke up. There was a sizzling sound, and then I saw a tendril of smoke followed by the smell of burning flesh. That was an even more intense reaction than what happened to wolves when they touched silver. Ouch.

The hunter held in the rest of his screams, his teeth grinding together in pain as he tried to keep his face as blank as possible. He stared at Wilder and Daxon, hatred etched into his gaze. I shivered despite the warmth of the room as I watched him plot their death.

"You're going to regret this," he snarled, and Daxon snorted.

"A little big for your britches considering I can see your bone peeking out from under that rope where all your skin has burned away."

The hunter roared and tried to break away from the chair, but the rope held tight. The liquid silver had sunk into the fibers of the rope and somehow hardened already, making it close to impossible to break. He wasn't going anywhere.

Daxon pulled his knife from his waist and dragged the tip of it across the hunter's throat, leaving a thin red line of blood. A few drops seeped from the wound. He then slashed down the front of his shirt, revealing the hunter's chiseled chest. It was littered with scars, like he'd been through hell and back before.

I couldn't find it in myself to feel bad for the guy, though.

"Why are you after her?" Daxon purred. I studied him as he walked around the chair making small slashes all over the hunter's skin. He looked like...he was enjoying himself. Daxon paid extra attention to the hybrid's chest, his slashes covering the entire thing until it was a bloody mess.

The hunter pursed his lips, not uttering a single word in response to Daxon's question.

"Tut, tut, tut," Daxon said with a grin. "Maybe let's try something simpler. How about you tell us your name?"

The hunter remained steadfastly silent, and Daxon didn't like that.

He pulled a small bottle of what looked like metallic glitter out of his pocket and unscrewed the lid.

He emptied a bit of it in his hand, laughing a little for some reason as he then blew the glittery substance onto the hunter. The hunter immediately started to scream, thrashing back and forth violently as the powder settled onto his skin. I realized what it was then. Silver powder. He'd blown the powder all over the hunter's cuts so that the powder seeped into his bloodstream.

Blood vessels burst in the guy's eyeballs as he continued to shriek in agony. I felt a little sick watching, but my wolf was pleased with Daxon's actions. I could feel her sitting at attention inside of me, savoring all the pain.

Daxon walked to one of the cabinets as if he wasn't torturing anyone and grabbed a glass. He filled it with water from the sink and took a long drink. I heard Wilder snort in annoyance, but Daxon pretended not to hear him. After his drink, Daxon walked to the hunter and held the half full glass in front of the hunter's face.

"Want any of this?" he asked innocently.

The hunter eyed the water desperately, the powder most likely making him feel like he was being burned alive from the inside out. The prisoner's breaths came out in gasps as he eyed the water.

"Please," he croaked. The word burst out of him, and he closed his eyes as he uttered it, a look of shame filling his features.

"Your name," Daxon responded.

The hunter let out another shuddering breath.

"Malik," he finally whispered, his shame growing so strong that it filled the whole room, combining with the scent of his burning flesh and making me want to throw up.

"Very good," Daxon praised. He gave the man a sip of water so small that I imagined it was almost worse than not having any at all.

Malik groaned, his entire body shaking as the silver

continued to pass through his veins. A wolf would eventually die without an antidote, but I wasn't sure about a hybrid. He certainly looked like he was dying. There was a fine sheen of sweat all over his skin and his color grew paler by the minute.

"Let's try another one," Daxon said with a grin, like he was a teacher praising his pupil. The pleasant facade abruptly dropped, and a psycho was suddenly staring out from Daxon's features. "Why are you after her?" he growled, pointing his hand at me.

Malik's shaking was increasing as he turned his head to look at me.

"Uh, uh, uh. I didn't give you permission to look at her." Daxon's dagger suddenly cut across one of Malik's eyes, and I yelped as blood splattered the room.

"For fuck's sake," yelled Wilder, wrenching the knife away from Daxon. "What the fuck is wrong with you?"

Daxon ignored him, grabbing the front of Malik's shirt and tipping him and the chair towards him. "Tell me," he roared, shaking him as Malik groaned. "Tell me!" Malik's head snapped as Daxon shook the chair violently once again.

"Jack and Jill went up the hill," Malik began to sing nonsensically, his one good eye rolling around the room. "To get a glass of waterrrrr. The queen fell down and broke her crown. And the king came tumbling after." His laughter grew manic and loud, spilling out of his mouth as a dribble of blood fell from his mouth. Malik turned his attention to me. "I found you," he told me in a squeaky voice.

"That's it," said Daxon, and a second later, Malik's head was rolling on the ground.

There was a beat of heavy silence and then Wilder roared. "You fucking idiot. He could have led us to the other hunters. We could have gotten something from him at least. Now we're back to fucking square one!"

He leveled a punch that Daxon took with a laugh, blood dripping from his lips as he just stood there.

"We weren't going to get anything from him. He'd already cracked."

"Yeah, because you poisoned him with fucking silver powder."

My head began to hurt as I listened to their bickering.

"Guys-" I began.

"Do you care about yourself so much that you couldn't do this one thing to help out Rune?"

The levity on Daxon's face disappeared, and the look he gave Wilder was so deadly...so cold that I took a step away from him.

"Don't you ever accuse me of not caring about Rune again. I would tear worlds apart for her, kill anyone who stood in my way. We both know you can't say the same."

With those cryptic words, he turned and walked past me, out into the night, leaving me with a still enraged looking Wilder.

"I feel like I'm missing something," I finally, carefully, said, as I wondered how we were going to clean up the carnage Daxon had left.

"I would do anything for you," Wilder suddenly announced, leaving my question unanswered. "You know that, right?"

"Yes-ss," I stuttered out. He gave me a longing glance and then picked up the hunter's head off the ground and threw it in a trash bag before striding out of the room, leaving me alone with Malik's body.

I collapsed into a nearby chair, not knowing what to

think. I surveyed the room. It was the epitome of a crime scene, blood everywhere.

Death and blood had become a far too frequent specter in my life.

The dread in my gut told me that somehow, this was just the beginning.

*N*ight cloaked the streets of Amarok, curling around the homes, the street lights, and the cars. Even Wilder and Daxon on either side of me were coated in shadows. I strolled alongside them, somehow feeling untouchable having these two powerful alphas by my side. I also realized how much shorter I was compared to them when wearing flats.

I scanned their faces, each looking at me with a smile, but their thoughts were miles away. Most likely with the hunter they just tortured and Daxon killed.

You see, we were headed to the town meeting that I'd been invited to, and both my alphas insisted that we needed to make a statement with us walking into the hall together. A scene that showed everyone Wilder and Daxon were no longer enemies, but working in harmony, and that I was the glue that brought them together. I wasn't sure if I thought that was the truth, especially after the whole hunter killing debacle, but I wanted it to be the truth.

Maybe we could at least call it a work in progress.

"Is it strange that I'm nervous?" I admitted. "Last time I

attended the town hall meeting, chaos broke out, and I'm sure some people still blame me for the fight that happened."

"That's why we're coming to them as a team," Wilder explained, always the logical one.

"And if they don't all agree," Daxon added. "I'm not babysitting anyone. This is one of those cases where we come down hard."

"I'll do the talking," Wilder replied, and I found myself agreeing on that point. Daxon was having more and more trouble putting on his "sunshine face," as I called it in my head, and I didn't think the townspeople would appreciate any heads rolling at the meeting.

Might be effective, though.

I counted down quietly, trying to quell my nerves as we crossed the road and the town hall came into view. It was a dark building with a pointy roof covered in green lichen. The long arched windows always reminded me of a human church.

"Who built the town hall, anyway? It could double for a haunted church," I joked.

"Probably the cult who lived in it before us," Daxon said casually.

I cut him a glare. "You're making that up."

He arched his brow. "Would I lie about that? I wish it wasn't the case, but stories from the elders say the building was here when the first settlement of wolves moved onto the land."

I was stuck for words at his confession.

"Don't scare her," Wilder reprimanded Daxon.

"If she's living here, she should know the history. Plus, it wasn't us who killed those humans."

I gasped. "There were remains found?"

"Bones," Wilder corrected. "Brittle, dusty bones from a long time ago."

I kept imagining a place covered in the bones from all the followers in the cult, and it made me sad to know that people were so easily corruptible and led with lies to follow a cult leader. Or maybe it had everything to do with fear. Scare someone enough that they begin to believe and do anything they were told. Maybe if someone had helped me see what Alistair was doing to me was wrong, I would have fought harder against him earlier. But I didn't know better, and I accepted the ugliest side of people because they told me I deserved it.

I swore under my breath for the millionth time that I would never find myself in that situation again, that I'd fight to the end.

At the entrance of the town hall, we stepped up to the closed double doors, and I couldn't shake away the fear that everyone would hate me even more once they learned of the danger lurking on their doorsteps.

I had a few friends in town, I reminded myself, and I wasn't this strange girl stumbling into their territory any longer.

Daxon flung open the doors, and the explosion of voices we heard chatting died instantly. Everyone in their seats turned to look our way, so many eyes judging, scanning me. They weren't even looking at Wilder and Daxon, just me. They'd been called to an impromptu meeting by their alphas, and I could just imagine the thoughts going through their minds at seeing me walking down the middle aisle between the mass gathering.

People were glaring at me as I passed them.

Wilder and Daxon stood tall in front of their pack members. Bitten and Lycan wolves mixed together, and no one had torn each other to shreds yet, so I figured the alphas' plan had worked by appearing they had joined together. The air grew thick with the scent of musk thanks to so many wolves gathered in one place together.

I remained between them just as they'd asked me to. No sitting down or hiding, Daxon had insisted.

I couldn't stop myself from scanning the crowd in search of familiar faces, someone to focus on rather than strangers. My gaze landed on Jim and Carrie, the most generous people I'd ever met. The older couple accepted me into their motel the moment I stumbled into town, and have been nothing but angels to me ever since. They sat in the second row from the front, and both smiled at me with reassurance.

Miyu sat a couple of rows behind them with her husband, who seemed to be twitching in his seat, shifting, and keeping his head low. Miyu was trying to help him, saying something. She'd mentioned to me that something was up with him, and I frowned as I watched the strange way he was acting.

"Thank you for your prompt attendance," Daxon began, drawing my attention. He had no intention of sitting back and letting Wilder lead this. I didn't expect anything less from him. "It is urgent that we bring the town up to speed on a new development."

Wilder cleared his throat, his chin high. The room fell into dead silence like everyone was holding their breath in anticipation of the news. So he pushed forward and said, "There's no reason for alarm. Daxon and I are working as a team to ensure your safety is our priority."

"Just tell us what's going on?" a man yelled from the back of the hall.

"We need to be ready," Daxon continued. "Prepared as a unified front."

"On a recent outing, we encountered wolf hunters," Wilder stated, his voice full of steel, but it made no difference.

Instantly, the rise of panicked voices spread like wildfire across the hall. An older woman was crying out in terror, and those around her had to quickly fan her and try to calm her. Only when someone moved out of my direct line of sight, did I notice it was Daniel's mother. The town gossip, from what I could tell. But it was Daniel who glared at me. He still blamed me for Eve's death, and now I'd look even more guilty of bringing death to their town.

My stomach tightened, and I stared at the flailing arms of the crowd as they tried to stand up and push past others, many of them wearing panic-stricken expressions. They must know all too well how dangerous these monsters were. I had nightmares remembering the chase away from those bastards on the freeway. The way just a hint of my scent caused them to shoot at us without hesitation was a massive problem.

"How close are they to our town?" one person asked.

"You want us to fight them?" another cried out.

"Settle down," Daxon said, bringing everyone to silence. "Like Wilder said, this is not the time for panic. We are safe for now, but the time for complacency is gone and—"

"How did they find you?" Daniel's mother asked, clutching a hand to her chest. She looked horrified. And how could I blame her? Those hybrids scared the hell out of me too.

"It's her!" a man with bushy eyebrows and bent nose shouted accusingly, pointing directly at me. "Isn't it obvious? The smell in the air in town the past few days had changed. She's been in heat and it's drawing the hunters to our doorsteps."

"Yes, it's her," Daniel called out.

Shit! I sucked in a strangled breath, but my inhales came too fast, and I blinked back the angry tears. So much rage, and it burned through me.

The explosion of voices was instant, and I shuddered in my shoes. Coming here was a mistake.

I was going to be sick, and I curled my shoulders forward, wanting to vanish.

"Enough!" Wilder bellowed, his voice heavy and reverberating across the room, a growl slowly following his words. The kind of sound he'd make to remind his pack members of their place. He was an alpha and they listened, but it didn't change the cold hard facts that some of the audience were glaring at me with death in their eyes.

"We have addressed Rune's scent, and it's no longer an issue," he continued. "But hunters could have been drawn to our town, closer than we ever wanted, so we need to all be aware of the potential danger and of anyone new coming into town."

Several people were already on their feet, yelling at the risk I put them in, and I hated standing in front of them, hated their anger, hated that I had no choice in this happening to me.

The same man protested. "She needs to leave our town tonight in case they can still smell it...or we just give her to them!"

Those around him were nodding, their voices climbing with their fury.

On the inside, I was trembling. Their anger swallowed me, but I didn't blame them for how they were feeling. Maybe I should just be given to the hunters. I brought harm to everyone I was around.

Ok...stop with the pity party, I told myself harshly.

Rage spread quickly in the hall, as more people were arguing, their shouting deafening. I tried to imagine that I was wearing a suit of armor, and their words couldn't sink in.

"She needs to go! You're putting all of us in danger for her!" More voices joined the chanting for my eviction.

"Shut the hell up," Miyu finally shouted from across the room, getting to her feet. "The only ones we should fear are those of you who forgot what a pack means."

Others turned their attention to the haters in the back, and the arguments blew out of control, with yelling and finger-pointing. It all became too much, and my head was spinning. Except, as I listened closer, I realized that the majority were suddenly fighting for me, taking my side. I'd never had anyone stand up for me in Alistair's house, so it was strange to have my men, Miyu, and so many others support me.

Having them on my side was heartwarming and made me want to cry.

But it didn't stop the darkness of the man's words from striking me as he shouted over the others. They hit me like a hot branding iron to my skin. His hatred sliced me apart. Doubt filled me again. Maybe he was correct. What right did I have to put them all in danger?

Daxon stepped forward, shoulders broad. The man reared back, well aware that he shouldn't piss off Daxon. But it also scared me because I didn't want Daxon to force people to fight for me, to risk everything.

I wouldn't allow it, and when I stepped after him, Wilder placed an arm across my stomach. He gave me a small nod that held me back. This wasn't just about me after all, was it? It was them showing the authority over their pack and not being challenged.

"Sit your asses back down," Daxon growled. "You fearful cowards would demand one of your own be thrown to the hybrids? That's an insult to our packs, a disgrace. Is that the treatment you want next time you're in trouble? For that matter, why are we living as a pack if we aren't here to protect each other?"

"She's not one of us," the man spat. "We all know she's an outsider, and this is why we rarely let others join us."

When the man with bushy eyebrows glared at me, instead of fear, the instinctual urge to snarl at him came instantly, rolling past my throat. My wolf was trying to rear up inside of me, to show everyone she wasn't weak.

Wilder had said he was going to make me a warrior. I was petite and slimmer than many, but the fire burning inside me roared. My jaw clenched, and I held his stare until he looked away first. I needed to keep reminding myself of this. *I am a warrior.*

It was only then that I glanced over to the corner where movement caught my attention, and I did a double-take. Two young girls, dressed in white dresses and kerchief head coverings. My first thought was why their mother had dressed them that way, but the longer I watched them whispering and playing a game where they held each other's hands and spun in a circle, the more I was convinced they were actually ghosts. Just like Lillian had been back at the bar.

They didn't notice me. And no one saw them... except me.

Daxon had been talking to the crowd who hadn't backed down, and I missed most of his conversation. Wilder was talking too. When I glanced back at the ghost girls, they were gone. I blinked and scanned the room to find they'd completely vanished.

Refocusing, I turned to the grumbling that grew louder from the small portion of the crowd.

Jim climbed to his feet. "I'm with Wilder and Daxon. Rune is one of us, and we fight for each other. Otherwise, are we any better than the hybrids?"

"Sit the fuck down, old man," a younger guy across the aisle shouted. "We'll be the ones fighting, not you."

"The hunters won't discriminate, and they'll come for all of us equally," Jim said. And then, gradually, the others stood up and voiced the same. "We're with Rune."

My heart sang, and my gaze darted around, cataloging that more people had joined me than the haters.

Miyu was smiling crazily at me, waving even.

"It's good to see most of us have our morals in the right place," Wilder stated. "Rune is staying with us, and we will fight to protect her. There's nothing to argue with here."

"Bullshit," the bushy-eyebrow man called, pushing past others to head to the doors. He wrenched them open, but Daxon had moved like lightning, grabbing his arm.

"Let me go."

I hated the thickness of the air, hated that I'd brought out tensions between my men and their packs.

Dread twisted in my stomach as I watched Daxon pull open the door and shove the man outside. He stood by the door like a guard.

"Daxon," Wilder said. One word and it carried enough warning for Daxon to tread carefully. Then he continued addressing the room. "We didn't pull you together to start pointing fingers. We're in this together. Of course our last resort is fighting, and we're working on solutions to help avoid this. You need to trust us, but also do your due diligence and be cautious around town. Report anything suspicious to us immediately."

Several townsfolk huffed and groaned under their breath. The small mob of angry haters marched right out of the town hall. The ones who remained left me smiling.

"We're with you," Marcus added, followed by more people.

I wanted to hug them all. But I remained at the front of the room near Wilder.

"Thank you," I said, my eyes pricking with tears. "You don't know how much it means to receive your support."

"Thank you. You're all free to leave," Wilder said.

As everyone moved about, Wilder and Daxon helped funnel the crowd quickly out the door. Out of the masses, Daniel appeared, coming right toward me. I was convinced he'd vanished with the haters.

I straightened and felt for the Wilder's blade hidden under my shirt, wondering if I'd have to draw it.

He paused two feet from me, his eyes dark, his expression hard. He set off an explosion of emotions inside my chest. Mostly anger and wanting to shove him out of my face.

"What do you want?" I demanded, holding my ground.

"Bitch, you brought death to our homes." He scoffed at me like I was worth nothing. "How will you live with yourself with all the deaths that will be on your hands once the hunters arrive?"

His accusation felt like someone had just lit me on fire. It engulfed me with terror, regret, and guilt.

A horrible sorrow cut through me, and I hated that he was right. Everyone who died at a hunter's hands would be my fault.

He stepped back into the crowd, vanishing with them outside into the night.

I hugged my middle, feeling like the worst person in the world.

When I finally looked up, Wilder, Daxon, and I were left standing alone in the enormous room with a lot of empty chairs. And a huge black hole in my heart. I hated that I could be leading all these people to their deaths.

"Some of them hate me so much," I murmured.

Wilder was shaking his head. "They're fucking scared cowards. We'll unite and fight as one if it comes to hunters finding our town. That's what pack life is. No one is alone." His expression darkened despite his words. He knew as well as I did the danger I could have brought to the packs. But I still adored the hell out of him and Daxon for standing by me, for loving me unconditionally.

Daxon took my hand. "Let's go home. It's been a hard night, and we'll talk about this more once you've rested."

And yet, I couldn't help but feel the heavy cloud looming over the town. All because of me.

The three of us walked out in silence when the hairs on the back of my neck stood on end.

I glanced back over my shoulder and found the two young girls standing in the middle of the room, staring right at me with a heavy intensity like they knew something I didn't.

12

"*T*wo cinnamon buns, three coffees, and a chocolate muffin," Mr. Jones said as he distributed the plates of food between Wilder, Daxon, and myself. The owner of the cafe smirked at me, his white hair tucked under his bowler hat. His huge blue eyes held only warmth. From the first time I'd met Mr. Jones, he'd been nothing but amazing to me. He was dressed in a pristine pinstripe suit, and all he was missing from his 1920s appearance was a gun at his belt to fit into a gangster movie. I wouldn't be surprised if he had a toy one at home to finish the look. He was quirky enough to be into that.

"Thank you," I replied, greedily sliding the plate with a cinnamon roll in front of me, my mouth already salivating. I've been starving since waking up this morning.

Last night, Wilder and Daxon couldn't decide who'd stay with me during the night to watch over me, so they both ended up staying, more out of stubbornness than anything else. They took the floor with spare blankets, but in the morning I found myself cocooned between both of them in bed.

They snored like bears, so I slipped out and headed into the shower. When I heard their growls and a large thunk from the bedroom, I laughed to myself, picturing them waking up to find it was only them sleeping and sharing the same bed.

"Let me know if you need anything else," Mr. Jones said, bringing me out of my thoughts. His smile grew wide for his alpha, Wilder. Then he swung around and strolled back to the front counter where I kept eying the cakes and pastries in the glass cabinet. Did I mention I was hungry this morning?

The guys were already digging into their breakfast, and I smiled as I tore apart my cinnamon roll, then stuffed a big piece into my mouth. Despite all the ugliness with Alistair, there was a positiveness that came out of all that darkness. Wilder and Daxon weren't trying to murder one another for a change.

The sunlight pouring in from the window glistened in Daxon's eyes. He licked the crumb from the corner of his mouth, and I instantly grew jealous of that tiny morsel, wishing it was me he licked.

His smile melted me from across the table, his legs tangled with mine, while Wilder on my left was close enough for our elbows to constantly rub. Here I thought I was the only one who loved to be touchy-feely. I was practically desperate for it, but they seemed to love it as much as me.

"I'm ordering more, Rune?" Wilder states, already getting to his feet.

"Pancakes," Daxon said. "More coffee too."

"I'll get right on that," Wilder replied sarcastically.

"What about you, baby?" Wilder placed a hand on my shoulder as he shifted behind me, and I leaned back against him, staring up at him, batting my eyes. "Maybe a Danish pastry."

"You got it." He blew me a kiss and strolled over to the counter across the room. My gaze fell to his strong legs and that perfect ass hugged by his jeans. Everything about him made me swoon. Apparently, I was a sucker for overprotective men who were drop-dead-gorgeous in anything they wore.

"You really like him, don't you?" Daxon asked, then gulped down the rest of his coffee like this was a marathon to finish breakfast.

"And I really like you too."

He wiped his mouth with a paper serviette. "I know you do. But sharing a mate with another wolf goes against everything I've always been taught...everything I feel."

I straightened in my seat, surprised by his words. Though I shouldn't be. "And what if these feelings I have for you and Wilder are unlike anything I've experienced before? What if I can't change what my heart wants? You two are the perfect combination of the man I desire."

He paused for a moment, studying me, and I was expecting a growly response, something caveman-like, but he surprised me. "Things between Wilder and I have been complicated for a long while. I don't think we can ever get to a stage where we'll be close enough to share. Too much bad shit has passed between us. And I won't lie, it destroys me seeing the way you look at him."

"Even when you know I look at you the same way?"

"To me, you're all mine, and only mine. I'll do anything for you, sweetheart. But I'm really struggling with this trio thing we've got going on here."

I swallowed hard, worry simmering beneath my skin. I

loved his honesty, but I hated where this was going. And I refused to choose between them.

He leaned back in his seat, brushing the crumbs off his black button-up shirt. My heart drummed fast, and I couldn't ignore the fact that Daxon wouldn't back down on this point. And I doubted Wilder would, either. But this was a sticking point for me too because I'd choose neither before selecting just one. And he had no idea how stubborn I could be.

I opened my mouth to respond when I spotted the man with bushy eyebrows from last night's town hall meeting entering the cafe with a buddy. I stiffened.

The man paused in the doorway, his attention locked on me, then shifted over to Daxon. Wilder turned to both the men on the way back to our table, muttering something, and the duo retreated instantly and stormed out.

"What'd you say to scare them?" I asked Wilder when he returned to his seat, his arm around my back, drawing me closer to him. He kissed the side of my head.

"Not a damn thing."

"I'll talk to Dean and Paul," Daxon growled under his breath, which I took to mean those men were Bitten and under his wolf pack.

That familiar tension ripened the air once more, stealing the most calming morning I'd experienced in too long. And I wasn't ready to lose it when I craved some peace and quiet for a change. So I brought up a new topic. "I just realized, this is our first joint breakfast together. We should do it more often." I reached for my cup of coffee, and Wilder grinned at me like he was well prepared to go along with the distraction.

Daxon, on the other hand, was too busy staring at the

doorway into the cafe. "I'm fucking pissed at Dean," he finally announced, not hearing a thing I said. "He knows better. I saved his wife from hunters many years ago."

"He's scared," I suggested. "If he almost lost his wife once, this might have brought back old memories."

"It's been irritating me all damn night." Daxon didn't wait for our response, he stood up, and stormed right out of the cafe just as Mr. Jones arrived with our orders.

"Someone's in a rush," he joked and set the plates down, then turned to a customer calling him from across the room.

I glanced over to Wilder, who slid Daxon's pancakes across the table and started eating them.

"Aren't you worried what Daxon will do to Dean?"

He shrugged. "Dean's a Bitten, and I have no say over his pack members. They can sort out their own shit. As long as it doesn't impact you and me, then it's not my problem."

As tempting as it was to argue, I understood it would lead nowhere. He placed a hand on my thigh and shuffled even closer, if that was possible, and I bathed in the way he held me tight while eating his pancakes with one hand.

Into my second bite of my Danish pastry, a loud thumping of footsteps drew my attention to the sidewalk outside the cafe. People were running like mad down the street. At least a dozen. Several others from within the cafe rushed outside.

"Fuck!" Wilder jumped to his feet. "Stay here," he told me, then sprinted outside.

What the hell just happened?

I was on my feet just as quickly and hurried outside, half expecting to find Daxon and Dean in a brawl, rolling across the middle of the road. That wouldn't surprise me in the slightest, except I found no such thing.

People were rushing past me. My head spun with confusion and a rising panic.

I grabbed someone's arm to stop them, needing to know. "What's going on?"

The woman looked at me, panic-stricken, and pulled free from my grasp, still hurrying down the road. "Someone's been killed," she said over her shoulder. "Goddess, it better not be Arcadia. I haven't seen her in days."

Arcadia was missing?

But as more people brushed past me, the realization that someone had been found dead plunged through me like a searing knife. The ache was deep, and before I could think straight, I was running with everyone else.

What if it was the hunters who'd done it?

Please don't let it be them. Please. Please. Please.

Although, if not the hunters, that meant it was most likely the monster who'd murdered Eve. And that wasn't any better.

By the time I reached the end of the street and sprinted across the bridge with everyone else, sweat had gathered across my nape. Like others, I just followed, needing to see this for myself, to understand what we were dealing with. Desperation drove me. Each step grew heavy, my heart pounding against my ribcage.

Don't let them find me.

I crossed the field and trembled as I curved around a small single-story brick home. Frantically, I scanned the crowd of people converging in one spot, trying to see what was going on.

Daxon's voice boomed from within the chaos. "Back the fuck up, everyone, now."

When I spotted the top of Wilder's head bopping in the center too, and he was silent, I could only think the worst.

I shoved myself into the crowd, madly squeezing in between the gaps, having to see who died. I prayed with everything it wasn't someone I knew.

An older man I didn't recognize wailed and collapsed to his knees, his head cupped in his hands as he cried. Others gathered around to hold him up, to console him.

The bursts of terrified whispers in the crowd grew, and I felt their fear like a noose around my neck.

I pushed forward, breaking free from the masses, and stepped into the open circle.

My breaths see-sawed out my chest rapidly, my heartbeat thumping in my ears.

I saw the woman at once, laying in a ditch on the ground, her legs and arms twisted like she'd been dumped into the crevice of the earth. No one would naturally fall that way.

Blood pooled around her from the open gash on her neck. My arms shook as I hugged myself. Half her throat was gone, and my breakfast hit the back of my throat.

I drove back the gagging reflex and instead stared incredulously at the pale face splashed with blood.

"What are you doing here?" Wilder hissed, his shadow falling over me, his hand grabbing hold of my arm. He glanced down at me, his gaze fierce and protective. Warmth spread through me at the way he looked at me, but it was overshadowed by the horrific incident. "You shouldn't see this," he continued.

I laughed faintly, the laugh not humorous at all. "I've seen far worse," I murmured. I shook my head and pulled free from his grip. "I have to be here." I stumbled forward and fell to my knees beside the poor woman who'd lost her life.

The man behind us must have been her husband. His

cries filled the air, the sound of his grief like bullets peppering me in the back, threatening to swallow me whole. In my mind, images of my mother flashed forward. The way she'd been thrown out into the driveway by Alistair, with a huge blade sticking out of her chest.

So much blood.

Just like this woman. Blood kept seeping from her wound, oozing down her flesh and collecting in the ditch beneath her.

Someone behind me screamed, "Hunters. They're here. They found us." After that, the pandemonium around us became a chorus of terrifying voices and accusations.

But I couldn't look away from this poor woman because I'd seen this kind of death before. I'd laid witness to this horror when I found Eve, when I saw the other pack member killed behind the town hall.

Wilder and some of his pack members were bellowing orders for everyone to return to their homes. "Keep calm. There are no indications Mary died at the hands of a Hunter."

After that, I blocked out all the sounds.

Daxon crouched beside me. "The hunters didn't do this," he said.

"I know," I added. "It's exactly the same way the last two murders happened, with their throats ripped out."

Daxon leaned forward, taking a deep inhale, his nostrils flaring. "Why can't I smell the killer's scent?"

"Hmm. What gets close enough to a wolf shifter to kill them but doesn't leave a smell at the scene?"

"Fuck if I know," he growled. "But someone in town's been preying on us."

"A serial killer," I whispered.

"Perhaps," he responds begrudgingly.

Around us Wilder had successfully dispersed the crowd away from the murder scene, members of his pack keeping everyone at a fair distance and sending them home.

Daxon took my hand and lifted me to my feet. Wilder was next to us. "This is fucked up."

"I think it's someone in town," Daxon snarled. "And I'm going to rip them to shreds when I find them."

"Agreed," Wilder muttered. "Same killing style. They always do it near the woods to give themselves a quick getaway. I'm going to take a group of trackers out with me and scour the forest. But shit, this couldn't have come at a worst time."

"Bet you anything, the killer was in the town hall meeting last night and counted on everyone panicking and blaming the hunters."

"Then we need a trap," I suggested. "Something to draw them out." The persistence of panic wriggled over my skin that perhaps the killer was watching us right now, enjoying the chaos they created.

But I refused to let myself explore that notion, or I'd fall into the same state of alarm as the others in town. I swallowed the need to vomit and pretended that it didn't affect me, which meant focusing on something else. Something like finding out who the hell was targeting us. All while dealing with the terrifying notion that I still hadn't stopped my body from going into random bouts of heat, or that hunters could track me down if they didn't find a permanent solution.

Wilder growled and stalked over to his men.

Daxon cupped the side of my cheek. "Are you alright after seeing this?" His words are gentle, his eyes searching my face for a response.

"Yeah, I'm good, just worried for us, for everyone."

He wrapped his arm around my shoulders and drew me under his arm. "There's a shitstorm coming, and we need to find a way to stop it before it hits."

His words didn't comfort me one bit, but it was what all of us were thinking. We were in so much trouble.

13

*W*ilder and Daxon were nowhere to be found, and I needed to go pick up a few snacks, figuring if the guys were going to bunk with me every night, I might as well make a movie night out of it.

I intended to inject as much normality into my life as possible. Looking out for hunters, dealing with a murderer in town, and some of the local pack members hating me was no way to exist. I lived with terror my entire life and couldn't do that again. So, if it meant accepting that things were shit, then I'd adapt.

I stepped out of Daxon's cabin and into the bright morning sunlight, then made a quick turn and hurried along the street and finally reached the grocery store. I grabbed a shopping basket and made a bee-line for the chocolate aisle. Pausing in front of the shelves of sweets, I pondered if I was in a nutty or fruity mood. Who was I kidding... Only monsters ate chocolate with fruit.

I reached for the nutty M&Ms when a cold breeze blew across my back. So cold, I could have sworn someone just opened a freezer door behind me. Except for the fact I wasn't anywhere near the frozen foods aisle.

"Boo!" a female voice yelled in my ear.

I flinched, dropping the basket and accidently pulling on the plastic lip holding all the chocolates in their place on the shelf. It snapped, coming right off in my hand. Candies suddenly slipped off the slanted shelf, piling up in the aisle from the entire freaking shelf.

"Shit!" I spun around, dropping the broken shelf, and came face to face with Arcadia in my personal space.

"What the hell?" I blurted.

She stood with her hands gripping her hips, her glare ready to destroy me. Except...wait. I blinked, unsure if I was seeing right. Something was really wrong with her. She looked pale, like sickly pale, but not only that... Were those the shelves of flavored popcorn behind her that I saw right through her body?

I blinked again, convinced I was really losing my mind. It had finally happened. I had snapped and was hallucinating.

"Of course, I'd find you buying chocolate," she sneered and pretended to yawn. She studied me head to toe with a narrowing gaze, full of contempt. "You really have let yourself go, haven't you? So go ahead and gorge yourself, Miss Piggy."

Stupidly, I let her words get to me, and I looked down at my blue summer dress. Was I really putting on weight? Her laughter had me lifting my gaze, and I glared at her, except I could see right through her head. "Are you feeling alright?" Or maybe it was me who was sick.

I couldn't help myself and reached out to touch her, to see if I was hallucinating or if she was real.

"Don't touch me," she snarled, smacking my arm away, except her hand went right through mine.

A small cry spilled from my lips, and I jerked backward into the shelves, terrified of what I'd just seen. Slipping over a candy bar, my hands flung outward, frantically grabbing for purchase, but ended up bringing more candy to the floor as I fell onto my ass. Crap, the aisle now resembled Willy Wonka's factory. All that was missing were those orange oompa loompas to rush in here and dance because I was losing my mind.

Arcadia crouched in front of me. "Listen up, bitch. Just because I'm dead or whatever the fuck this floating in life shit is, you can see me and that means karma is coming to bite your fat ass. And that's in the form of me."

"Y-you're dead?"

"Ding ding! Hell, you're slow. Look at me, I'm freaking transparent. I seriously don't know what Wilder and Daxon see in you. I guess those two buffoons are just as fucking stupid."

She kept on rambling as I got to my feet, while I attempted to make sense of what was happening. If she was dead and became a ghost, it made sense that I saw her as I had seen the other ghosts, but I sure as hell did not need my lovers' psycho ex haunting me.

"Who killed—"

"Aha." She flung her hand between us, clicking her fingers. "Knew you'd ask that question, and that's why I've been dying to tell you." She burst out laughing. "O.M.G. I am so hilarious."

This girl had some serious issues.

"I'm listening," I answered, noticing an older woman turning her trolley to enter the aisle. One look at the river of chocolates and then me standing in the middle like a lunatic, and she slowly backed away. *Smart move, lady.*

"Wilder and Daxon, those fucking morons finally did it. They had threatened me but I never thought they'd have the balls. I even told them to do it. But in the end, Wilder chickened out and got Daxon to kill me." She cackled like somehow that was funny. Clearly, I was missing the joke.

"You wanted to die?" I asked, trying to actually believe that my men took her out. If they did, they better have a damn good reason, right? Daxon was crazy, I accepted that when I fell for him hard, but Wilder. Nope, that was a hard pill to swallow. Something didn't ring true here, but I also suddenly realized how little pity I held for Arcadia being dead.

"Shit, how brain-dead are you?"

I rolled my eyes, knowing exactly why I felt no sympathy for her. But the shock of her actually being dead tightened my chest. "You aren't exactly making sense. Stop rambling," I said.

"You stop rambling," she snapped, acting like a child, and I flinched at how loud she spoke. "Of course, I didn't want to die. Idiot. Do you think I'd choose to spend eternity dressed in this leopard pajama jumpsuit? I was naked when I died. Too bad I couldn't have stayed like that." She flicked her perfectly styled hair over a shoulder and lifted her chin with that insulting look she used to give me every time I ran into her. But in truth, that was the first time I really noticed her clothes, what with being distracted by her being transparent and dead!

"But I have something to tell you," she bragged in a sing-song voice.

"I'm waiting," I answered because she was just as annoying and irritating dead as she was alive. I spotted a

couple at the end of the aisle watching me talking to myself.
Geez, this wasn't going to end well, was it?

"You're a selfish bitch," Arcadia spewed the words, and I
swung my attention back to her.

"Excuse me?" My shoulders reared back, and I couldn't
help but feel like I was suddenly on a Jerry Springer show
about to get into a hair-pulling fight with my man's ex.

"You waltz into town and steal not one but both Alphas
in town. Who the fuck does that? They were mine!" she
yelled, her face shaking... in fact, all of her was blurring in
and out like static.

"Um, I think you need to calm down," I suggested, to
which she huffed at me. Her mouth opened with what I
could only imagine was another slew of insults when she
just vanished. Just like that, she popped away. Thank the
moon goddess.

Except as I stood amid more chocolate than I could eat
in a lifetime, the truth of what she told me sunk in.

Wilder and Daxon had killed Arcadia.

My chest tightened, and I struggled to draw in a breath.

I turned and ran out of the grocery store empty-handed.
All I could think about was finding Wilder and Daxon to
demand they tell me the truth. It's not that I didn't trust my
own eyes, but I needed to hear the truth. Sure, the girl was a
major bitch, but death... that was a very extreme reaction to
someone pissing you off.

Then again, I was talking about Daxon. Except Arcadia
insisted it was Wilder who got Daxon to finish her. With my
heart drumming in my chest, I was running faster, making a
line right for Wilder's place. He was located farther behind
the town, backing onto the woods. Not too many other
cabins lay nearby.

I knocked on the front door, but when he didn't

respond, I retreated and went toward this backyard, though with his lofty fence, it was impossible to see anything. I listened carefully but didn't hear any sounds; I guessed he wasn't home. Turning on my heels, I went back to the main road, waving to Mr. Jones as I hurried past his cafe. Next stop, Daxon's cabin, as he could have returned home for all I knew.

Daxon's cabin lay empty too. I turned on the spot and huffed. Where the heck were they? I tracked my way back toward town, figuring someone was bound to have seen them somewhere.

On the way there, I passed the town hall, and something about it paused me in my tracks. Everything I'd encountered in that place had come with trouble, but now I was remembering the two ghost girls from the other night. They'd been haunting the building for a long time, and well, that left me curious about a few things. Like could they have seen what happened outside the building? Could they hover through town like Arcadia seemed to be doing, tracking me down in the grocery store?

The murders hadn't left my mind, and what if the ghosts saw who killed the poor guy who had been butchered just behind the town hall?

I marched across the road and grassy field. Up on the front steps, I pulled at the door handles, but they were locked. Making my way toward the back, I wondered if the rear door was open.

Shadows from the building darkened the yard, but I found no luck there either.

I glanced into the woods backing onto the town hall when a flicker of blue caught my attention. A bright electric blue that shouldn't be in the woods, right? Every inch of me trembled with thoughts about hunters and killers. But with it came a deep, heart-wrenching feeling that someone else was hurt.

Looking around, I saw I was alone. Staring back at the blue, I decided to check it quickly because it sat just on the edge of the woods. And I was no fool to go too deep into the forest on my own.

I stepped closer.

A piece of fabric flapped in the light breeze.

I squinted, unable to make sense of what I was looking at. At first glance, it almost appeared like someone was on their hands and knees with the way the shirt was spread out. Shadows didn't help, and it took me a few more steps to finally see that it was just a stupid abandoned shirt.

I exhaled loudly, breathing easily as I scared myself for nothing. "Geez. Stupid shirt." I snatched it from the shrub and noticed the spray of blood on the front.

Looking closer, it looked rather fresh, and my hands were shaking. My thoughts narrowed in on the fact that something terrible had happened to whoever owned this shirt.

The scrape of footsteps sounded from somewhere in front me, and I lifted my gaze to the woods. Darkness shifted through the dense forest, the branches thick with large, green leaves rustling from the breeze.

I dropped the shirt instantly, and my hand fell to my boot where I stashed Wilder's blade this morning. My heart throbbed in my ears as I wrapped my fingers around the hilt.

My eyes were glued to the woods when something shifted between two trees in the distance.

Strong, wide shoulders came into view, but it was too dark to see their face or even the color of their clothes.

I was frozen in place, dread building in my chest.

Someone grabbed me by the arm from behind, and panic burst through me. I screamed and swung around, brandishing the knife through the air

"Whoa," Wilder called out, his other hand snatching my wrist with the weapon before I slashed him across the face.

Daxon was there too, both of them glaring at me. "What are you doing out here? Shit, Rune!"

"I-I..." I twisted back around toward the person in the woods, but they were no longer there. "Someone was just standing there." I pointed to the location.

"Are you fucking kidding me?" Daxon growled, then he threw himself into the woods.

"What's going on?" My gaze followed Daxon until he vanished into the forest, swallowed by shadows.

Wilder, still grasping my wrist, quickly walked me to the front of the town hall and looked at me with exasperation "Put your knife away."

Which I did. "Will you tell me what I just walked into?"

"We set a trap for the killer."

My mouth dried, and his words hit me like a blow to my gut. The shirt, the blood. "Oh shit. That was him, wasn't it? The killer. At least, I think it was a he, because they had broad shoulders and seemed like a pretty large build."

My words were rambling, but my heart was still beating from what I'd just experienced.

"You've just described every man in town. Rune, you can't go wandering off on your own anymore, please. We've told you this a million times." The ache in his gaze grew heavy, and the way he held my arm, his thumb stroking the inside of my wrist, I knew he meant each word.

My feet were locked to the ground, and I stared back toward the woods, understanding that not even walking around in broad daylight was safe. Someone was watching us all the time.

Wilder kept looking over his shoulder and into the forest.

"You better go," I told Wilder. "Go hunt down that son of a bitch!"

"Head straight to the inn so you're not alone." He kissed my brow and swung around, then darted into the woods in the same direction Daxon disappeared.

And I stumbled in the opposite direction, unable to shake off the feeling of darkness following me. Or maybe it was the sensation of being watched.

Fast footsteps took me down the main road where other people wandered around. Having them around made me feel partially safer, except it didn't stop me from looking over my shoulder every few seconds.

Quickly, I rounded the Inn and hurried down the small alley that led out to the back entry that overlooked the river. It was quiet here today, and picturesque, with the sunlight beaming brightly above me. The scene was quite deceiving, as you'd never suspect a killer skulking in the woods surrounding such a perfect town.

I shook myself, hating how my skin crawled. "Stop freaking out."

A shadow fell over me, and my thoughts flew to Wilder, coming back to check I'd made it to the Inn in one piece. I smiled as I twisted around to greet him, but it wasn't his face that I found. The man who stood inches from me wore a sneer, his eyes almost glowing. He wore all black, and a cap on backward, his teeth too white, too perfect, with longer canines pushing over his lower lip when he grinned.

His nostrils flared as he sniffed the air... sniffing me. "You've concealed your heat."

He was a hunter. Fuck me!

"I've been watching you..." His fist connected with my gut so unexpectedly that I expelled a gurgled sound past my throat.

Terror thundered through me as I bent forward, clutching my middle and feeling like I was about to vomit the contents of my entire stomach out on the lawn. A horrific pain deepened where he hit, and I cried out, falling to my knees.

He crouched in front of me, his face in mine, his putrid breath across my face, then grabbed the hair on top of my head, fisting it. "Fucking filthy mutt. You think you could hide from me?" He spat in my face and got up, yanking me by my hair and dragging me with him as he made his way to the river's bank. Death flashed before my eyes.

I awkwardly reached for my boot, hopping on one leg to do so, but my fingers thankfully gripped onto the hilt of Wilder's blade.

I was dragged faster, my feet barely keeping up while my stomach still hurt so bad.

Anger and fear twisted my insides.

I screamed for help, and I thrust the knife forward desperately, shoving it deep into his side. It went into his flesh so much easier than I expected.

He bellowed, the back of his hands striking me across the face. His knuckles were like being struck by a bag of stones.

I cried out, clasping the side of my face with trembling fingers as I stumbled backward. My vision blurred in and out, and terror surged forward at how much trouble I was in.

"Fucking cunt!" The hunter yanked the blade from his side, snarling, his face tight.

But I spun and tried to rush away. He looped an arm

around my waist at the last second and wrenched me off my feet.

A horrific desperation clung to me, and I punched and kicked my heels back into his legs, but nothing worked. He was a giant made of iron.

"Get off me," I bellowed, but with it came a familiar feeling rushing down my arms. And I embraced it instantly, jutting my hands toward his side just as he tossed me at the water's edge.

A spark of white light shot out from my hands regardless, going haywire as I dropped to my ass after losing my footing. Power struck him in the arm, then zapped past him into thin air.

He flinched, then raised his injured arm, the flesh burned like he had it in a fire. His face contorted, and he growled, the pain in his expression terrifying.

Frantically, I scrambled up and sprinted down the river's edge, screaming for anyone to hear me.

The heavy thump of my heart pounded in my ears.

I tore across the land.

But when a heavy hand snatched me by my hair and yanked me backward, I cried out, my world darkening, fear embracing me that I'd die here. And no one would be the wiser.

Tripping over my own feet, I fell, my head smashing against the hard ground.

The monster stood over me, staring down with ferocious anger. He set a foot on my chest, the weight overwhelming me; I could barely draw a breath into my lungs.

"How did you do this?" He stared at his charred arm.

Even from my position laying flat on the ground, I already saw the dark edges of his flesh fading away, replaced with perfectly smooth skin. Shit, he was healing that fast?

How in the world were we meant to fight these hybrids?

An unexpected growl pierced through the commotion, savagely ringing through the air.

Next thing I knew, the hunter was ripped away from me, the weight of his foot lifted from my chest. I could breathe again, and I drew in deep gasps of air as I scrambled to my feet.

The terrifying explosion of grunts and screeches came from the fight in front of me. I couldn't even see at first who attacked the Hunter, but I welcomed it. *Please Moon Goddess, keep me safe.*

I almost cried out loud at the joy streaming across my chest that someone had come to my rescue.

Fear and relief collided inside me, and my entire body shuddered as I watched the battle nervously. I wanted that monster taken out, to see him take his last breath.

In an instant, the bastard was flying across the lawn and crashed in a heap. All I saw at first were twisted limbs, and so much blood pouring from the open gash in his throat that he had to be dead. But he couldn't be dead... not when he groaned and started to get up.

Shit! How can he move after that?

That was when my sights swung to the man who saved me.

North!

The man who worked as a mechanic at Dentworks with Daxon. Everything I'd seen of this man had been scary-as-hell, including the last time Daxon got physical with him to keep him locked up before he lost control of his wolf from the full moon.

He was a Fenrir, another breed of wolf, just like Wilder was a Lycan, and Daxon a Bitten. But Fenrir were more feral from what I could tell. His kind carried the blood of the berserkers and were aggressive beasts, but they didn't fully transform, just their eyes. They were dominated by their wolf more than their human side, which explained why I rarely saw him in town mingling with others.

But who gave a shit when he was my savior. He towered over me with his six foot six size and was a formidable opponent against the hunter. Wild, brown hair frayed around his face, streaked with gray. He was wearing grease streaked gray overalls over a white tee in desperate need of a wash.

He looked my way quickly. "Get to safety, I'll take care of this mongrel."

He heaved for breath, his chest pumping in and out. Everything about it was huge. His height. His muscles. His aggression.

Blood was smeared across his cheek and brow, more dripping from the side of his mouth.

I trembled at the hulking warrior.

Tilting his head back, he unleashed an ungodly sound that sent shivers down my spine.

Then he lunged toward the hunter, leaping forward on all fours like in one of those horror movies.

The hunter cried out a brutal scream, dragging himself backward while clutching his bleeding neck with a hand. In the other, he gripped a blade.

I was locked in place, unable to move if I tried.

But he didn't stand a chance, I saw that now.

North collided with the man, shoving him flat to the ground, and ripped into him savagely. Screams and the slashing sound of flesh tearing rang through the air, the blood splattering the grass around them.

Every punch and slash of the blade the hunter delivered was useless. North felt nothing.

He tore the hunter apart with his bare hands. It was the only way to describe what I was watching. He bit into the hunter's neck and seconds later came back up with the man's jugular dangling from his mouth.

Sickness stuck to the back of my throat at the sight of blood, flesh, and bits of sinew.

I was going to be sick.

People were streaming out from the Inn, others showing up from the street, their shocked whispers growing louder. I was surprised it took them this long to finally come after all the screams and commotion.

Everyone stayed back, in shock judging by their wide eyes and gaping mouths, but how could I blame them? North was a fucking beast and tearing a person limb from limb. Hopefully they figured out soon that North was doing everyone a huge favor.

North suddenly paused and twisted his head back around to the gathering crowd. Blood painted his face. His upper lips peeled back over fangs dripping with blood, and a threatening growl erupted from his throat for everyone to stay away.

Without hesitation, he whipped back to his victim, snatched the dead, limp man into his arms, and sprinted out of there in a disturbing, hunched run.

My heart rattled in my chest in utter shock as I watched him vanish behind the homes in the distance. Screams followed him everywhere he went, and I could only guess he was looking for a place to devour the hunter.

I gagged, and that time I couldn't hold it back any longer. I bent at the waist and hurled the contents of my stomach onto the lawn. It hurt right in the solar plexus with how quick everything came rushing out.

Terror gripped me from knowing that a hunter had been

watching me long enough to know what I looked like, even with my scent cloaked.

That shook me down to my bones.

"Rune, dear, are you alright?" Jim asked, his voice shaken.

I wiped my mouth with the back of my hand and straightened, turning to face him. But he was blurry behind my tears.

A true fear ripped through me that I would never be safe ever again. I couldn't find the words to respond, but tears rolled down my cheeks. Unable to stand all the eyes on me, I ran right into the Inn and up to my room, locking the door behind me.

My heart seized, and I slid my ass to the floor, the door at my back. I couldn't stop quivering at how much trouble I was in. Heaviness pressed in on me, and everything was just too overwhelming.

I couldn't keep doing this.

Couldn't keep running.

Couldn't keep being terrified.

Something had to change.

"I have one of my men outside, keeping watch," Wilder reassured me, his huge, sexy-as-hell frame filling the doorway to his cabin.

My chest tightened as I knew he was about to leave me alone at his place, and I hated it.

After the hunter attacked me in broad daylight in town, every sound now had me jumping. Talk about paranoia, but there was only so much one could take. And apparently, a hybrid trying to murder me again had been my breaking point.

Wilder gave me a wan grin, clear he knew exactly how unsettled I felt. Without another word, he collected me into his embrace, and I laid my cheek against his rock-hard chest, looping my arms around his middle, a sense of calmness radiating from him. I listened to the thumping of his heartbeat, and he gently rubbed my back.

"I miss you already," I murmured.

When I glanced up, a painfully desperate ache flashed across his face, and I watched the battle behind his eyes as if he was dying to say, *fuck it, I'm staying.*

"Rune, this kills me, but I promise I'll try not to be long. I just can't sit around while there are fucking hunters around. We never found the serial killer in the woods, so he's still out there too. Daxon and I are striking hard tonight and hunting down every last son of a bitch." He stroked my cheek and raked his fingers through my hair.

I trembled, thinking of the figure I had spotted in the woods, staring at me, stepping toward me. How close had I been to him that he could have attacked if Daxon and Wilder hadn't shown up. And he was still out there on the loose.

Wilder tilted my head back. His mouth was on mine, and I softened against him, inhaling his musky wolf scent, loving the way he tasted. My hands pressed flush to his chest, and I fisted his shirt. My life had completely flipped from feeling alone to having two possessive men, and I loved it all so much.

It wasn't the first time since I ran from Alistair that I'd found myself with these two guys, craving them. I always fought to survive for a chance at a normal life. Now I had two more reasons to make sure I stayed alive.

Wilder broke away from my lips and the cold settled over them quickly. He held me close as he glanced over his shoulder into the night outside, then nodded to one of his men who stood in the yard.

"Keep the doors locked. I left you a treat in the fridge," he said with a wink.

A quick kiss, and I leaned toward him even as he retreated from me, his hand sliding out of my grasp.

"Be in my bed when I return," he reminded me with that wicked, gravelly voice that drove me crazy with need.

His grin was the last thing I saw before he shut the door. I hit the dead-bolt and shut myself inside.

Then I turned to his empty home.

"Well, it's just you and me then," I said to no one in particular, but it made me feel less alone.

His place was huge... two story, modern and simplistic, and it had a grand staircase just off the entry. It had the bare essentials like any bachelor pad. When I first came here, he didn't even own a television, but he'd borrowed one from a friend just for me.

Yep, he was a keeper.

Of course the first thing I did was track down the fridge in a kitchen that had barely any appliances. Just the counter with a long table and benches running down the middle of the room.

I opened the fridge. Aside from half a dozen bottles of water and a huge raw steak, in the middle of the top shelf sat a plate with an oversized slice of cheesecake. My mouth salivated, and I grabbed it, the whipped cream from the shelf on the door, and one of his bottles of water.

I flopped down on the black leather couch in the living room and started searching for a movie to watch. Something funny and completely distracting. I settled on The Hitman's Bodyguard as I'd heard some amazing things. With cake in hand topped with a mountain of whipped cream, I settled on the couch, folded my legs, and forgot everything else.

I hadn't laughed so loud in ages. I don't even know how long I'd been watching, but my cake was done, and part of me was toying with the idea of doing some snooping to see what secrets Wilder held.

Setting the empty plate on the table near the couch, a picture in a simple black frame caught my attention. It shone under the lights like it had been recently polished. I reached over and picked it up.

It showed a much younger Wilder, a child maybe five or

six. He wore a goofy smile and was adorable, while he stood next to an older woman who had the same eyes and mouth as him. It had to be his mother. It was strange how they stood next to each other but they weren't hugging, rather standing there like strangers for a photo. Something in my chest tightened at the sight.

I set the frame back down and took the dirty plate back to the kitchen, switching on every light in the cabin. It gave me a sense of security to eliminate all the shadows.

Rinsing the plate in the sink, I glanced outside the window when out of the blue, movement caught my attention in the yard. I froze and leaned forward, trying to make sense of what I saw... but there was nothing there.

"Stop being so paranoid," I murmured to myself. There's a guard in the yard, and that was what I'd seen.

I finished washing the plate when another blur had me snapping my head up to the yard. Why were the guards running around anyway? That single thought had my heart racing, and I recoiled from the kitchen, needing to find out.

A sickly sweet smell of gasoline filled my nostrils. It was faint, but definitely hadn't been there earlier.

"Where's that coming from?" Maybe someone was using gas heating in the neighborhood?

Just to be on the safe side, I double-checked the locks. But when the smell of gasoline intensified, I was convinced it was coming from somewhere in the house. A surge of panic struck. And I hastily unlocked the door, then tugged at the handle.

But it refused to open.

"What the fuck?"

Would Wilder have locked me inside? I didn't remember hearing him do so. I checked the locks again, clicking them on and off, and the sound was there as if it was doing its job.

But the harder I yanked at the handle, the more I realized it was stuck.

When the gas smell deepened, I did a quick check of the kitchen just in case something had been switched on. I was about to take off to the back door again when suddenly, movement caught my attention again from the kitchen window.

And for a split second, I locked eyes with Arcadia, who hovered in the yard.

My stomach dropped.

Then she was gone.

"You've got to be fucking kidding me." I sprinted to the back door and unlocked it, but it wasn't opening either. It felt like the door had been glued to the doorframe.

I might have just half cried, half screamed.

The gasoline smell grew, and after seeing Arcadia, who'd promised to get me back...well, I wasn't an idiot. I lunged for the phone sitting on the wall, but the reception was dead. Not a sound.

Fucking bitch.

I darted to the windows in the living room, shoving aside the curtains. No sign of the guard. The windows were jammed shut too.

Of course they were.

"Shit. Shit. Shit."

Doing a small turn on the spot, I decided there was no way in Hell I'd be letting Arcadia kill me.

I sprinted upstairs, going from room to room, checking the windows for any sign of the guard to get his attention so he could at least break down the door or something. But only when I got to the spare room and looked outside did I find him.

He was sprawled on the yard, arms outward, legs twisted, and he looked knocked out cold. Fuck!

If Arcadia could lock up this house, then hell, she could easily knock him out.

Bile hit the back of my throat, and I shivered, feeling the terror of being trapped in the house swallowing me.

A tremendous explosion came from downstairs, and I jumped in my skin.

"What the hell now?"

Halfway down the stairs, my worst nightmare came to life.

Dark smoke curled in from under the front door, the smell acrid, stinging my nostrils.

She was going to burn me alive.

I scrambled down the stairs and raced into the kitchen, where I grabbed a chair and rushed with it to a window. I ripped back the curtains, only to be greeted by a wall of flames.

"Oh, crap. Please no!"

Dread pulsed in my ears, my heart pounding. I had to get out. Dumping the chair, I raced to every window again. There had to be a way to get out of here.

Except, fire blazed in every direction. The cabin was engulfed by a circle of flames.

I was trembling. That psycho was serious about taking me out.

Where the hybrids failed, an insane ghost might just succeed.

"You're not going to kill me," I yelled. "Do you hear me, Arcadia?"

I sucked in heavy, smoky breaths that left me choking. I stumbled to the front door, smashing my fists against it. When that did nothing but increase my frustration, I slapped a hand across my mouth and nose as the acrid stench grew worse.

Frantically, I ran from window to window for any opportunity to escape. There was no basement in this house that I could find. Finally, I decided to drag the chair upstairs and try smashing open a window there. The height might give me enough space to jump over the fire.

There was no way I'd die today. Not when I had so much to look forward to.

In Wilder's bedroom, I raised the chair and flung it at the window. It smashed through, glass shattering and spewing outward. I cried with relief, but the flood of fresh air was snatched away almost instantly.

In its place, a wall of flames burst upward, blocking the entire window like someone knew I was attempting to escape.

I reeled from the intense heat, the licking of fire that already caught on the curtains spreading through the room.

The room tilted around me as I cried out for help.

I couldn't breathe from the smoke and couldn't think straight.

So I sprinted out of the room, shut the door behind me, and crossed the hallway before sprinting back downstairs. I covered my nose and mouth with my folded arm, struggling to take in air.

I dropped to my knees and stayed low. Smoke rose, and I crawled quickly across the living room near the couch and held myself still, rocking back and forth.

Each breath was like barbed wire being dragged through my lungs.

Smoke filled the room, and my mind searched for a way to get out. I had to get out. I didn't survive Alistair and the hunters and everything else to die like this.

"Get up," I muttered under my breath. "You need to get out."

I'd never given up before, so I wouldn't now. I wouldn't.

I pushed up on unsteady legs when the front door burst open, coming right off its hinges and breaking apart into shards thrown in every direction.

Terrified, I swung away from it and threw myself back to the ground, half landing on the couch, half on the dining table, its legs breaking beneath me.

I tumbled, hitting the floor hard, while the picture frame whacked me right in the face. I snatched it just as someone grabbed me by the back of my shirt and yanked, forcing me on to my feet.

"Rune," Wilder cried out. "I've got you."

Next thing I knew, I was thrown over his shoulder, and he rushed us out of the house.

Flames sparked and cracked, the heat overbearing, and my vision blurred in and out from the smoke I had inhaled. More of it curled up into the night sky, blotting out the moon.

I was coughing uncontrollably, my throat raw and stinging.

When my feet finally touched the ground outside the burning cabin, I stumbled back into Wilder's arms, where he held me...right where I belonged.

"Rune, are you okay? What the hell happened?" He held me by my shoulders and forced me to look up at him.

His gaze fell to the picture frame I still clutched with a death-grip to my chest. I handed it to him, and he stared at the photo of him and his mother for a long time before taking it from me. The one thing I saved from his burning house with all his belongings was a photo.

"I'm sorry," I croaked, my insides shrivelling up to think I caused him to lose everything. It took me a moment to find my balance and stand on my own, to actually draw in breath that didn't cut into my insides. "I never wanted anyone to get hurt or for you to lose your home."

He's holding me, the hurt and conflict in his eyes deepening the ache in my heart. "It's just a cabin. I can rebuild. What matters is that you're safe. Who did this?" he asked, his voice heavy.

Behind him, I finally noticed that half the town was putting out the fire with buckets and hoses, including Daxon, madly hosing down the out-of-control flames. They were racing around wearing masks over their mouths and noses, yelling instructions at one another.

It broke me to know that I continued to bring so much trouble to this town for everyone.

"Rune, talk to me," Wilder asked, and I turned my attention back to him.

"A-Arcadia," I stuttered. "She did this. She tried to kill me."

He blinked at me, the shade of his face paling instantly. He paused for a long moment, and there was only silence between us. Then he was shaking his head. "No, she couldn't have." His tone tightened, and he sounded adamant, and of course he was. He and Daxon had killed the girl.

"It was her," I insisted. "She's a ghost, and she threatened me earlier at the grocery store. Apparently, I can see spirits now, and I have no idea why. But I guess she was coming for her final revenge against me from beyond the grave."

Wilder wasn't responding, and the wheels behind his eyes were spinning as he tried to piece everything I'd told him together.

"She told me what you and Daxon did to her."

He sighed heavily, his gaze tracing my face, a haunted look twisting his expression. I saw the pain on Wilder's face...mixed with a bit of regret. "She had it coming to her. I won't change my decision."

"Why did you do it?" I implored, needing to understand. Just then, Daxon stormed up to us like a hurricane. He grabbed me instantly and wrapped me in his arms, lifting me off the ground. His breaths raced, and he smelled of smoke, but beneath that was his musky, sexy scent that drove me crazy.

"Don't ever scare me like that again, sweetheart. You cannot die...this shit has to stop." He was kissing me, peppering my face with soft kisses, and I heard the ache of his pain in his voice.

"I'll try my best," I answered, then broke into a cough.

He set me back on my feet when Wilder interrupted us, gaining himself a guttural growl from Daxon. "She knows about Arcadia. The bitch came to her as a ghost and burned my house down with Rune in it."

"Are you fucking kidding me? That psychopath," Daxon growled, his body tensing. I raised a brow at his choice of words, considering how much I knew he enjoyed killing, but he wasn't the one trying to off me. Unlike his ex.

"Why did you kill her?" I asked again, staring at both men, my back stiffening. I tried to hold my impatience inside, but panic turned my heart into a beating drum at the thought of discovering Wilder was just as much a loving murderer as Daxon. And I already had a feeling I only knew the tip of the iceberg when it came to Daxon. I loved him, but I also loved Wilder just as he was.

Daxon's chest puffed out. "Because the bitch sold you out to Alistair. She told one of your ex's enforcers about you. That's how he found you in town. And there was no fucking way she was going to walk away from pulling that shit."

My world spun, and I stumbled at his words. Wilder caught me before I fell over. I winced, Daxon's words welling in my chest like someone had punched me over and over.

"She sold me out," I cried, the words shaking with anger.

"After that, she lost the right to live," Wilder growled, the anger on his face darkening. "She wanted you dead and away from me. That wasn't going to happen."

I lifted my head, tears filling my eyes from the anger burning through my veins. There was a part of me that wanted to just scream and go find her. Perform a seance so I could bring her back from the grave and kill her again myself. But what more could I do to her that the men already hadn't? She was a ghost for the rest of eternity, and I had no pity for her. Because of her selfish actions, the woman I'd always thought was my mother had been killed. Not to mention losing the answers to who my true parents could be.

She deserved everything she got.

Still, I was shaking furiously at her, while Daxon rubbed my arm soothingly.

I closed my eyes and my world spun. Maybe I'd inhaled too much smoke, but I felt myself slipping, and the next thing I knew, I opened my eyes and was cradled in Daxon's arms.

"You've been through too much, sweetheart. And you're no longer staying at the Inn. It's not safe. You're moving in with me."

"Like fuck she is," Wilder snapped, drawing attention from a few of the locals fighting the blaze.

I cringed on the inside, tired of their incessant arguing, especially when we already had so much against us.

"And you're going to stop me?" He laughed for show and to mock Wilder. "What do you suggest? That you'll move in with her at that run-down Inn?" Daxon snapped.

Well, the place wasn't that bad, in all honesty. Jim and Carrie made it feel cozy and welcoming.

"There are other temporary homes I can move into, and she's coming with me." Wilder stepped closer, and I was pinned between two Alphas ready to tear each other apart.

Anxiety flared, my heart rate spiking, and after everything, I barely held it together to not cry. I was exhausted by their jealousy.

"Enough," I roared with my last ounce of energy. "Please, no more fighting. I think I'm going to pass out."

My head pulsed with a growing headache, and exhaustion carved through me. I broke into a coughing fit, my lungs straining.

Wilder and Daxon exchanged glances, growling, and if I wasn't in Daxon's arms, they would already be in a brawl.

The death glares deepened, and they broke out into an argument about where I should live and who deserved to be with me, their voices rising in anger. I blocked out most of it as my head thumped; I'd heard it all before.

The power struggle.

The ego.

The loathing for one another.

I really didn't have the energy for this, and my words came flying out loudly. "Either we all live together, or I'm going back to the Inn on my own. I get final say on what happens to me," I snapped and waited.

My heart banged in my chest, and my breaths came faster, each one painful and raspy as I dragged air into my lungs.

Both of them were silent, their massive forms on either side of me like mountains.

I know they didn't have plans to hurt me... that I was sure of. But with how the dynamics were going between us, one of them would end up dead very soon if something didn't change. And I sure as hell couldn't live with that.

Daxon was studying me, and I couldn't work out what he was thinking.

"Sure. Why the fuck not," he said suddenly, his voice dripping with sarcasm. "We'll all live together like one big fucking happy family." His quick response took me completely off guard. "Just stay the fuck out of my way, Wilder. And no one goes into the basement."

I threw my arms around his neck, tucking my face against the curve of his neck. "Thank you."

I had no idea if this would end up with them murdering one another, but I was hoping it might be the solution to them finally healing some of the wounds that had started years before I'd arrived in town.

When I looked over to Wilder, shadows crept under his eyes, and he hadn't responded. His attention lowered to me, and I smiled at him softly, needing them to make this happen. For me. For their packs. For us to survive.

"Appreciate it," Wilder answered with a dark voice. "And got it. No basement. You sure the serial killer isn't you?" He barked, but there was no laughter.

Was he being serious?

Daxon groaned in response. "I'm taking Rune home." Then we were gone, walking across the lawn and onto the sidewalk.

When I looked back over Daxon's shoulder to Wilder, he was studying his burning home.

My heart hurt like someone had jammed a blade into it and twisted it.

I did that to him. I caused his cabin to go up in flames. I took everything from him, and I had to find a way to make it up to him before the guilt swallowed me.

15

I was glued to the window from inside the car, staring at the oversized fair. We'd been driving for an hour to reach Highville, a nearby town, because everyone insisted I needed some *fun* time. Especially since we were in the month of October and that meant all things Halloween, a holiday that used to be my favorite when I was a little girl.

I got caught for a moment in memories as we got closer, remembering the decorations my mother had put around the house, the costumes she'd lovingly sewn into the early hours of the morning. I remembered it all as if it had happened yesterday.

A feeling of love seeped into my veins, and for a moment I felt warm, bathed in a golden light. She'd loved me even if she hadn't created me. Had my real mother?

I pushed aside the issue of my real birth parents for another day and tried to psych myself out to at least pretend to have fun.

Bright lights from the fair glinted against the overcast day, and there were people everywhere, making their way toward the *Spook-tacular Fair*, as written on the huge banner flapping in the breeze over the entrance. Small town fairs were evidently a big part of life around here, with all the big cities hours and hours away. I wasn't complaining.

Beyond the gates, there were rollercoasters and carousels, and I couldn't help but remember the fair we attended weeks ago that somehow felt like years ago, and the kooky fortune teller. There better not be one at this fair.

Coming to a complete stop in the parking area, I scrambled outside, where the cool air swished through my hair and ruffled the skirt of my yellow dress.

"This looks like fun!" Miyu squealed, rushing over to me. She grabbed my hand and was so giddy, it made me laugh and jump up and down with her.

"I love fairs," she said. "Rae, hurry up."

He curved around the car, taking his time walking, his head low, and looked as excited to be here as Wilder and Daxon who were standing a few cars away waiting. They both insisted on attending, which was perfect for me. As long as they didn't break into an argument, it would be a perfect day.

Since moving in together, the jealousy between them had skyrocketed. And I wouldn't lie that it was starting to get on my nerves.

Was it too much to ask for the two men I loved to get along?

A flicker of guilt tore through me, because of course it was.

Having multiple mates wasn't that big of a deal in the shifter world. The chance of meeting your fated mate was rare, non-existent usually, so wolves made the best of their situation. Alphas didn't share though. Alphas were possessive. If you looked under the definition of Alpha, there was probably something there that said: *doesn't share well with others.*

What I was asking of Wilder and Daxon went against everything in their genetic makeup.

But I still couldn't resist wanting it with everything inside of me.

Miyu and Rae were holding hands, and we all headed toward the entrance, Wilder and Daxon taking a place on either side of me.

"Are you excited?" Wilder asked me, his smile contagious, and my hand slid into his, our fingers intertwined.

"You know it," I responded, feeling Daxon's hand taking mine, and my chest radiated with heat from being with them. The fair was full of humans who wouldn't understand this strange relationship, but I didn't care what they thought. I just wished I didn't feel like the rope in a tug-of-war battle.

I smiled regardless, allowing myself for today to put everything aside and just enjoy the fair. No fights. No arguments. Just us.

Lifting my gaze to Daxon, he watched me, his golden eyes hooded and brimming with temptation. My heart flared in response, and I became hypersensitive to the way Wilder and Daxon stroked my hand with their thumbs, how they looked my way, wanting my attention.

My breath caught in my chest because for a moment, I let myself believe how perfect things could be with us three together, with them agreeing to share me, with only our futures to worry about. They'd been friends once before, hadn't they?

Yeah, Rune, before a woman got between them.

I inwardly flinched at the reminder but decided to remain steadfastly stubborn about this. I wasn't like Arcadia.

Maybe I believed in fairy tales too much, or maybe I'd endured so much sorrow that my heart had no more space for suffering.

"Did I tell you I'm the king of apple bobbing?" Daxon informed us out of the blue.

"Is that so?" I said. "Well, I'll hold you to it if we find the game."

Wilder was chuckling.

"You think you can beat me?" Daxon challenged.

"I have no doubt."

"Okay, settled then," I butted in. "The apple bobbing showdown is on."

Miyu looked at us from over her shoulder, smirking. "Oh, did I mention that this fair runs the state's annual apple bobbing championships? And it's today."

"That's perfect," I said, half-laughing and expecting them to back out.

"Bring it on," Daxon stated.

"I'm ready," Wilder said.

I shook my head, but as long as the only competition came in the form of retrieving apples from a bucket of water, then I welcomed it.

Once we entered the fair, the explosion of people, sounds, and colors was overwhelming. But it didn't take long to find familiar faces from our town here too, which made everything feel a little more normal. Some of them even smiled at me as we passed them.

Progress.

"Okay, where to go first?" I asked.

"First," Miyu said. "I'm going to sign these two up for the apple bobbing tournament. I need to see them do this." She was laughing hysterically as she and Rae vanished into the crowd.

Daxon was shaking his head as the three of us wandered in the opposite direction, mostly following the flow of the masses.

Of course, the first ride we passed was the Love Tunnel, and as corny as it sounded, I paused. "Let's go on that," I said, already dragging both guys with me.

Each of them groaned.

But I didn't care as I stared at the small boat with a red heart on the front and a cherub cutout behind the seat. The couple in the boat were kissing as they sailed right into the arched doorway with a blinking love heart sign flashing above it.

I couldn't help but smile at the notion that I finally understood the true power of love. "I really want to try this out, please," I pleaded, already pulling the guys alongside me.

"Yeah, that's not going to happen," Daxon said.

"Why?" I turned to him, pouting.

"Don't look at me that way. You're breaking my heart, sweetheart. We're not all going to fit."

"You're welcome to stay behind," Wilder offered, and drew me to his side by my hand.

Daxon snorted a laugh. "I don't think so. Let's go. I'll make us fit." The determination on his face sort of scared me.

By the time we made our way to the front of the line and scored our very own love boat, Daxon might have been onto something about the whole fitting thing.

The guys were practically glued to each other, side by side, and, well, that had me sitting on their laps. When the young man at the ride booth insisted that wasn't permitted, Daxon had a small chat with him privately and suddenly we were allowed to do anything... even swim the whole length if we so chose. I'd be passing on that thought; the water underneath the boats was a rancid yellow color...who knew what was growing down there.

Wilder had his arm looped around my middle like a seat-belt while Daxon lounged back and kept a hand on my thigh.

"Well, this is fun," I said, being completely genuine. Sure, my seat was bumpy, but I loved being up close and personal with my guys.

And we were off, entering the tunnel.

Everything went dark very quickly, and a coldness crept up my arms, which I guessed they did on purpose to encourage snuggling. I leaned back into Wilder's arm, while Daxon's hand crept up my thigh and under my skirt.

"I like this ride," Daxon said, his fingers brushing over the fabric of my underwear, so softly that I had to hold a moan in.

Wilder, taking that as a response to his embrace, kissed my shoulder, and suddenly, I was thrown into a fantasy of these two Alphas claiming me at the same time. Of course, it also slightly terrified me with how it might play out considering both were incredibly dominating and competitive.

A flash of red light flicked on in the tunnel, and I squinted until my eyes focused.

We were gliding past a fairy tale scene. Snow White lay in her glass case with her prince charming kneeling by her side. The fake woods surrounding them were swaying, birds on wires swung back and forth in the air, and a soft classical ballad played. The animatronic characters had the prince moving in closer, his mouth touching hers, then he jerked back just as Snow's eyes flipped open. That led to the seven dwarfs breaking into a skipping dance.

"This is ridiculous," Daxon grumbled.

"Hush," I said. "I love this." To be fair, I'd never experienced rides like these, but I'd read about them. And I was catching up on all the things I missed.

"You're adorable," Wilder whispered, his lips on my neck. The lights switched off again, and we were thrown into darkness.

Instinct kicked in as both men were all over me again, their mouths, their hands, and you didn't hear me complain. I just hoped they didn't have those infra-red cameras in here.

Okay, I was freaking loving the ride. A moan rolled over my throat achingly, a hand on each of the men's legs, holding on.

Wilder groaned in my ear, while Daxon's fingers wriggled under the elastic of my underwear.

Another flash of light, and he growled. I hastily pushed his hand out from under my skirt.

"For fuck's sake, this ride is never-ending," he snarled, I'm sure wanting to pull me off somewhere to act on the charged energy in the air.

Wilder chuckled and dragged me to lean against him.

We passed the display of Rapunzel in her tower, where she threw down her long, golden hair for her prince. Seeing all these scenes, as ridiculous as they were... they touched a part of me. I never expected to experience my own fairy tale. Sure, what I had with Wilder and Daxon wasn't even close to a perfect happily ever after yet, but it was a love I never expected. My heart was close to bursting whenever they looked at me, touched me, made love to me. They were my prince charmings... or maybe more like the big bad wolves. But I'd take it.

The next scene we passed was that of Little Red Riding Hood. The girl in the red cape was running from a vicious wolf lunging after her, his sharp teeth inches from snapping the back of her ankle. In the background of the wood scene stood a hunter, looking like he'd come to rescue her, and he gripped a shiny axe.

"Wait, I don't recall that from the original story," I said.

"Well, that's original. The wolf as the enemy," Daxon drawled. He jolted up in his seat, rocking the entire boat from side to side.

"Whoa," I called out, latching onto the side.

Wilder's grip tightened as I slipped down into Daxon's spot to gain some kind of balance.

Next thing I knew, he'd leapt from our boat and onto the Red Riding Hood scene, then went about madly rearranging things. Which mostly included decapitating the hunter, then laying Red on her back, with the wolf on top of her in what strangely looked like a humping position.

I burst out laughing while Wilder groaned.

"Well, I wasn't expecting that to happen," I muttered.

"Nothing he does shocks me anymore," he said, disgruntled. Daxon still shocked *me* though. I was still caught off guard trying to understand who Daxon was. The affable, golden god that I'd met at the beginning, or the slightly manic heartthrob who didn't care what anyone thought that he seemed to be now.

Our boat sailed right past the scene, with Daxon left behind when the lights went out.

Wilder hastily curled an arm around my back and hauled me up onto him. I instantly straddled him across his lap. The darkness was an illusion of the forbidden, a temptress that had butterflies beating their wings feverishly in my stomach that maybe we'd get caught.

I found his face and mouth with my hands. But he was quicker and kissed me hungrily, his fingers digging into the small of my back. I panted, feeling the hardness in his pants, and I rubbed myself against him.

"I want you all to myself," he whispered. "Mine."

"Yes, yours," I moaned, lost in the lust and ignoring the underlying meaning of what he was saying.

I clawed at his shoulders and plunged my tongue into his mouth, tangling with his. A distinct growl vibrated from his chest, a sound I knew all too well as his wolf needing me as much as Wilder did. Heat overwhelmed me.

I lost myself to him, wanting to hear the husky growl in his throat.

But just as quick as it started, a blinding light snapped on, and it took me seconds to realize it was sunlight. I gasped and scrambled hastily off Wilder's lap as I realized we'd just exited the Love Tunnel. Everyone was watching us, a few clapping.

Breathless, I pushed down my skirt over my thighs, my face on fire. Wilder ran a hand through his hair, not appearing bothered.

"Hey, where's Daxon?" I asked.

Wilder climbed out of the love boat at our stop and offered me his hand. I took it and got up, glancing back to the tunnel but finding no sign of him.

"He's big and ugly enough to look after himself."

I snorted. I don't think anyone could ever call either of them ugly.

Just as we left behind the Love Tunnel, Miyu emerged from the crowd. "Geez, where the heck have you been?" Her words were only for Wilder. "You're going to be late. And where's Daxon?"

"Late?" I asked.

"The apple bobbing. It starts in five minutes, and they need to be there or they are disqualified."

"Daxon is occupied with some redecorating in the Love Tunnel. Where's the event?"

Miyu turned to Rae, who was staring off into the crowd like he wasn't even with us. "Rae, babe, are you listening?" She touched him on his arm, and he snapped around from his daydreaming. "Can you try and find Daxon? He's going to miss the competition."

Next thing I knew, Wilder, Miyu, and I were carving our way through the crowd at a mad pace. Miyu wasn't kidding when she said she needed to see the guys participating in the tournament.

By the time we had Wilder at the booth, and we'd found front row seats to the event, I was gasping for air. "I need to find a way to start running again," I moaned.

Miyu kept looking around anxiously. I touched her arm. "Is everything okay?"

She glanced back at me, her lips pinched to the side. She looked like she wanted to tell me something, but was torn if she should.

"I'm sure Daxon will be fine if he misses out," I reassured her, just as Daxon strolled onto the stage and a handful of women behind us cooed and started talking about the delicious looking specimens on the stage. A shot of jealousy jolted through me at hearing them talk about my men.

Daxon took the last empty spot amid the ten entrants. A lanky man stood between my two men. Everyone kneeled in front of a large metal tub filled with water and floating apples. They all placed their hands behind their backs.

I caught the eyes of Wilder and Daxon, both looking my way, and a flare of their competitiveness sparked in their eyes.

This should be interesting.

"It's Rae," Miyu suddenly said, drawing my attention from the judge spelling out the rules of the tournament.

That was when I noticed Rae wasn't actually with us or on the stage. "Where is he?"

She shrugged, and when she lifted her gaze to me, her eyes were rimmed with tears. "Something is wrong with him. Maybe it's me. It has to be me."

My chest tightened, and I took her hand in mine, holding her, needing her to know I was always there for her. "What's going on?"

"I don't know. That's the problem. But for weeks he's not been himself, and it's been getting worse. He hardly speaks some days, or he just goes out and doesn't return until nightfall. When I ask him, he gets angry and brushes me off. I think he's cheating on me." Her voice croaks like she might burst out crying.

"Oh babe, no, he wouldn't." I'm rubbing her back. "I've seen the way he looks at you. How much he loves you. You just had your mating ceremony. I saw how he looked at you there. He's crazy about you. Maybe something happened with his friends or a family member and it's hard for him to talk about it?"

She wiped a loose tear away. "I don't know. Maybe I'm just expecting too much."

"Stress puts an unimaginable toll on people. Give him some time so he feels your support and he'll open up. I mean, you know guys. Some of them would die before sharing their feelings."

She laughed and leaned in against me. "They really would, wouldn't they?"

I hugged her. "It'll be okay, and if he hurts you, then I'm kicking his butt all the way to the freaking moon."

"Deal." She smiled, but it was forced and didn't reach

her eyes. Worry flickered in my gut. They would be fine. They had to be fine.

A whistle blew that had us both jumping in our seats.

We jostled to look up at the stage where the battle had commenced.

I leaned against Miyu, holding onto her hand. "Always here for you."

"Thanks, lovely." She cleared her throat. "Now, who are we betting on winning?"

"I'm hoping neither to be honest."

She gasped in an over-exaggerated manner.

"Girl, if one of them wins, they will lord it over the other for eternity, and I don't need that when they are already like two giants at war."

She chuckled. "It's all for you. They each want you for themselves and you're making them share. That's got to be killing them."

"Yeah, I know." That ache surged through me again, as I had no idea how to begin resolving this between them.

But I shook it away and instead focused on watching the battle in front of me. This was my day off after all.

Every participant was madly plunging their face into a watery tub, fishing for an apple. But I had to give it to Daxon and Wilder. They were scooping out twice as many as everyone else at a rate that had even the judge standing behind them, cheering them on. One poor kid at the end of the line looked down at the two apples he'd spat out next to his bucket, and then sighed and gave up once he saw the speed at which my guys were going at it, more than ten already sprawled around each of their tubs.

"Wow, it's like they've practiced this before," Miyu mused, unable to take her eyes off them either.

"How many apples are in those tubs?"

"Twenty, I think."

The audience was roaring. The other contestants had basically given up by this stage, while Wilder was collecting those apples and spitting them like a madman. Water splashed everywhere each time he came up for air, his hair plastered on his brow, and he spat out another apple.

Daxon kept glancing over at Wilder, and he must have assumed he was falling behind because I was certain he just growled.

My stomach tensed. "They are going batshit crazy," I said.

Miyu was nodding, but watching the show obsessively. All she was missing was a bucket of popcorn.

"Done!" Wilder finally splattered, the last apple dropping from his mouth.

The crowd exploded with cheers, while Daxon dropped the last apple moments later. Water dripped off his face as he cut Wilder a death glare.

I rolled my eyes. "Hey, let's go and avoid the aftermath of their arguing," I said.

She nodded instantly, and before long, we were darting through the crowd and away from the men. "Maybe we should have come here, just the two of us," she suggested.

"I'm starting to think the same thing." With a laugh, I yanked her directly for the House of Horrors. "There. I want to try that."

Miyu might have squealed with excitement, and we rushed inside.

Green smoke wafted through the dimly lit corridor like somehow we'd just stepped into a creepy-ass house. Picture frames lined the wall, with old black and white photos of freaky families who all had white eyes. The faint light overhead kept flickering on and off, when a sudden scream had us both jumping into each other's arms.

I erupted into laughter.

"Geez, Rae will never stop teasing me if he sees us scared like this."

"Yep, we're werewolves, not chickenwolves. Let's go."

With a small group of teens entering the house behind us, we moved to the door at the end of the hallway, which swung open in our presence.

There were three hallways before us with a number above each entry, and I glanced over to Miyu for her decision.

But in that exact moment, the kids behind us brushed right past, nudging us aside aggressively.

"Hey, watch it," I called out, stumbling, while they screamed and ran into various hallways.

An inhuman snarl came from behind us, and I jostled around to where a six-foot zombie, clothes torn from his body and pus leaking from his wounds, was coming right for us.

I flinched.

Um, he looked so freaking real.

Miyu screamed, and when I whipped back around, she was gone.

"Miyu?"

The growl behind me rose in volume, so I sprinted into hallway number three, as it seemed like a good number, and I didn't want to be caught.

I was running, scared and laughing at the same time, calling out, "Miyu! Where are you?" I kept turning left and right, taking any passage I came across, but when I found myself mostly alone and feeling like I was going in circles, I started to worry this place was a maze, and I was lost.

So, I fast-walked back the way I came, figuring I must have taken a wrong turn.

The moment I turned another corner, a shadow fell over me from behind.

I screamed instantly.

Strong hands grasped me around the waist, and I was off my feet in seconds. Everything happened too fast. One second I was in the haunted corridor, and in the next second, I was brought into a small storage room filled with props like curtains and plastic skeletons.

Fear tripped through me, and I fought to be let down.

When my feet kissed the floorboards, I swung around, my fist flying through the air.

Daxon captured my wrist and tsked at me.

His gaze fell to my lips, a predatory grin spreading his mouth. He liked my fear, that was obvious.

Daxon made me lose all control with a single look as his gaze told me all about the myriad of filthy, dirty things he wanted to do to me. My heart thumped like crazy in my chest, adrenaline still skyrocketing through me from being scared.

But I slapped his arm with my other hand. "You scared the crap out of me."

"You thought I wouldn't catch you after you ran from the tournament?" He grinned, and his wolf peeked out from behind his eyes.

"I didn't realize we were playing a cat-and-mouse game," I gasped back.

He laughed like I'd somehow missed the obvious.

Before I could respond, he came at me, his intensity seeming to fill up the entire small room. I was in his arms in a second, my back hitting the wall as he pinned me in place.

Our mouths clashed as his hands tugged up my skirt.

His hunger was ravenous, dominating, and I gasped as he took me like he owned me.

He curled a finger under the band of my thong and ripped it off me.

I moaned at his aggressiveness, but he was unrelenting, his mouth on my neck, his hand between my thighs.

I softened, whimpering at the way his hands stroked my clit perfectly.

"You got me so fucking hard on that damn boat ride." His touch slid along my drenched pussy. When he pushed two fingers into me, I moaned, my head thrown back, and I lost all thoughts.

If I thought I had any control of myself, I was very mistaken. Daxon made sure of that.

"Is this what you want?" he asked.

I nodded, grabbing at his shirt, tearing it apart, buttons flying everywhere.

He laughed, loving that. I frantically yanked at the buttons on his jeans.

His cock popped out, thick and heavy in my hand. It made me feel dirty to be in this room, hidden away with the public right outside the doors, grasping onto his huge dick, not caring if anyone walked in on us. It also made me feel a little bit alive.

Daxon growled savagely as I palmed him up and down.

He pulled at my dress; the straps sliding down my shoulders, and with a final tug, he freed my breasts as I tried to keep my cries soft.

"I want to see all of you," he growled. "I want to hear you. I want everyone else to hear you too, to hear how you scream for me."

His hand grabbed a breast and squeezed, his other

cupped my ass, his fingers grazing along my crack, teasing me.

"Get your ass on the floor. Hands and knees," he commanded, and I hesitated for a second because the floor was a bit...dirty.

Daxon slapped my ass, and I squealed. The sting of his strike sent a shiver to my pussy, and I bit my lower lip, squeezing my thighs together.

"You liked that, didn't you?"

I couldn't find my voice, but instead did as he ordered me because I was weak when it came to Daxon. And I was desperate to feel him inside me.

Using his discarded shirt as a blanket, I kneeled down on it. He came in from behind me, nudging my legs open, and pushed the dress up to my waist.

I'd never thought I'd like to be dominated during sex. In fact, I'd always thought I'd hate it after what I'd been through with Alistair. But something about the way Daxon and Wilder did it was freeing. Like I didn't have to make any decisions, I could just live in the moment, feel all the sensations, just enjoy the pleasure.

Daxon didn't give me a chance to second guess my position, his cock was already pushing into me.

My heart raced, and I fisted his shirt, moaning. "I love this."

He growled, the sound echoing through the room as he pushed into me, stretching me.

"Tell me what you want, sweetheart," he growled.

I whimpered at how good he felt embedded deep inside me, filling me completely. "I want everything. I want to come. I want to have you fuck me. Hard. Make me scream. Please," I croaked the words. "Fuck the hell out of me."

"Yes, my dirty girl," he growled. He dragged out of me, then thrust back in, hard.

I moaned, clawing at the floor, taking all of him into me. He drove harder and deeper. Just how I loved it.

Our breaths grew heavy, and he picked up speed, his growl filling the room. My knees skidded on the ground as he thrusted, the sharp bite of pain adding to the sensations of pleasure somehow.

"I'll never get enough of you, of this. I'm going to be the guy who makes your heart and wolf forget they were ever broken."

He fucked me harder, and I was breathless, but his beautiful words pushed me over the edge. I screamed out my orgasm.

Closing my eyes, I let myself float away, my pussy clenching over his cock.

Daxon groaned his pleasure, gripping my hips, finding his own finish inside me.

He looped an arm under my stomach and lifted me up onto my knees, my back pressed flush to his chest.

I was shuddering, floating, every inch of me crying for more while he buried his face into the curve of my neck, kissing and nipping at my skin softly.

He had me wrapped up in his arms, and I moaned as my body continued to buzz.

I opened my eyes, then froze.

Wilder!

He was standing in the doorway. His features lit up from the eerie, flashing light coming from the haunted house.

Trembling.

His hands fisted by his sides.

The hurt on his face, the ache of seeing me with Daxon, twisted his lips into a snarl.

Daxon's head snapped up from my neck, but he never said a word, only held me tight against him possessively.

Dread iced through me at the haunting sorrow flaring in Wilder's gaze.

It wasn't like he didn't know I spent time with Daxon. They'd agreed to this, after all. But there was definitely something different about it this time. I'd fucked up. Bad. The guilt coursing through me were overwhelming. I'd come here with both of them...what had I been thinking?

I hadn't been thinking. That was the problem. They both succeeded in making me lose my head, no matter the situation.

I wanted to cry as we just continued to stare at each other. What was only a moment seemed like an eternity as I looked at the heartbreaking pain written all over his features.

I'd done that to him.

I wanted to cry, to scream, to apologize...or somehow beg him to join us.

Wilder growled, his lips peeled back. "Of course I'd find you two sneaking off to fuck. It's what you're good at, isn't it? I'm such a fucking idiot," he hissed.

He turned abruptly and stormed out of there.

"Wilder, wait," I called out, struggling to get up and run after him.

"Forget him," Daxon whispered behind me as he helped me to stand. Except, how could I?

He was written all over my heart, just like Daxon was.

And I may have just ruined everything.

I looked around the diner, frowning when I saw that Wilder wasn't anywhere to be found. I was pretty sure it was his day to be here. Daxon had a pack thing he'd had to attend, so Wilder had told me he was hanging around. Maybe something had come up. I set down a plate in front of Mrs. Rosenbachen, ignoring the frown she gave me as she stared down at her food.

"I ordered the country fried chicken, waitress," she sniffed as she pushed the plate away from her.

Mrs. Rosenbachen knew my name. I know she did. She'd been in here what felt like a million times since I'd started working here.

But she refused to use it.

I pasted a smile on my face and counted to five before answering, so I didn't throw the plate in her face.

"That is country fried chicken, Mrs. Rosenbachen," I told her patiently, grabbing a pitcher of water to refill her drink.

She sniffed, eyeing the food disdainfully. My gaze slipped out the window, hoping to see Wilder and quell the feeling of dread curling down my spine.

He'd been off for days, ever since the Halloween fair thing, if I was being honest, when I'd been a complete fool. Wilder had brushed off my attempts to apologize, but I knew he was still hurt. He'd been quieter, moodier, disappearing for hours at a time without an explanation. I'd been trying to get him to talk to me, but nothing was working.

"It's the gravy! I ordered the cream gravy, this is brown gravy. You got my order wrong," she announced loudly, slicing through my glum thoughts.

I knew for a fact that she'd ordered the brown gravy, and that she in fact hated the cream gravy. But as Marcus was always trying to drill in my head, the customer was always right.

"Let me just get you a new one with cream gravy then, Mrs. Rosenbachen," I told her, lifting the dish off the table and holding it tightly so that I didn't drop the damn thing right on her head.

She sniffed and looked away from me without a thanks, and I rolled my eyes as I trudged to the kitchen.

"I need another one of these, Rae," I told him as I walked into the kitchen holding the plate.

"What the fuck is wrong with that?" he growled, taking me aback with the fierce glint in his eyes.

"Ms. Rosenbachen evidently wants cream gravy now," I told him, shrugging my shoulders. Usually we would both laugh about her crazy demands, but there was a heaviness in the air and the way that Rae was banging around the pots and pans in the kitchen told me that we wouldn't be joking about it today.

"Yeah, yeah," he spat as he grabbed a new fried chicken filet that had been cooking and plopped it onto a plate. Rae grabbed a spoonful of cream gravy and threw it on the dish before pushing the plate back at me without another word.

I opened my mouth to try and say something, anything, to make him smile or relax, but then he cursed at something on the stove, and I decided to try another day.

"Thanks," I finally said, before grabbing the plate and walking back out to the dining area.

Marcus stopped me before I made it back to Ms. Rosenbachen's table. "It's slow today. You can cash out whenever," he told me. He gazed around the room with a frown. "Wilder isn't here yet?"

"Something must have come up," I said with a shrug, pretending I wasn't worried about it.

"Need me to walk you back to the inn, or to Daxon's house?"

"No, that's alright. I'll be fine," I told him.

He looked torn for a second, but then someone called from a nearby table, and he patted my shoulder before striding away to see what the guest wanted.

"I'm starving to death over here," screeched Ms. Rosenbachen suddenly, and I realized I was just standing there holding her rapidly cooling food.

I walked over and set the food down. She pursed her lips in dismay, ready to say something, probably that she hadn't asked for cream gravy.

"Enjoy your food," I hurriedly told her before striding away and ignoring her answering grunt. Marcus could handle her. I was so done with Ms. Rosenbachen and her country fried chicken.

I cashed out my tips and waved goodbye to Marcus before leaving the restaurant. I shivered as I stepped outside. It was rapidly growing colder, and I knew there would be snow soon. The bite in the wind went right through my thin coat. I really needed to order something warmer. I was used to the cold from growing up in Chicago; the wind coming off

Lake Michigan tore right through you, and for a few months there, Chicago was like hell in frozen form. But I was still hoping that Amarok would give me a milder winter.

I walked a few steps outside the diner before stopping, not exactly sure where to go. Daxon and Wilder had been my constant shadows lately, and it was a little bit disconcerting to not have one of them around. I finally decided to head to Daxon's house. One of them would eventually be there, and it seemed the safest place to be without one of them...unless Arcadia decided to burn the place down.

I walked through the town towards Daxon's. People milled around the streets, going in and out of stores. There was a heaviness in the air from the recent death and the threat of the hunters. The townspeople were hurrying along much faster than usual, not sticking around to chat. I waved at a few familiar faces and they gave me tight smiles in return. Sighing, I stopped trying to be friendly for the rest of the journey, not having the energy to deal with fake niceties. Maybe someday that would change.

I walked up the steps to Daxon's front porch, sniffing the air for the scent of either of them. I caught the faint wisp of Wilder, and I smiled and unlocked the door, hurrying inside to look for him. But he wasn't anywhere to be found.

Movement caught my eye through the massive glass doors that led to the back deck, and I sighed in relief when I saw that Wilder was sitting outside on a couch that was set up out there, staring off into the woods that surrounded the place.

I walked over to the glass, relieved to see him even though I had just seen him a few hours ago, right before my shift.

A flicker of unease curled in my gut when I got to the

glass doors though, and my hand hovered above the handle as I looked out at Wilder.

He was seated on the couch, hunched over, a crumpled up piece of paper in his hands. I saw an envelope lying on the coffee table in front of him; the top torn off. There also looked like there was some kind of newspaper clipping on the table as well.

I felt like I was intruding on something as I stood there, and then I scoffed at myself. Wilder had certainly been there for me through some dark times. Whatever had happened, I'd be by his side.

No matter what.

Taking a deep breath, I slowly opened the glass, not wanting to startle him.

He didn't even look up as I stepped out.

"Wilder," I whispered, and a shudder went through his body at the sound of my voice. I walked over to the couch and softly touched his shoulder. He flinched like I'd shocked him. I quickly withdrew my hand and then stood there awkwardly for a moment before finally sitting down next to him, careful to keep a few inches away from touching him.

We both stared out into the woods that surrounded the property, the sounds of our breathing melding with the sounds of the animals coming to life in the woods now that dusk was falling.

I desperately wanted to ask him what was wrong, but I held my tongue, absorbing the feeling of his pain swirling around us. I could feel it sinking into my skin, becoming a living, breathing thing inside of me that combined with my own pain that was ever-present.

"I got a letter today from my half-brother, Samuel," Wilder finally said quietly in a raspy voice.

I stayed silent, waiting for him to say more.

"He was writing to tell me that my mother had died." I flinched at the news, the loss of a mother hitting me far too close to home since I'd just experienced the same thing. Wilder said the words succinctly, like they were just everyday words, but as I finally allowed myself to turn my head away from the dark forest and look at him, my breath hitched at the bleakness in his gaze.

A devastating laugh slipped from Wilder's beautiful lips, and he hung his head.

"Wilder," I whispered, not knowing what to say. I knew he hadn't seen his mother for quite some time, that she'd left when he was young and started a whole new family. But even with that betrayal, there was nothing that could take away the pain of losing a mother, the person who'd brought you into the world.

He picked up the newspaper clipping on the table in front of us and tossed it at me. It fluttered in the breeze, moving away from me until I grabbed it.

It was her obituary. I read through the glowing tribute, inwardly flinching when I saw there was no mention of Wilder in the surviving family section of the article. I frowned when I got to the bottom and realized that the funeral had already passed. It had happened over a month ago. A quick glance at the torn envelope told me that the letter had just been mailed three days before.

"She was a selfish, terrible woman, I realized that years ago. But you know what my last memory of her was? Besides the phone calls from time to time when the guilt of leaving me behind led her to give me a pity call?"

"Wilder, you don't have to-" I began, wondering if it was best if his pain just breathed for a bit, but he continued on.

"I remember her standing at the front door, three suit-cases with all her belongings scattered around her. My father was somewhere in the back of the house, refusing to see her off. He'd come into my room that morning, told me my mother was leaving, and that if I wanted to say goodbye, I needed to go downstairs."

His voice broke off, and he clenched his fingers into the couch, his knuckles turning white from how hard he was squeezing.

"I was in green dinosaur pajamas. We'd just gotten the set at the store the week before. I was obsessed with them. I walked down the steps to go downstairs, not understanding what was going on. The wood was cold under my toes. I had this plastic T-rex that I was holding in my hand, my parents couldn't get me to part with it. I remember seeing her dashing around downstairs, grabbing odds and ends off the shelves, some fancy silver tea set that my parents had been given at their mating ceremony. Anything she thought was valuable she took."

I could hear the words he didn't say. That she hadn't thought he was valuable, so he'd been left behind.

"I finally made it to the bottom of the stairs, and she noticed me. She was dressed up, like she was going to a party. She was wearing this blue silk dress, and her makeup and hair were perfectly done. She looked at me, and she patted my head." Wilder tore the cushion, the sound ripping through the peaceful night air. "She fucking patted my head. And she told me to be a good little boy, and she'd see me again real soon."

He swallowed a hiccupped sob, his gaze wide and unseeing. Tears were streaming down my face as I watched him. My heart was breaking for him. Whatever pieces that had been somehow left untouched from my own betrayals were shattering for him.

"I didn't get to say goodbye. She walked out before I

could wrap my little brain around what was happening. I remember that door slamming shut behind her...and that was it."

He pulled a shaky hand through his hair before slamming it down on the coffee table, and I jumped in surprise at the sound.

"I didn't get to say goodbye then, and I didn't get to say goodbye now. But I guess that was what my mother wanted."

All the words I wanted to say disappeared because I could see Wilder's wounds far clearer now. We'd had heart to hearts before, but this was different...this was more.

Hatred wound its way insidiously through my veins. I found myself hating his mother for living, and for dying. Alive, she'd left a festering hole inside of him that all terrible mothers did when they broke their children's hearts. But at least alive, there was a chance for the wound to heal. Her death meant that the wound would stay with Wilder forever. It might scab over in time, but it would never go away.

"I've never been good enough," Wilder said suddenly, as he turned his head to look at me. His green eyes pierced into me, making me ache as they begged me for a relief that I'd never be able to give him. "My whole life, I could never be enough. You know, when I met Arcadia, I thought she was my good thing. I thought she loved me. And then at the first sight of golden boy Daxon, I was forgotten. And then you came around. And even though I knew you liked him, I couldn't stop myself. I had to try to get you to love me."

He grabbed my hand, his skin trembling against mine.

"I knew when I met you that you would break my heart. I knew out of all the things I'd lost in life, that losing you would be the thing that hurt me most."

"Wilder, you haven't lost me," I breathed in a shaky voice,

the sadness and hatred swirling inside of me rapidly changing to fear.

"I can't be chosen second again. I can't watch you love him and eventually decide that I'm not enough. I'm not strong enough."

"What are you saying?" My chest was tight, and I was struggling to form words, to form thoughts.

He glanced at the obituary, his face hardening as if he'd come to a decision and was steeling himself for the reality of it.

"I'm going to say goodbye this time. If she taught me one thing, it was that I need to do that. I have to do that."

He stood up, letting go of my hand abruptly as I scrambled with what to do, what to say.

"Wilder, please. We can talk about this." My words came out in pleading gasps.

He bent over and grabbed the obituary, crumpling it into his hand along with the letter. He took two steps away, and then turned back towards me.

My heart leapt with illogical hope that he'd changed his mind already, that everything he'd just spoken were words born of grief, not of truth.

"You'll always be the wild I was looking for, Rune," he murmured. "And I'll always be the one that wasn't good enough."

He walked away then, and the night quickly swallowed him into her depths.

And I swore I heard my soul breaking, shattering like glass.

I'd been rejected by the one the goddess had created just for me.

And I didn't think that had hurt as badly as this.

17

*T*he house felt empty without Wilder. I'd stayed on that porch for the rest of the night, staring out into the forest, waiting, just waiting, for him to come back.

I could sense him out there, and it felt like that had to mean something, that he hadn't completely disappeared when he knew I'd be alone for the rest of the night without him.

Eventually I drifted off, on that couch, my exhaustion one that was soul deep and my dreams filled with a nonstop reel of me running through the darkness looking for Wilder, and never finding him.

I came to when a pair of strong arms picked me up and began to carry me inside. I flinched before inhaling the comforting, familiar scent of Daxon.

"What are you doing out here, baby?" he grumbled tiredly. My eyes flickered open, and I stared into Daxon's exhausted looking face. Looking over my shoulder, I could see the sky starting to lighten, meaning that Daxon had been out all night.

It took a second for everything to come rushing back, and when it did, it felt like I was dying all over again.

"Wilder," I moaned the words, and Daxon stared down at me worriedly, carrying me to the couch in the living room and gently setting me down.

He frowned, looking around the house like he expected Wilder to suddenly walk out. "Where is that bastard, anyway?"

"He's gone," I answered in a hollow voice.

"He was supposed to be here all night with you. That was the only reason that I even said yes to helping find the McCarthy boys." Daxon was furious, and I was actually glad that Wilder wasn't here right at that moment because he would have attacked him for sure.

Daxon's words sank in. "Wait, did you find their sons? Did the killer get them?" Fear sliced through my pain, but Daxon quickly shook his head before my panic went out of control.

"The brothers got stuck in the quarry. It just took so long because neither of them were supposed to be in the quarry in the first place, so no one knew to look there." He pulled me close to him and ran his fingers through my hair soothingly. "Baby, it's alright. I should have phrased that differently." Daxon pulled me a bit farther from his body and grabbed my chin gently. "You still haven't said where Wilder is."

"I don't know where he is," I answered softly, tears filling my eyes as the truth rolled over me for the millionth time since he'd left. "He got a letter that his mother had died...and then he started talking about how every woman in his life leaves him. And then he said he had to say goodbye. I don't even know how it all happened."

I pulled my arms from where I'd had them around him

and buried my face in my hands, heavy sobs erupting out of me. Daxon rubbed my back soothingly. "He'll be back, sweetheart. As much as I wish he won't be, and he really is done, he'll be back. He loves you too much to leave for good."

"You didn't see him, you didn't hear the words he said. He was done, Daxon. I broke him."

The words sounded very melodramatic as I said them, but I believed them. It felt like there was a golden thread that had been connecting Wilder and Daxon and me, that I hadn't even realized was there. But when it was severed...there was no missing that.

I'd thought long and hard about what I was feeling all last night, wondering how it could hurt so badly when he wasn't my fated mate, when I hadn't accepted his bite at all. The answer was pretty obvious once I'd thought about it. I'd never truly loved Alistair; I'd never had a chance to. I'd been in love with the idea of him, and when he rejected me, it was my wolf that was truly hurt. It was the promise of him that destroyed me. He hadn't actually broken my heart, because there had never been a chance for him to have it in the first place.

I was destroyed by Wilder's rejection because I'd actually loved him. We'd had time and room to build something, something so pure and beautiful that the loss of it would stay with me forever.

I examined Daxon's beautiful face. He was looking at me so earnestly, like he couldn't stand the sight of my tears. Somehow I'd fallen in love with them both, and even though I'd known that for a while now, the depth of it was just sinking in.

I hadn't wanted to fall in love with them. But it had

happened as easily as breathing. Slowly at first, and then all at once, until it wasn't a choice anymore. It was a need.

I never knew what love was, not really. I had no memories of my father and mother's love...or at least the fake mother and father I'd had. I'd never had real interactions with pack members to see what their relationships were like. What I'd thought was love had been twisted and wrong, so ugly that the moon goddess herself must have averted her gaze from it.

But what I'd built with Wilder and Daxon was going to be beautiful. It had a million roadblocks, and I'd been willing to overcome them all.

I just couldn't do the one thing that both of them wanted from me: pick one of them.

Daxon held me close in the broken silence. "He's a bloody fool, Rune," he finally whispered. "Only a fool would willingly lose a girl as perfect as you."

"I'm tired, Daxon," I whispered to him reluctantly. "Sometimes it feels like the whole universe has conspired against me, that I'll never just be allowed a moment of peace. I haven't even had a chance to start and try and figure out who my real parents were with everything that's been going on." My voice broke, and I had to take a deep breath before I could speak again. "I feel like I can't breathe with him gone. And here I am, crying in your arms for another man when you're everything I could ever want."

I pulled away from him and moved off his lap onto the couch. I tucked my knees against my chin, rocking back and forth slowly.

"Rune," Daxon said gruffly. It was a struggle to meet his eyes because I was so afraid of what I would see. Would this be where he left too? I wanted desperately to be this strong, powerful woman...a strong, powerful wolf, but it was so fucking hard. I'd been put through fire, and what should have made me fierce and unbreakable had instead left gaping cracks in my psyche that I wasn't sure I could ever fix.

"I love you, Rune," Daxon said softly, taking my hand and holding it against his chest so I could feel his heart beat against it. "My heart is yours for as long as you want it, and it will still be yours even after that. I have a million fucking scars wrapped like barbed wire around my heart, and somehow you've drawn stars around them all, filled in my jagged edges with something I'll do anything not to lose. He'll come back, Rune, because he's not a fool. You don't get a taste of perfection and then give it up."

A hiccuped sigh slipped out of me as I tried to get ahold of myself.

"And if he doesn't, I swear to you, you'll never lose me. And if somehow something takes me away from you, I swear to do everything in my power to always come back."

Maybe a better woman would have said something in return and then asked to be alone so that she could continue to mourn her lost love.

But I wasn't a better woman. And I took what Daxon offered me with everything I had. I leaned in to kiss him fervently, and he kissed me back desperately, like we only had tonight instead of forever.

Our kisses soon became more. Clothes were slipped off and our bodies soon moved together. Soft sighs and silent declarations. Daxon soothed my soul with his touch, and it should have been enough.

A better woman would have been happy to just have Daxon in her arms.

Instead, I wished with everything in me that Wilder had been there too.

A better woman, I was not.

~

I DANCED THROUGH THE TREES, my paws padding almost silently through the decaying leaves and the soft, cold ground as I ran. I left silver, glittery footsteps behind me as I went, and the cold breeze soon made them disappear. This was how I should be living every day, wild and free to be whatever I wanted. I owned this world. No one could stop me.

Wait, this wasn't right. My consciousness perked up suddenly, my wolf growling at me to go back to sleep, or wherever it was I'd been while she'd taken over and gone on this run. I struggled to think about where I'd been before this. I'd been at the coffee shop with Miyu, right? With Wilder gone to wherever it was he'd disappeared to, Daxon had a million pack responsibilities. He'd dropped me off to spend the day with Miyu...and then what?

It was all blank after that.

My legs pushed forward, my wolf refusing to relinquish control. She was heading somewhere purposefully, her breath pushing steadily and easily out as she ran quickly through the woods, as if drawn by something. I pushed against her, trying to figure out how to shift back, but it didn't work. Although a part of me knew I needed to get back to the safety of town, something inside of me told me that I was safe. That my wolf would make sure nothing happened to me.

The forest began to thin out up ahead, and I saw that we were coming up to a clearing. There were voices up ahead, so my wolf slowed down until she was practically creeping, her body close to the ground as she went to investigate.

Except the voices became more familiar to me the closer we got to the clearing. My wolf clearly recognized Wilder's voice as well because she wasn't sneaking around anymore. She was flat out sprinting towards his voice as fast as she could.

We burst into the clearing and then came to a sudden stop. Wilder was standing there with Daria, his arms wrapped around her desperately, kissing her passionately like she was everything to him. Like I was sure he'd once kissed me.

My wolf dropped to the ground like she'd been shot, and I immediately shifted, laying there in the mud naked like the forgotten cast off that I was. They were so wrapped in each other's embrace that it took a full minute for them to notice me there after they finally ended their kiss.

A whine ripped from my chest. I'd thought I was dying when he'd left and said it was over, but this...something got lost inside of me, a coldness moving in and absorbing everything around it.

Wilder gazed at me impassively while Daria smiled like she'd won everything.

I jumped up from the ground, filthy and naked, feeling utterly betrayed. Maybe I should have asked for answers. But Wilder didn't seem inclined to want to say anything.

So instead, I ran away, shifting back again as I did so, my human heart unable to bear what had just happened.

Wilder didn't come after me. And maybe that was all the answer I needed.

18

RUNE

I don't remember the trip back to Daxon's house. Everything was a blur, a mess of images with Wilder and Daria's kiss interspersed as a highlight through them all. I shifted and stumbled up the stairs to Daxon's front door, truly unsure what I was supposed to do now. Once inside, I walked immediately to the bathroom numbly, turning on the shower to a temperature that was scalding and then getting in, letting the water's heat bite at my skin and take the edge off the pain.

I didn't cry, the tears wouldn't come. The coldness was still there despite how hot the shower had been, spreading rapidly.

I stood in the shower until the water turned cold.

My body felt beaten down, ruined, as I got out of the shower and into a pair of sweats. Drying my hair, I walked out to the living room to curl up on the couch when something that sounded like a muffled scream came from somewhere in the house.

Frowning, I walked down the hallway, listening for the noise again. I heard what sounded like Daxon laughing, and

I continued forward until I realized that the sounds were coming from behind the door at the back of the hall that led to the basement. I faintly remembered him saying something about not going in the basement, but I think at the time I'd thought he was making a joke. Daxon had a weird sense of humor like that.

But he was definitely down there, when he was supposed to be still out doing pack duties. Now that I was shifted back, I remembered that I was supposed to stay at Miyu's until he came to get me. I still had no idea how I'd ended up running in the woods as my wolf, but I definitely remembered Daxon staying out late.

Doubt flushed through my mind. Was he cheating on me, too? Was he downstairs in some kind of sex den with a girl? I hadn't doubted him before, but I'd never doubted Wilder either.

Was everything in my life a lie?

I stumbled down the hallway to the door and reached out to grab the handle.

It was locked.

Of course it was locked.

The sound of someone moaning came through the door again, and I lost it. I ripped open the door somehow and practically threw myself down the steep wooden steps.

And then I came to a screeching halt once I got to the bottom and peered into the room.

A shirtless Daxon was standing over a man who'd been chained to a long metal table.

There was blood everywhere, like some kind of horror movie.

Daxon had been hunched over whoever he had chained to that table, holding a pair of pliers near the guy's mouth.

He dropped the pliers when I got to the bottom of the

stairs, and I realized the only reason he hadn't heard me before was that he was wearing headphones, rock music blasting out of them loud enough to rouse the dead.

"Rune," he said cautiously, but my attention wasn't on him. It was on the man behind him.

It was Rae. A low moan sounded from him right at that moment, and I faintly realized that he was missing his tongue. Daxon must have cut it off.

Shock was hitting me quickly as I backed away slowly, as if in a trance, right as Daxon began to approach me, still holding the pliers.

I'd known Daxon had been changing, that there was a sense of violence laced through his makeup that I hadn't noticed before.

But this was so much more.

Daxon was the killer, or if not *the* killer who'd been haunting the woods, he was something else...maybe something worse.

"Let me explain," he murmured soothingly, like it was possible to have some kind of good explanation for having the love of my best friend's life on a torture table.

Without another thought, my wolf emerged.

And I attacked.

Continue the story with Wild Love...

WILD LOVE
BOOK 4

Real Wolves Bite. Continue the Wild series...

Get your copy of Wild Love today!

WILD SERIES

Wild Moon

Wild Heart

Wild Girl

Wild Love

AUTHOR'S NOTE

So...how are you feeling? Did you scream? Throw your Kindle?

You're welcome, hehe.

That being said, I know that was brutal. Our adrenaline was pumping the entire time we were writing. Some parts of it literally destroyed us.

Just stick with the process. Trust us to get Rune and her men where they are supposed to be.

And remember...

Maybe it's not about the happy ending...maybe it's about the journey it takes to get there.

Just Kidding. It's always about the happy endings.

A huge thank you to Jasmine Jordan for coming in to proof for us. Another huge thanks to Leah Steele for being the best beta ever. Much love to our PAs Caitlin, Anna, and Sarah.

And of course, thank you to you. Thank you for making this series such a success and falling in love with Rune, Wilder, and Daxon.

XOXO,
    Mila and C.R.

ABOUT C.R. JANE

A Texas girl living in Utah now, I'm a wife, mother, lawyer, and now author. My stories have been floating around in my head for years, and it has been a relief to finally get them down on paper. I'm a huge Dallas Cowboys fan and I primarily listen to Beyonce and Taylor Swift...don't lie and say you don't too.

My love of reading started probably when I was three and with a faster than normal ability to read, I've devoured hundreds of thousands of books in my life. It only made sense that I would start to create my own worlds since I was always getting lost in others'.

I like heroines who have to grow in order to become badasses, happy endings, and swoon-worthy, devoted, (and hot) male characters. If this sounds like you, I'm pretty sure we'll be friends.

I'm so glad to have you on my team...check out the links below for ways to hang out with me and more of my books you can read!

www.crjanebooks.com

BOOKS BY C.R. JANE

www.crjanebooks.com

The Fated Wings Series

First Impressions

Forgotten Specters

The Fallen One (a Fated Wings Novella)

Forbidden Queens

Frightful Beginnings (a Fated Wings Short Story)

Faded Realms

Faithless Dreams

Fabled Kingdoms

Fated Wings 8

The Rock God (a Fated Wings Novella)

The Darkest Curse Series

Forget Me

Lost Passions

The Sounds of Us Contemporary Series (complete series)

Remember Us This Way

Remember You This Way

Remember Me This Way

Broken Hearts Academy Series (complete duet)

Heartbreak Prince

Heartbreak Lover

Ugly Hearts Series Contemporary Series

Ugly Hearts

Hades Redemption Series

The Darkest Lover

The Darkest Kingdom

Academy of Souls Co-write with Mila Young (complete series)

School of Broken Souls

School of Broken Hearts

School of Broken Dreams

School of Broken Wings

Fallen World Series Co-write with Mila Young (complete series)

Bound

Broken

Betrayed

Belong

Thief of Hearts Co-write with Mila Young (complete series)

Siren Condemned

Siren Sacrificed

Siren Awakened

Siren Redeemed

Kingdom of Wolves Co-write with Mila Young

Wild Moon

Wild Heart

Wild Girl

Wild Love

Stupid Boys Series Co-write with Rebecca Royce

Stupid Boys

Dumb Girl

Crazy Love

Breathe Me Duet Co-write with Ivy Fox (complete)

Breathe Me

Breathe You

Rich Demons of Darkwood Series Co-write with May Dawson

Make Me Lie

ABOUT MILA YOUNG

Best-selling author, Mila Young tackles everything with the zeal and bravado of the fairytale heroes she grew up reading about. She slays monsters, real and imaginary, like there's no tomorrow. By day she rocks a keyboard as a marketing extraordinaire. At night she battles with her mighty pen-sword, creating fairytale retellings, and sexy ever after tales. In her spare time, she loves pretending she's a mighty warrior, walks on the beach with her dogs, cuddling up with her cats, and devouring every fantasy tale she can get her pinkies on.

Ready to read more and more from Mila Young? www.subscribepage.com/milayoung

For more information...
milayoungauthor@gmail.com

BOOKS BY MILA YOUNG

www.milayoungbooks.com

Shadowlands

Shadowlands Sector, One

Shadowlands Sector, Two

Shadowlands Sector, Three

Chosen Vampire Slayer

Night Kissed

Moon Kissed

Blood Kissed

The Alpha-Hole Duet

Real Alphas Bite

Kingdom of Wolves

Wild Moon

Wild Heart

Wild Girl

Winter's Thorn

To Seduce A Fae

To Tame A Fae

To Claim A Fae

Shadow Hunters Series

Boxed Set 1

Wicked Heat Series

Wicked Heat #1

Wicked Heat #2

Wicked Heat #3

Elemental Series

Taking Breath #1

Taking Breath #2

Gods and Monsters

Apollo Is Mine

Poseidon Is Mine

Ares Is Mine

Hades Is Mine

Sin Demons Co-write with Harper A. Brooks

Playing With Hellfire

Hell In A Handbasket

All Shot To Hell

To Hell And Back

When Hell Freezes Over

Hell On Earth

Haven Realm Series

Hunted (Little Red Riding Hood Retelling)

Cursed (Beauty and the Beast Retelling)

Entangled (Rapunzel Retelling)

Princess of Frost (Snow Queen)

Thief of Hearts Series Co-write with C.R. Jane

Siren Condemned

Siren Sacrificed

Siren Awakened

Broken Souls Series Co-write with C.R. Jane

School of Broken Souls

School of Broken Hearts

School of Broken Dreams

School of Broken Wings

Fallen World Series Co-write with C.R. Jane

Bound

Broken

Betrayed

Belong

Beautiful Beasts Academy

Manicures and Mayhem

Diamonds and Demons

Hexes and Hounds

Secrets and Shadows

Passions and Protectors

Ancients and Anarchy

Subscribe to Mila Young's Newsletter to receive exclusive content, latest updates, and giveaways.

www.milayoungbooks.com

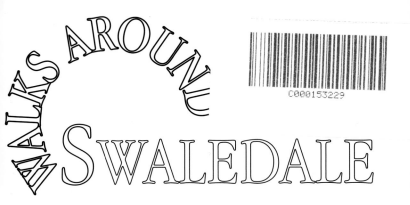

10 WALKS OF UNDER 6 MILES

Sheila Bowker

Dalesman

First published in 2008 by Dalesman
an imprint of
Country Publications Ltd
The Water Mill
Broughton Hall
Skipton
North Yorkshire BD23 3AG

Text © Sheila Bowker 2008
Maps © Guelder Design & Mapping 2008
Illustrations © Christine Isherwood 2008

Cover: Thwaite by Mike Kipling

ISBN 978-1-85568-251-1

Printed by Amadeus Press

PUBLISHER'S NOTE
The information given in this book has been provided in good faith and is intended only as a general guide. Whilst all reasonable efforts have been made to ensure that details were correct at the time of publication, the author and Country Publications Ltd cannot accept any responsibility for inaccuracies. It is the responsibility of individuals undertaking outdoor activities to approach the activity with caution and, especially if inexperienced, to do so under appropriate supervision. The activity described in this book is strenuous and individuals should ensure that they are suitably fit before embarking upon it. They should carry the appropriate equipment and maps, be properly clothed and have adequate footwear. They should also take note of weather conditions and forecasts, and leave notice of their intended route and estimated time of return.

Contents

Walk 1	Keld to Swinner Gill	5
Walk 2	Muker to Ivelet Bridge	7
Walk 3	Gunnerside Gill	10
Walk 4	Gunnerside meadows	13
Walk 5	Surrender Bridge to Healaugh	15
Walk 6	Thwaites to Reeth swing bridge	18
Walk 7	Arkle Beck from Reeth	21
Walk 8	Grinton circular	24
Walk 9	Arkengarthdale	27
Walk 10	Marske to Orgate Force	30

Introduction

Swaledale is, for the majority of its twenty-two miles (35 km), convoluted, narrow and steep-sided. The most northerly of all the Yorkshire Dales, it has probably the remotest landscape and most haunting, rugged wilderness of them all.

The moors above the upper dale plummet downwards, without pausing for breath, before rebounding back up again. The high moorlands are undulating patchworks of heather, whinberry and pale-coloured reeds; immense mosaics of peat and bog. Man has been, and is still to some degree, scarring and marking these uplands: from his tracks, stone quarries and coal pits, and the hushes, pits and smelt mills of the lead mining of yesterday; to his shooting lodges, grouse butts and well-worn footpaths of today.

As the valley begins its downward tilt, towering grey-white limestone outcrops and scars edge the moorland. Below these, endless marches of drystone walls thread their sinuous lines through wildflower meadows, which in summertime stir the senses with their glorious colour.

Swaledale has its own side-valleys – ravines such as Swinner and Gunnerside, Arkengarthdale and Marske. Each beck empties into the River Swale as it wriggles and wiggles its way along the valley floor.

But the Swale's flow has not always been easy and Kisdon Hill, situated between Muker and Keld, is actually a geological deviant. Kisdon was formed during the Ice Age by glacial boulder clay which blocked the river's course down the western side of the hill and forced the creation of a new route on the eastern side – leaving Kisdon Hill in the middle.

The River Swale emerges on the Pennine hills of High Seat and Nine Standards Rigg and, from the dramatic waterfalls, or forces, near Keld down to the broader pasturelands around Richmond, is the dale's dominant factor. As one of the fastest-flowing rivers in England, the Swale has aptly been described to "Rusheth rather than runneth".

The Ordnance Survey OL30 Northern & Central map covers all the walks in this book.

Keld to Swinner Gill

Length of walk: 2½ miles (4 km)
Time: 1½ hours
Terrain: broad stony tracks all the way.
Start: privately owned car park at Park Lodge Farm in Keld
(signposted through the village, and with an honesty box for the
small charge made); grid ref: 892011

Keld is at the crossing point of probably the two best-loved, long-distance footpaths in England: the Pennine Way and the Coast to Coast Walk. The dream of Tom Stephenson since the 1930s and opened thirty years later, the 270-mile Pennine Way was the UK's first national trail, and the first attempt at travelling north-south along the ridge rather than across it. The Coast to Coast Walk, devised by A Wainwright, traverses northern England from St Bees Head (near Whitehaven) on the Irish Sea to Robin Hood's Bay by the North Sea, and most who complete the 190 miles celebrate in Wainwright's time-honoured way by dipping their boots in the sea at both ends!

There's no need for an apology that this is almost a 'there-and-back' walk – it is vintage, with stunning views, thrilling waterfalls and sites of industrial heritage. It also starts on the Coast to Coast route and is joined briefly by the Pennine Way, so offers the chance of a taster of these two famous routes. The village closest to the head of Swaledale and situated at an altitude of 1050 ft (320m), Keld boasts a setting amongst flawless fells, a selection of aristocratic waterfalls and two chapels – but no public house!

Walk straight ahead away from the car parking area at Park Lodge Farm, to take the stony track signposted to 'Muker'. Bordered by either walls or hedges, the track drops down to the left and is signposted 'Pennine Way, Public Bridleway'. Descend down a series of steep, rocky steps and cross the River Swale via the footbridge to reach a beautiful grassy haven beside East Gill Force waterfalls.

Bear left uphill on a rough, stony track which then heads to the right and crosses the top of the waterfalls as they tumble down to join the River Swale. You leave the Pennine Way here as it heads north up to Tan Hill.

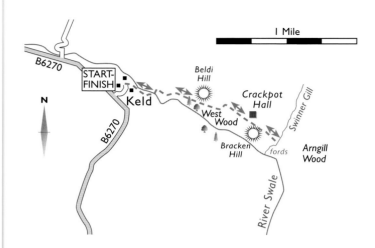

The Tan Hill Inn, standing 1,732 ft (528m) above sea level, is the highest licensed premises in Great Britain.

Turn right, signposted 'Public Bridleway', to go through a wide, wooden gate and along the very obvious track (actually an old cart track from the lead mining era), which rises gently above the Swale's wooded valley.

The view down to the steep-sided banks of the Swale's wooded valley reveals limestone scars that have been exposed by the river's action.

After walking approximately ¾ mile (1.2 km) along the track from the gate, two well-worn tracks that are quite close together head up to the left. Take the second one, leading to Crackpot Hall.

In Wainwright's book on the Coast to Coast Walk he describes Crackpot Hall as a 'decaying ruin'. The hall may have deteriorated, but the view down Swaledale towards Muker certainly hasn't.

Retrace your steps from Crackpot Hall to turn left when you reach the main track and continue as it descends down Bracken Hill, through a wide gate and on down to Fair Yew End. Here, beside old buildings rooted in the lead mining days, a footbridge crosses East Grain Beck as it flows down Swinner Gill before merging with the Swale. A very pretty waterfall is just upstream, and the whole area makes a very picturesque half-way point in the walk.

Excluding the section up to Crackpot Hall, retrace your steps back to Keld.

Muker to Ivelet Bridge

Length of walk: 4½ miles (7 km)
Time: 2½ - 3 hours
Terrain: mostly field and riverside paths, with short sections on bridleways and lanes.
Start: public car park in Muker; grid ref: 910979

In its picturesque setting beside Straw Beck and surrounded by lofty fells, Muker has to be one of the prettiest villages in Swaledale. Its place-name has Norse origins: Meuhake, which means a small or narrow cultivated field.

Prior to St Mary's Church being built in Muker around 1580, the only parish church in the Upper Dale was at Grinton, hence the coffins of the deceased from Keld, Muker etc, had to be carried to the graveyard at Grinton (see the start of Walk 8 for further details). Both the village of Muker and its church grew in size and stature early in the 19th century at the height of the lead mining industry.

The innovative Victorian naturalists, Richard and Cherry Kearton, came to the school here in Muker from their home in Thwaite. Cherry was a photographer and Richard a writer and lecturer, and the brothers received great national acclaim when they published the first wildlife books to feature photographs taken from the remarkably-constructed hides they built – including one in a stuffed cow!

From the public car park in Muker, head east over the bridge spanning Straw Beck for just a few strides before taking the track going off at a gentle angle on the right, signposted 'Occupation Road, Bridleway 1½ miles'. The walled, stony track rises up to a summit between a pair of barns before dipping down to cross an easy ford, immediately after which are two gates on the left. Take the second gate (unfortunately, the one with the small beck flowing beneath), to follow a narrow trod that keeps a wall on the left.

The footpath becomes well-walked as it rises up through a gate and fords another shallow beck. A wall stays on the left until it dog-legs down and away for a short while, leaving the path to maintain altitude under holly

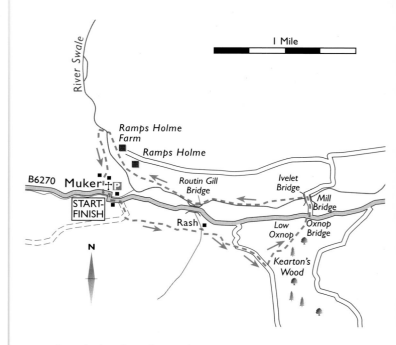

trees and continuing through a gap in a cross-wall. The wall on the left soon reappears and the footpath fords a number of small becks.

A 'Footpath' sign confirms the route just before the tiny hamlet of Rash, where the path leads up through a metal gate and across in front of the garden at Rash Grange. Continue along the driveway to another wide, metal gate and straight ahead in front of Rash View. Follow the track down to the bridge (which bears the initials NWH and the date 2007) over Routin Gill as it tumbles down small, pretty waterfalls. Turn right through yet another wide, metal gate and rise up on a track with the beck on the right. Follow the track as it swings left away from the beck, and our route continues via a narrow gate on the right just before another property. Walk past an electricity pylon and across a narrow field to a stile situated at the point opposite where a wall changes to a fence. The narrow path continues with a broken wall on the left before rising up to cross a step-stile over a fence, then follows the direction of a yellow arrow pointing to a gap-stile on the left a little further on. Soon the path divides by a barn; take the right-hand one heading uphill and keep ahead through two wide gates in quick succession which lead out on to the tarmacked lane and turn right uphill.

The tarmacked lane rises between Oxnop Side and Oxnop Beck to head over and down to Askrigg in Wensleydale. If you turn around, its elevations offer good views down to the typical Swaledale landscape of fields, stone walls and barns. The village of Ivelet is just across the river, the impressive proportions of Gunnerside Lodge on the hillside above, and the equally impressive limestone outcrops at High Scar overlooking Gunnerside Gill further up still to the right.

If you look west, you'll see Muker and Thwaite hugging the valley floor, Kisdon Hill above to the right, and then the River Swale as it curves down from Keld. Kisdon Hill is the geological deviant that was created during the Ice Age; the full story is explained in the Introduction.

After walking approximately ¼ mile (0.4 km) up the tarmacked lane, turn left through a wide, metal gate beside a 'Footpath' sign and head for the left-hand corner of Kearton's Wood. Don't actually enter the woodland itself (which is private), but go through a gap-stile in the wall heading away to the north, and across meadowland in the direction of a sign. Maintain altitude for a while, then drop steeply down the saddle of the field to the corner of a modern barn at Low Oxnop. Cross a fence via a step-stile, then a wall via a gated gap-stile almost immediately after.

Oxnop Beck splashes beneath the trees on the right, and is especially attractive where it gurgles over a couple of waterfalls.

Bear right and, keeping a fence on the right, descend down to follow Oxnop Beck's course along to Oxnop Bridge. Climb the stone steps leading from the meadow up to the main B6270 road, and turn right for just a few paces, then left on the lane past the characterful, old Mill Bridge just downstream. Follow the lane down through the trees and cross the River Swale via Ivelet Bridge.

Turn left on to the riverside footpath, signposted 'Footpath to Muker – walk single file across meadowland'. The distinct path leaves the bank briefly to rise up to a gate at the top corner of the second meadow, but after that it hugs close to the river for most of the way. Yellow markers and 'Footpath' signs appear at times to confirm the route, as it goes through gap-stiles and up and down a little, but it's always obvious – and constantly delightful! The path leaves the riverbank after Ramps Holme to head up to the right and pass in front of Ramps Holme Farm. Soon after entering the trees of Ivelet Wood, the footbridge at Ramps Holme Bridge comes into view and the path divides. Take the left-hand one heading downhill to cross the bridge. Turn right after the bridge, then up left through a gap-stile, and walk along the pavement slabs across the meadows back to Muker.

Gunnerside Gill

Length of walk: 4¼ miles (7 km)
Time: 2½ hours
Terrain: steep uphill section on a tarmacked lane to start,
then field and beck-side paths all the way.
Gunnerside Gill is quite a deep ravine, hence the land drops
steeply down from the path at times.
Start: Gunnerside village, where there are numerous road-side
options for parking; grid ref: 950982

The pull up from Gunnerside might stretch the calf muscles, but it's grand, and the walking is fairly easy after that – and more than worth the effort. If you do this walk in the morning, you could always treat yourself to the gentle stroll round Gunnerside Meadows (Walk 4) after lunch to really feel the contrast between the two areas.

From Gunnerside, walk across the bridge over Gunnerside Beck on the main B6270 road in the direction of Low Row and, after passing the houses around Lodge Green, bear left uphill on a tarmacked lane accessed via a gate beside an electrified vehicular entrance gate. Follow the lane as it rises steeply and veers left round a hairpin bend.

Keep on up the lane for approximately ½ mile (0.75 km) as it passes various properties, and leave it at a sharp right-hand bend to strike ahead on a stony, rutted track with a stepped wall a little way off to the left. Follow the track as it contours round to the right and crosses a shallow ford. The track then divides and, although the left one leads to almost the required place, the right one is a dead cert, so go for that.

Go through a wide gate and follow the track (which becomes more grassy than stony), as it winds up and through another wide gate before swinging left in front of a property named Pot Ing (Potting on the OS map). Head through a gap-stile situated at the far end of the property, and follow the faint path to a gap-stile in a cross-wall. Go straight up and across this field in the direction of a short cross-wall above, where a gap-stile is quickly visible. Proceed through, after which the route becomes a better-defined old, grassy track that drops and rises up to another gap-stile, with the property named

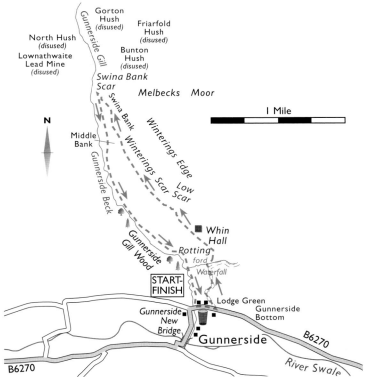

Whin Hall a little distance away up to the right. The green track is easy to follow as it leads across fields dissected with stone walls and easily-observed gap-stiles, and a derelict barn on the left will be passed before reaching Winterings.

Man's industrious activities have marked and scarred the barren, breezy landscape around Winterings, where there appear to be remnants of stone, lime and lead workings. The exposed limestone outcrops up to the right are aptly named High Scar and Low Scar.

Head directly towards a long building – Hugill House – to go through a gap-stile immediately in front, and continue almost up to the front of the building before turning right and crossing a narrow wooden step-stile beside a gate. Join a track and follow it left to walk round behind the house. The track is broad and obvious as it initially heads down between dilapidated walls then

11

continues as a more linear route across Winterings Pastures' large fields, before veering up round a sharp bend to the right. The view down to Gunnerside Beck suddenly opens here, revealing the gorge in all its mystical beauty.

Continue on the obvious, though narrowing, track to just beyond where the stone screes come down really close on the right, where the track divides beside a very conveniently-placed lime kiln. Take the left-hand option: a narrow, descending path, below which the land falls away quite sharply. Walk down to the division of paths at Swina Bank Scar, marked by a cairn, and turn left, continuing downhill.

Just beyond Swina Bank Scar are a number of hushes, including Bunton Hush, Friarfold Hush and Gorton Hush. Hushes, appearing today as barren gashes on the hillsides, were an early method of revealing veins of lead ore.

Remains of Dolly Lead Level workings are on the opposite side of the gill as the path descends, with a wall coming in on the right for a while. The route is clearly-defined as the path descends Middle Bank and continues close to Gunnerside Beck for the rest of the walk. It is a delightful beck-side walk with ample opportunity for a pleasant picnic.

The path passes further industrial heritage sites of interest, including the Sir Francis dressing floor and storage chambers, named after the son of Sir George Denys, owner of the mining rights. This was a venture which began in 1864 as an attempt to tap deep-lying deposits of galena (lead ore). The galena was crushed and sorted on the dressing floor before being smelted.

Keep on the obvious path as it descends through a gap-stile to continue directly beside the beck for a while, before rising slightly through Gunnerside Gill Wood. Although delightful, the path twists and turns over exposed tree roots, and progress may be slow.

Gunnerside Gill Wood Pasture (and Elias's Stot Wood a little further west) survive as precious reminders of the wooded landscape hereabouts before clearance by man. Indigenous trees including holly, birch and rowan provide shelter for primroses, Ramsons (wild garlic), bluebells and wood anemone. Both areas are being regenerated and protected for the future.

The trees eventually give way to fields as the outline of Gunnerside village comes into view and, once back amongst the houses, a walled track leads between gardens to a set of steep, stone steps. The steps lead to the unmade track adjacent to Gunnerside Beck where you turn left and walk back into the centre of the village.

Gunnerside meadows

Length of walk: 1½ miles (2.5 km)
Time: ¾ hour
**Terrain: a short, easy walk through meadows and along a
riverside path, but with a number of gap-stiles to negotiate.**
**Start: King's Head public house in Gunnerside
(there are road-side parking opportunities around Gunnerside);
grid ref: 950982**

*There seems to be a choice of answers as to why Gunnerside is so called,
but the consensus appears to be that there was an old Viking settlement
hereabouts, and 'Gunnar' was some sort of Norse warrior or hero who came
to the dale about 1000AD. What is without any doubt though is that from the
17th century Gunnerside was a major lead mining area with large numbers
of miners living here. Beside lead mining and farming, another local
industry was knitting, and miners would knit as they walked to work.*

*John Wesley, the founder of Methodism, spent time in Swaledale before
moving on to Wensleydale in 1790. Gunnerside, therefore, was staunchly
Methodist and its first chapel – reputedly costing £600 to build in 1789 –
was one of the earliest Methodist chapels to be built.*

*Swaledale is a narrow, steep-sided affair before it reaches Gunnerside, so
here is the first opportunity for a valley-bottom walk without steep climbs to
negotiate. Although a short, simple stroll, when the hay meadows are in
flower this is a joy, and one of the quintessential walks of Swaledale.*

Walk down the side of the King's Head public house and along the paved
path that leads to the public conveniences and picnic area. Turn left just

Meadow flowers are one of Swaledale's greatest treasures

13

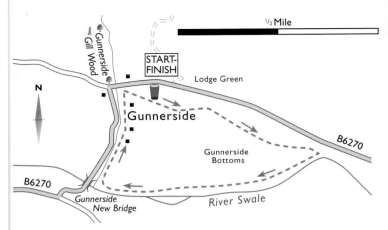

before the loos and go through a gated gap-stile. This is the first of a few, as it's then a succession of small meadows intersected by gated gap-stiles through each cross-wall. In the growing season, signs usually ask walkers to proceed across in single-file so as to minimise damage to the hay crop.

Most of the fields that border the River Swale are traditional hay meadows and therefore a picture in late spring and early summer when they team with wild flowers. You may see buttercup, bloody cranesbill, wood sorrel, scabious and vetch.

The River Swale comes closer as you reach the last meadow (which is made obvious by a wide track leading up to the road). Bear right across to the riverbank and through a gate giving access to the riverside path which is confirmed by a 'Footpath' sign. Turn right (although there's nothing else to do unless you want to get wet!), and follow the path that runs between the river and the meadows. Sadly, erosion by the river when in flood is slowly wearing away the bank so a little care is needed in places.

The path continues across Gunnerside Bottoms, to stop abruptly where Gunnerside Beck flows into the Swale. Do walk to the end to see the sloping aspect and double arches of Gunnerside New Bridge, before turning back for a few strides to head back to Gunnerside. Leave the riverside path via a wide metal gate beside a small barn, and follow the footpath north across meadows and through narrow gap-stiles identified with yellow markers. The route is confirmed by yellow arrows as it passes to the right-hand side of a modern barn, then the obvious path leads through two more gap-stiles (one is almost too narrow to negotiate, but fortunately a farm gate is just beside it), and you're back at the start beside the public conveniences in the village.

14

Surrender Bridge to Healaugh

Length of walk: 4 miles (6 km)
Time: 2½ hours
Terrain: old mining tracks, high-level moorland footpaths, field paths and a short section on a quiet lane. Fording Bleaberry Beck may prove challenging – particularly following rain, and route finding may be difficult in poor weather.
Start: Surrender Bridge, where there are numerous off-road parking options; grid ref: 988998

From Surrender Bridge, head north uphill towards Langthwaite for a short distance to the topmost of the numerous grass tracks heading east; the one you want is the only one marked with a 'Footpath' sign. It is a wide track that soon passes a rock painted with the number '8' on it (presumably a shooting position) and continues along to the left of the old smelting mill.

Today, Surrender Bridge is an area of quiet, haunting beauty, making it difficult to believe it was once part of a lead industry so large that it's said half a million tons of ore were mined in Swaledale, including the lead for the roof of the Vatican. There have possibly been smelt mills here from as early as the 1670s, but the remains that we see now date from 1841. Surrender Bridge Smelt Mill had three furnaces (or hearths) where the ore from the surrounding mines was smelt, and another furnace used for re-smelting slag. Production ceased around 1870 as the industry declined.

As it heads on from the mill, the track soon narrows to a footpath and crosses peaty ground that may be boggy after rain. Where a couple of routes appear ahead, keep to the left-hand, higher option marked with a cairn (ignoring the one leading to the top of the gorge on the right, which is actually the return route). The cairn probably appears somewhere up on the skyline, and you pass it as the land rises over Novel Houses Hill.

The views widen from the openness of Novel Houses Hill, revealing the wilderness of this stunning moorland landscape. You may see and hear curlew, grouse, skylark and golden plover. These birds are ground-nesting: building their nests amongst the heather in spring and early summer. It is recommended that dogs are kept on leads at this time of year.

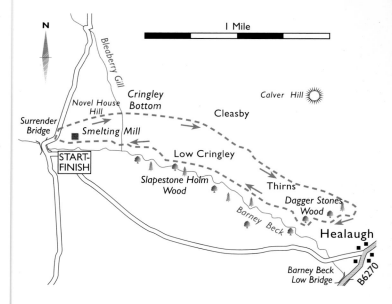

Continue along the obvious, stony path, and follow it as it descends steeply left down Bleaberry Gill to ford the beck. It's a good idea to have a good look across to the far side of the ravine to locate the onward route before descending to the beck, and then it's everyone for themselves to find a safe place to cross as the rocks will be slippy if wet. You may find it best to work your way upstream to cross, so knowing where to head once you're on the other side is a worthwhile exercise. The footpath ascends out of the gill to meet a cross-wall with a gap-stile just to the left of a wall heading in the same direction as the widening, obvious path. Keep the wall on the right across Cringley Bottom (just how do these names come about!). The path goes through a wide gap in a fence where the wall ends immediately following some sheepfolds on the right. The path widens to a clearly defined track and, though lesser impersonators leave and join it, just stick with the most distinct and obvious route.

(Please note – the route marked with the green dotted line on the OS map is now virtually unused, and this one appears to have taken its place.)

The track passes just to the south of the barn and three walled fields at Cleasby, and has started to slowly descend by the time a wall comes in on the right. Soon after that wall ends, another joins up on the left, and then the track drops to meet and join a better surfaced lane coming in from the right. Bear left and walk downhill past Thirns farmhouse on the right, where the lane becomes tarmacked. Just as the lane begins to descend steeply, a 'V' of grass drops down to the right to a wide gate marked with a yellow route arrow at the bottom. Drop down the 'V' of grass and through the gate, before swinging down right to another wide gate. The rooftops and chimneys of Healaugh can be seen down to the left, with the River Swale wending its way down the dale just beyond.

Another yellow marker points the way between a wall and a derelict building, and ignore any doubts that you've gone wrong as the path is leading you through the grounds of a new property, as further markers confirm you're on a public footpath. Go through a gate on the left before walking in front of the property and crossing to the wall opposite and through a gated gap-stile identified with a yellow marker. Keep close to a wall on the right as the path descends slightly to two wide gates. Take the right-hand one, and rise up a small knoll to locate a narrow gap-stile beside a barn/garage. Bear left in front of a house and walk along the driveway as it curves along the southern edge of Dagger Stones Wood. Turn right at a t-junction to walk in front of an elegantly proportioned property, and keep ahead on the broad track through the woods, with Barney Beck below on the left. As the track bears sharp right, leave it to strike ahead through a narrow gap-stile and follow the footpath leading uphill out of the trees. The path widens to a broad green sward and all the while keeps fairly close to a wall separating you from the trees and beck down to the left.

A footpath sign on the left confirms the route back to 'Surrender', and the heather-clad moors begin to appear up in front again. There are more 'Footpath' signs where the path changes over to the other side of the wall, and, for a short distance, is narrow with the land dropping away to the beck, but is soon grassy and more level – and makes a delightful walk. As you leave the woodland, a gap-stile appears ahead on the right, but ignore it and keep on the left-hand side of the wall along a distinct path through bracken.

Follow the footpath as it drops steeply down through a gated gap-stile to ford Bleaberry Beck and, again, it's everyone for themselves to find a safe place to cross as the rocks will be slippy if wet. It's a short but steep pull up the other side of the beck and as the land levels it's quite a surprise to find you're back on the moors again. Follow the obvious path back past the old smelting mill to Surrender Bridge.

Thwaites to Reeth swing bridge

Length of walk: 3¾ miles (6 km)
Time: 2 - 2½ hours
Terrain: an easy-to-follow, linear walk along riverside footpaths for the majority, with a short road section at the start and a quiet lane towards the finish.
Start: rough parking area at Thwaites adjacent to the B6270 between Feetham and Healaugh; grid ref: 012985

There are two choices for the start of this walk. The first (Option a) involves fording Barney Beck just as it joins the River Swale and, although there are some large stepping stones, the crossing may prove difficult if the beck is high. The second choice (Option b) is to stick with the lane and cross the beck via Barney Beck Low Bridge and walk through Healaugh to join the riverside footpath a little further on. The ford is quite close to the start of the walk, so walking along the riverbank to check out the beck's condition will only take a few minutes.

Option a) From the rough parking area situated between the road and the river, walk east along the riverside path, following the signpost 'Footpath to Reeth 1¾ miles'. The path hugs the bank to reach the ford over Barney Beck and, if you decide to continue, ford the beck and continue along the easily-defined path and the village of Healaugh will soon be seen just up on the hillside to the left.

Option b) From the rough parking area situated between the road and the river, walk east along the road over Barney Beck Low Bridge and through the village of Healaugh. Leave the road to walk at a gentle angle, across an open grassy area on the right situated just where the houses end, to pick up the footpath signposted 'Footpath to Reeth and Grinton via riverside'. Drop down through a wide metal gate and then head straight for the river, keeping a wall on your left. When you reach the riverside path, turn left. (Please note Option b) adds approximately 200 yards (180m) to the length of the walk.)

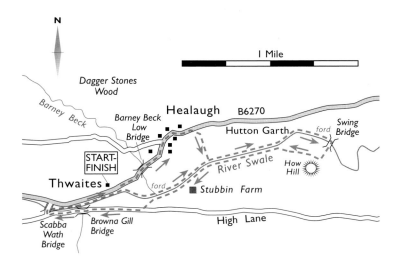

The place-name Healaugh means a 'clearing in the forest' as around the twelfth century the manor of Healaugh was the centre of a renowned hunting forest, and it is believed that John of Gaunt, one of the younger of King Edward III's thirteen children, had a hunting lodge here.

Options a) and b) are identical from this point.

Continue along the well-walked riverside path across the meadows, negotiating gates and small step-stiles along the way. After a small gate beside a wide, wooden gate, the path enters a pretty little dell where there is a division of routes. Take the right-hand, lower option, signposted 'Swing Bridge', which continues along the riverbank via a footbridge by a wetland area and on to the swing bridge spanning the River Swale.

The current Reeth Swing Bridge was erected in 2002 as a virtual look-alike to the original, which was severely damaged when struck by a floating tree during heavy floods on the night of 19th September 2000. The original bridge was built in 1920 using money raised by the residents of Reeth and Grinton and, during its eighty year life, survived numerous other floods. Although called a 'swing bridge' it doesn't actually swing, so offers a safe crossing for walkers.

After crossing the bridge, the footpath divides three ways. Take the right-hand option signposted 'Harkerside ½ mile' and, following the direction of

19

the arrow, walk up the meadow to the corner of a fence. Bear right over a footbridge crossing a tiny beck, and right again when you meet a stony track. A wall comes in on the right and ends again quite soon near two gates just on the right. Cross back over the tiny beck and take the left-hand gate where a 'Bridleway'

Grey wagtails can often be spotted running along the riverbanks of the Yorkshire Dales

sign indicates the footpath as it crosses diagonally over a meadow towards the south bank of the river. Rise up to join and follow the well-traversed riverside path, crossing stiles and gates highlighted with painted circles: blue ones at first and then the more traditional yellow ones.

The River Swale is one of the fastest flowing rivers in England and, where a cobbled section of the path drops down to virtually water level, the speed of the flow can really be appreciated. The height of the water when the river is in flood is indicated by the exposed tree roots at shoulder height just to the left of the footpath. Both banks teem with a variety of flora including Ramsons (wild garlic), bluebells and wood anemones; and fauna including pheasants, terns, oystercatchers and rabbits.

The painted circles have changed to yellow by the time the path goes through a gate beside a slightly hidden 'Bridleway' sign, leaves the riverbank to cross a narrow field and begins to rise up. A wall runs all the way along on the left as you pass Stubbin Farm. Go through a stile beside a wide, wooden gate, and you eventually come out on to the moor via another gate marked with a yellow dot beside it on the wall. Continue up the obvious path ahead beneath telegraph cables to reach High Lane, which connects Askrigg and Grinton, and turn right.

The elevated lane undulates between the bracken and reeds of the lower moorland and provides lovely views: up the dale ahead to Browney Moor, across the river to Reeth Low Moor, and to Fremington Edge above Reeth round to the right.

Follow the lane down over a cattle grid and turn right at the road junction to cross the three-arched Scabba Wath Bridge back over the River Swale. Where the lane joins the B6270 road, turn right to walk back to the parking area at Thwaites.

Arkle Beck from Reeth

Length of walk: 3¼ miles (5.25 km)
Time: 1½ - 2 hours
Terrain: along field paths, a bridleway, and short road sections.
Start: Swaledale Folk Museum, Reeth; grid ref: 039992

Reeth first became established as an edge-of-the-forest settlement inhabited by forestry labourers and officials, and was granted a market charter in 1695. By the nineteenth century, Reeth had become a small town and the nucleus for the hand-knitting and lead mining industries. With its cobbled lanes, interesting buildings and huge village greens which give an airy feel to the place, Reeth today deserves its reputation as the tourist honeypot for Swaledale.

Swaledale Folk Museum in Reeth is a treasure house of more than 500 objects and displays showing the dale's village life, religion and industries.

From Swaledale Folk Museum, walk down the cobbled lane to just before Holme Cottage – the last house prior to the main B6270 road – and turn left on a paved path running between the houses. The path is walled and narrow as it leads through a gate, then has a fence either side as it crosses a field, where a 'Footpath' sign confirms the route. Turn right through another gate giving access to the riverbank and walk under Reeth Bridge.

Arkle Beck flows beneath Reeth Bridge before it joins the River Swale a little further south near Grinton. The bridge was built in 1773 by architect John Carr from Horbury, who was responsible for much grander creations, including Harewood House, near Leeds, and Cannon Hall at Cawthorne.

Walk under the bridge and turn right up to road level, then turn back on yourself across the bridge and cross the road and walk towards Low Fremington for a few strides until you come to two 'Footpath' signs beside a gated gap-stile. Go through the stile and take the left-hand option to walk along a rutted track, which you leave where it swings right, to walk straight ahead along a narrow field and over a ladder-stile in a cross-wall. Continue in the same direction, passing to the right of a barn, and go through a gated gap-stile situated just to the right of two trees. Rise up to the right over a small knoll and keep on to a gap-stile in the top right-hand corner (the land

21

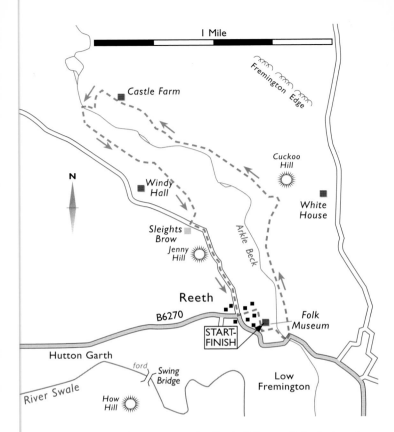

on the left drops steeply here, with derelict buildings a little further along amongst trees). Turn right through the gap-stile and then walk up two fields, keeping a barn in the second one just to your right. Continue on up and through a narrow gap-stile accessing the stony bridleway contouring around the bottom of Cuckoo Hill. Turn left and walk approximately ½ mile (0.8 km) along the bridleway, keeping a wall, dilapidated at times, on the left.

This section makes a lovely, undulating walk with grand views up towards Fremington Edge on the right.

After crossing a shallow ford, the track swings down and left, and a yellow marker post is situated on the right-hand side. A division of routes quickly follows by a 'Footpath' sign. Take the left-hand option which, for now, keeps close to the river. A wall comes in on the right almost immediately which you need to follow to walk up to and past the front of an empty house that would appear to have once been white-washed. The path keeps rising up and is broad and well-walked as it crosses over some collapsed stone walls, but becomes narrower through an area of shrubs. Keep on through a gated gap-stile and maintain altitude as you cross a field to negotiate a gap in another collapsed stone wall – marked with a yellow dot. Cross a narrower field and go through a gated gap-stile before walking between a barn (on the left) and Castle House. Go through a wide, wooden gate leading from the far end of the property on to a broad, green path which takes you down past the corner of a wall coming in on the left. Follow the path as it swings round the end of the wall and joins a rutted track coming in from the right and leads you down to a flat bridge spanning Arkle Beck.

Cross the bridge and follow the track as it swings up left through a wide gate with a 'Footpath' sign and yellow markers beside it. Walk up out of the trees to reach the junction of three footpaths, denoted by 'Footpath' arrow signs. Follow the left-hand route, marked 'Reeth', up to and through a wide gate on the skyline, and shortly after drop down off the track to pick up a narrower footpath to the left. Continue on the path as it roughly follows a line of pylons across the fields over Windy Hill, but take care where the path merges with a track for a while before leaving it again to descend left (beneath a pair of wooden pylons close together), to reach a fence-corner and cross an easy ford with a yellow marker and signpost to 'Reeth'. The path is then easily navigable and maintains a steady altitude as it crosses the rest of the fields, each divided by gated gap-stiles with yellow markers, to exit on the Langthwaite to Reeth road by a property called Sleights Brow. Turn left and walk down Jenny Hill back into the centre of Reeth.

Brown hares are widespread throughout the Yorkshire Dales. They are much bigger than rabbits and have longer legs and ears with a black tip

Grinton circular

Length of walk: 3¼ miles (5.25 km)
Time: 1½ - 2 hours
Terrain: beck and riverside paths, moorland tracks and short sections on lanes.
Start: Grinton Bridge (limited road-side parking options near Grinton Bridge and around Grinton village); grid ref: 046985

From Grinton Bridge head south along the road past St Andrew's Church.

Comparisons between the neighbouring villages of Reeth and Grinton have often been made, with Reeth referred to as the secular, market town of Swaledale; and Grinton as the sacred, with its mother church.

St Andrew's is also sometimes called 'The Cathedral of Swaledale' as this splendid building was, until Muker built a church in 1580, the only parish church in the Upper Dale. This meant that the coffins of the deceased from Keld, Muker, Ivelet and Feetham had to be carried to the only consecrated burial ground here at Grinton. The route inevitably became known as the 'Corpse Road', and at Ivelet Bridge and Feetham remains can still be seen of the roughly-hewn stone slabs pall bearers used to rest their load upon.

Grinton reputedly means 'green enclosure', but the village probably wasn't too green during its years as a lead mining centre, when Grinton Mill was owned by the London Lead Company.

As the houses end take a signed 'Footpath' on the right, accessed through a gate beneath a large holly tree, and walk along the narrow path beside Grinton Beck. Go through a gated gap-stile leading out on to Vicarage Bridge and up the drive straight ahead, still keeping the beck on the left. Follow the drive as it bears right uphill; it briefly becomes a walled track before transforming again into a green sward going through a wide gate and rising up beneath overhead pylons. A high wall soon comes in on the right, and the path continues ahead up and through another wide gate and out on to the open access moorland.

After approximately ¼ mile (0.4 km), turn right at a crossroad of paths to

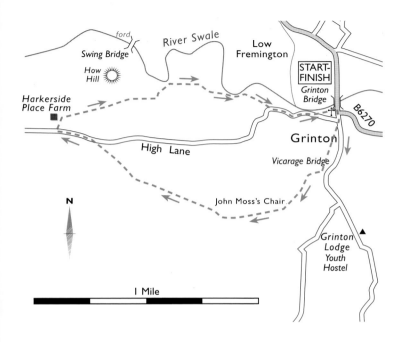

join the well-trodden route heading from the castellated grey building, Grinton Youth Hostel, which is roughly level with you over to the left.

Grinton Lodge was originally built as a shooting lodge, but became a youth hostel in the 1940s.

Keep Grinton Lodge behind you and follow the path across the quaintly named John Moss's Chair, to reach a gate in a fence where a wall comes close by on the right. You lose the wall on the right after a while, but others briefly take its place.

There are rewarding views to be enjoyed from this elevated moorland path: across the River Swale to Reeth, with Arkengarthdale rising above and Fremington Edge soaring up to the moors, whilst along the dale to the right is Marrick with its ancient priory.

Another wall is close on the right as the path swings right and down, shortly joining a track coming in from the left. Bear right along the track as it descends slightly and leads through a wide metal gate in a temporary fence (bearing a sign advising it was erected by the Nature Conservancy). Bear left as you swing down to another wide, metal gate, this one giving access to a tarmacked lane.

Turn left along the lane for a short while, before turning right down the farm track to Harkerside Place Farm, signposted 'Reeth 1 mile via swing bridge'. Go through a stile beside a cattle grid on the farm track, and turn right just before the farmyard following the footpath, signed again 'Reeth via swing bridge'. Walk along the track to turn left down through a wide, metal gate, signposted 'Grinton swing bridge' this time. Follow this descending track to just before a barn where you strike right, across the meadow, to go through a gate-stile in a cross-wall. Follow the obvious path down across this field, through another gated stile, before dropping down to join a wide track running along the valley bottom. Where the wide track bends left heading in the direction of the swing bridge, leave it and go straight ahead on the south-bank path close to the river in the direction of Grinton.

The lime-rich soil of Swaledale is perfect for hart's-tongue fern which thrives in shady, moist, rocky places

The path keeps fairly straight – more than can be said for the river which twists and turns, back and forth.

A fence comes in on the right, then another one on the left. Go through a gate virtually ahead leading you on to a walled, stony track. This is a delightful section of the walk, with the river playing 'Now you see me, now you don't' on the left! Follow the track all the way to its end where you are led out on to the tarmacked lane you joined briefly a little while ago. Turn left and follow the lane until it runs cheek-by-jowl with the river, and Grinton Church is just coming into view, to turn left beside a 'Footpath' sign and descend a steep set of steps leading to the riverbank. Turn right again past the burial ground, and straight ahead with the church on the right and, when you reach the road, turn left back to Grinton Bridge.

Walk 9

Arkengarthdale

Length of walk: 3½ miles (5.5 km)
Time: 2 hours
Terrain: along field paths, bridleways, and short road sections.
Arkengarthdale is fairly steep-sided, so the land drops steeply
down from the path for a short section.
Start: Langthwaite village car park; grid ref: 005024

Arkengarthdale is a narrow side-valley running south-east for seven to eight miles from Dale Head to Reeth in Swaledale. Man's scarring of the landscape, particularly higher up the fell-sides, is testament to this being the most productive region of the lead mining industry, with six mining grounds on the east of the dale and four to the west. The main community of the dale is at Langthwaite where, until 1730, the parson received an annual lead tithe of one tenth of all the ore that wouldn't fit through a one inch riddle.

Turn right out of the public car park in Langthwaite and walk up through the village to the far side of the church of St Mary the Virgin. Turn right again to go through a small metal gate beside a wide wooden one bearing a sign for 'Scar House'. Walk along what appears to be the tarmacked driveway for the house, but a sign reading 'Footpath only, no Bridleway' confirms your right to walk it. Follow the driveway, which resembles a tree-lined avenue as you pass West House, to swing right across a cattle grid followed by the bridge spanning Arkle Beck, with Scar House towering above you in the trees.

Scar House is an elegant manor house that is reputed to be a shooting lodge for the Duke of Norfolk. The sunken garden, to the right of the driveway just past the bridge, is exquisitely laid out and cared for.

Bear right immediately after the bridge on a soily path beside a stone wall, the start of which is slightly hidden beneath large shrubs. The route leads up to the corner of the coach house, before swinging up left on a gravel path heading to the left corner of Scar House itself. Drop down the driveway for a few strides before heading right up a gravelly track. Where this track bears right to continue to the rear of the house, keep straight ahead on Scarhouse Lane, a stony track leading up through woodland.

The woodland ends and the track enters open farmland after going through a wide, wooden gate. Leave the track via a gate situated at the far end of the first field on the right, and follow the obvious footpath as it rises up the field to the corner of the woods and on up through a gate giving access to the bridlepath called Windegg Lane. Turn right and keep along the elevation; there is a wall on the left and a footpath sign reading 'BP Fremington 4 miles'. Leave the bridlepath through an opening in the wall on the left, (there is a substantial barn just above), for enough paces to allow the wall to have changed to your right-hand side, and walk in virtually the same direction on a very faint trod. After a gap in a dilapidated cross-wall, the narrow path is a little more obvious as it crosses a field and meets a fence above the trees along Booze Common.

Cross a wooden step-stile and continue along the path through heather and whinberry. This is the section where the land falls away quite sharply to the right but, after crossing another step-stile angled a little to the left, a fence comes in on the right and the path is on more even ground. The fence

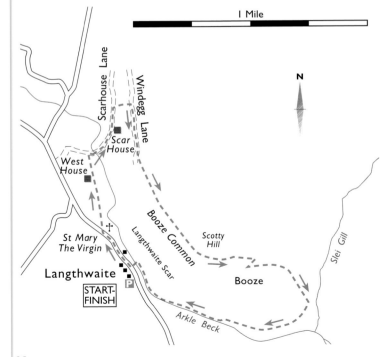

changes to a wall which curves away as the narrow path continues across rough fields. Where the path splits just before a wall running in the direction your walking can be seen ahead, aim to continue with the wall on your left. Numerous narrow paths run round the old quarries and pit workings on Scotty Hill, but if you keep close to the wall on the left all the way, you shouldn't go wrong. Where the hamlet of Booze comes into view ahead, leave the wall and join a wider footpath at a bend, and follow it right as it descends.

There are good views across Arkengarthdale from here: down to Arkle Town (all six or eight houses of it) and Fore Gill Beck's ravine separating Reeth Low Moor from Reeth High Moor above. The tiny hamlet with the intriguing name of Booze boasted forty houses at the height of the lead mining period, but it's a quiet backwater of just a handful of farms and cottages now.

Buzzards are now a common sight in the Dales skies, though they spend a lot of their time perched on fence posts or pylons

The footpath is more of a track as it loops down and round to descend through a wooden gate on to a tarmac lane with a grassy centre. Turn left along the lane, which becomes rougher and rutted for a while, then concreted by the time it meanders through Booze. Turn right off the track opposite Town Farm on a paved path through two wide, metal gates in quick succession.

The hillside to the left across Slei Gill bears strong scars of lead workings and hushes (details of hushes are included in Walk 3), but the views are beautiful, all the same.

After the two gates, the route is confirmed with a 'Footpath' sign pointing down the field, so follow its direction to a gap in the cross-wall ahead where another 'Footpath' sign points down the next field with a wall fairly close on the right. Keep descending on the broad green sward to where it joins another path coming in from the left, and bear right. As you go through a wide gate ahead, the path becomes a stony track, then enters woodland via another wide gate. Continue through the delightful woods and, after the track has zigzagged around a barn, it continues along the side of Arkle Beck all the way back to Langthwaite. Cross the road bridge over the beck and walk up to the road and turn left back to the car park.

Marske to Orgate Force

Length of walk: 3½ miles (5.5 km)
Time: 2 hours
Terrain: woodland and field paths, bridleways, and quiet lanes.
Start: small car parking area beside the beck in Marske
(voluntary donations to the upkeep of the church suggested);
grid ref: 103004

Swaledale is broad and gentle with verdant, lush farmland by the time it reaches the tiny hamlet of Marske, tucked away in a dip along the back road connecting Reeth to Richmond. Marske Hall was owned by the Hutton family, who produced two High Sheriffs of Yorkshire, an Archbishop of Canterbury and two Archbishops of York. The bridge spanning Marske Beck is of medieval origins.

The walk heads north following the course of Marske Beck and, beside Pillimire Bridge towards the end, passes a quite well-preserved waterwheel – a haunting memorial to the dale's past.

Walk from the car park to the road junction and take the lane signposted 'Whashton and Ravensworth', and 'Coast to Coast route'. Cross the bridge and carry on past the steps up to the church of St Edmund the Martyr, before bearing left in front of the telephone box on the lane to Newsham. The lane swings right and becomes a steep pull up through the woods, but is charming and worth the effort. Where the trees cease on the left-hand side, turn left through double metal gates beside a stone sign for 'Gingle Pot Farm' – as opposed to Jingle Pot as shown on the OS map.

The farm track begins with a wall on the left before it curves to the right across a couple of fields. As you reach the farm, follow the direction of a green arrow denoting the route between the buildings, and you're soon faced with two wide gates, one in front and one to the right. Take the right-hand one, again indicated with a green arrow, and follow a short track before turning right through another wide, metal gate leading out into a field. Head diagonally up the field to a gate in the far left corner, again marked with a green arrow (but take care to take the gate in the left-hand wall, not the one straight ahead in the top wall).

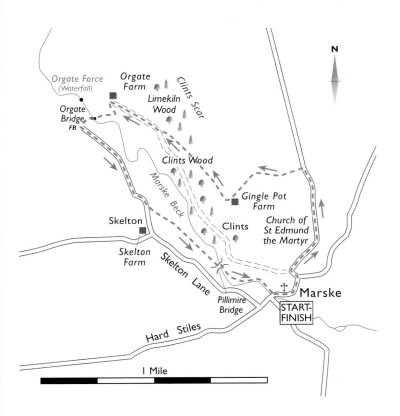

Turn right in the direction of the green arrow into Clints Wood, along a grassy path heading down through the trees. The path gradually becomes a stony, rutted track, and is confirmed by another green arrow on a post just before a clearing in the trees. Follow the track as it rounds a sharp left curve and descends to meet a bridleway coming through the woods from the left. Join the bridleway and turn right.

(Please note that the footpath shown on the OS map heading straight forward from the sharp left curve on the track seems to have disappeared and, from the numerous boot marks on the ground, staying on the track has obviously become the desired route.)

The bridleway leaves Clints Wood via a wide gate and appears to be an old route with a grassy surface.

This section of the walk is very picturesque, with views up to Clints Scar above Limekiln Woods to the right, to Telfit Bank to the left and down across Marske Beck to Skelton further left still.

Continue along the bridleway to Orgate Farm, and turn left down the farm track as it swings downhill to a footbridge beside Orgate Bridge.

Orgate Force, where Marske Beck tumbles down a pretty waterfall, can just be seen upstream from here.

Continue on to join the tarmacked lane and turn left, skirting a large barn. Continue along the lane as it rises and descends before passing the first of the few dwellings in Skelton. Leave the lane just beyond Skelton Cottage, via a stile on the left beside a small barn with a corrugated iron roof, marked with a 'Footpath' sign. Follow the obvious path as it diagonally crosses a field to reach and cross a step-stile at the end of a line of trees. The footpath continues with a fence and the ever-nearing Marske Beck on the left, till it descends down to the water and passes the old waterwheel just prior to the double-arches of Pillimire Bridge. Walk across the bridge and through a wide, metal gate to where the path splits. Bear right on the level option and you're very soon walking beside the beck again. Drop right through a small gate and follow the well-walked path through woodland before climbing the stone steps up to the road bridge and turning right back to the car park.

The poisonous fly agaric and the shaggy inkcap are two kinds of fungi which may be spotted on woodland walks between September and November